THE DAREDANCERS

The Daredancers

A novel

by

DOUGLAS ALAN WALRATH

Adelaide Books
New York / Lisbon
2021

THE DAREDANCERS
A novel
By Douglas Alan Walrath

Published by Adelaide Books, New York / Lisbon
adelaidebooks.org

Editor-in-Chief
Stevan V. Nikolic

For any information, please address Adelaide Books
at info@adelaidebooks.org
or write to:
Adelaide Books
244 Fifth Ave. Suite D27
New York, NY, 10001

ISBN: 978-1-955196-20-8

Printed in the United States of America

Once again to Sherry

Happenings

The heart has its reasons, which reason knows not of.

Blaise Pascal, *Pensees*

JOAN. I hear voices telling me what to do.

They come from God.

ROBERT. They come from your imagination.

JOAN. Of course. That is how the messages of God come to us.

POULENGEY. Checkmate.

Bernard Shaw, *Saint Joan*

Schuylerkill Falls, New York

August 1977

1. ON THE EDGE

First, he was annoyed, then, he was anxious. The digital clock read "1:45." Who would be calling at quarter to two on a hot August Sunday morning? Probably a wrong number . . . hopefully a wrong number . . . maybe the ringing would stop? He waited. It didn't.

He reached out in the dark and picked up the phone. "This is Walter Macdonald."

The caller spoke in a hushed voice. "Walter, this is Jack Rivenburg at the Grill. I'm sorry to be calling you in the middle of the night."

He sat up quickly. "Jack! Are you all right?"

"Yeah, I'm okay. I'm not calling about myself; it's about Ed Hutchins. He's been sitting here at the bar since ten 'clock. I stopped serving him at twelve-thirty; he'd had four drinks by then—that's the limit. He doesn't act drunk, but I know he wouldn't pass a breath test. He's just fallen asleep with his head resting on his arms. Everyone else is gone."

"You must be closed by now. Can't you wake him up gently and drive him home?"

"He wouldn't agree to it. He came in carrying a big blue cloth bag; it's on the floor leaning against the bar stool he's sitting on. After everybody else left he hinted that he's got a weapon in the bag. I don't know whether he really does, but he said I'd better give him all the money in the cash register. If I do that, he'll spend at least five years in prison."

"Can't you get the bag away from him while he's asleep?"

"I might, but you know he was Special Forces in the army. I don't want to risk waking him up and getting into a struggle with him by myself. I need backup. That's why I called you. He knows what you can do; he won't mess with you. Will you come?"

"I'll be there in five minutes."

As he sped through the deserted streets to the Schuylerkill Grill Walter's mind wandered back through some of the experiences he'd had with Ed and his family during his seventeen years in Schuylerkill Falls.

Ed's father, Bob, taught math at the high school. He was one of those rare teachers students remember long after they graduate. Sadly, his life was cut short by a sudden heart attack only a few months after Walter arrived in the village. He seemed to rally for almost two weeks, and then died early on a winter morning at the age of forty-seven.

Walter was a constant caller at the Hutchins home during the months following the funeral. He spent countless hours there—most of them with Molly, Ed's mother, a lonely widow schoolteacher at only forty-one. During the long days and nights, the beginning bachelor minister and the beginning widow became more than soulmates. They danced on the edge.

He was young then, a new pastor living alone and just beginning to find his way as a minister. On that spring morning he was awake at first light and out for a six-mile run. He showered, had breakfast, and was working at his desk when the telephone rang shortly after ten o'clock.

He recognized her voice right away. "Walter, this is Molly." She was obviously crying. "I crashed a little while ago at school. I had to come home. I'm in shambles. Can you come?"

"I'll be right there."

He ran through the shortcut alongside the manse carriage house, past Miss Simpson's garage, out her driveway and across Grove Street to Molly's house. Molly opened the door as he came up the steps onto her front porch. She reached out and touched his shoulder. "Thank you so much for coming." Her face was streaked with tears.

He followed her down the hallway and into the kitchen. He took off his coat and laid it on what he knew had been Bob's chair. She sat down in another chair and motioned for him to sit opposite her. She collapsed into tears. He reached across the table and held her hands in his while she sobbed.

After a while, the sobbing subsided, and she withdrew one of her hands and wiped her eyes with her sleeve. She returned her hand to his. She gripped his hands tightly, bent her fingers and dug her fingernails into his palms. "Why us?" she demanded. "Why did God do this to us?" She was almost shouting. He held her hands tightly. Finally, she shook her head and sighed, and looked straight into his eyes, and spoke softly. "I'm done in, Walter. I don't know whether I can go on. I don't know whether I want to go on."

"I'm so sorry, Molly. I don't know why it happened to you."

She shouted again, "Why don't you? You're the expert on God; you're supposed to know. Why the hell did God let it happen? He could have made him better, but he didn't! Why didn't he?"

He shook his head back and forth. "I don't know the answer, Molly. I wish I did, but I don't. All I know is how much God cares for you."

"I don't mean to be ungrateful, Walter, but that's not good enough." She pounded her fist on the table. The lid on the sugar bowl rattled loudly. She shouted, "IT'S JUST NOT GOOD ENOUGH!" The tears flowed out of her eyes. He reached out, took hold of her hands, and sat quietly with her. After a while he let go of her hands, reached into his back pants pocket, and took out his handkerchief and gave it to her.

"Thank you." She sighed deeply. "I'm sorry. I know I shouldn't talk like that, but I'm losing it, Walter, and I don't know what to do."

"Just try to be quiet. Just sit quietly with me." He reached out and put his hands around one of hers.

After a while she became calmer. She withdrew her hand and wiped her eyes again with his handkerchief. She smiled at him. "If you keep giving me handkerchiefs, people are going to talk."

"Let them!"

She laughed. "I love that about you. No matter who might be watching, you're your own person."

He relaxed against the back of his chair, "Thanks, so are you."

She had begun to collect herself. "So, now that we agree about that, would you like some coffee? There's still some left in the pot from this morning."

"I would, thank you." She stood up and placed the pot on one of the burners on the stove. "Sorry, but I don't have any of Mom's rolls to give you."

"I can't afford to eat any more of your mom's rolls; if I do, I'll outgrow all my clothes!"

"I know what that's all about!" Her voice was steady now. "Life can be pretty rotten, Walter. Bob and I were so happy. I never expected to be a widow at the age of forty-one."

"No one does, Molly. We never think something like that will happen to us."

The coffee in the pot began to sizzle. She stood up and took two mugs from the cupboard. She poured the warmed coffee into them. She gave one to him and placed one by her place at the table. She looked directly at him. "May I ask you a personal question?"

"Yes, I don't mind."

In spite of his answer she could tell that her request made him uncomfortable, but she continued. "Have you ever been in love, really in love, so much in love with someone that you would do anything or go anywhere to be with that person?"

He wasn't sure how to respond. Finally, he said, "Yes, I think I have."

She shook her head. "I'm sorry, Walter. If you only think you have, then you haven't. I loved Bob so much that I would have done anything for him. I would have given up my work, left my family, even left my church, even compromised my morals for him. I didn't have to do any of those things, but I would have. I hope you don't think I'm wicked."

"No, I don't think you're wicked. You remind me of an old proverb: 'Omnia vincit amor.' 'Love conquers all.'"

"And you haven't yet found a love that conquers your all?"

He hesitated. "Not yet," he said finally.

She looked into his eyes. "I hope someday you do."

They sat for a while and said nothing. The way she looked at him made him feel uneasy. He looked down into his coffee cup; it was nearly empty. "I'd like a little more coffee, if there's any left in the pot."

"There is; it should still be warm." She stood up and walked to the stove. She turned and looked at him. "Do you ever lay your hands on someone and pray for healing, like they ask elders to do in the Bible?"

"I never have," he said, "but if someone wanted me to, I would do it."

She brought the pot over to the table and refilled his mug. He took a sip of the warm coffee as she set the pot back on the stove. She turned at looked at him again. "Would you pray like that for me?"

The look in her eyes frightened him, but still he said, "I would. When would you like me to do it? Would you like me to do it sometime when you can come to the church?"

"No, I don't want to wait. I would like you to do it right now, here in my kitchen. I want to kneel down right here, right now. I think it would be good for me to feel the hard floor under my knees. Maybe if you lay your hands on my head and ask God to take away my pain, it will go away."

He hesitated, but finally he said, "We can do it here. We can pray to God anywhere." He pushed his chair back from the table and started to get up.

"You don't need to stand up; just turn your chair sideways to the table and I will kneel in front of you." He turned his chair and sat back down carefully. She pushed her chair to one side, placed one hand on the table, and knelt in front of him. Her head was at his knees; she pressed her forehead against them. Gently he laid his hands on her head and closed his eyes.

"Oh, God," he began. For a moment he couldn't find more words to say. Then he spoke haltingly. "Please be close to Molly . . . because she hurts . . . I know you know she hurts . . . Lay your comforting hands on her hurt and heal her pain; fill her loneliness with the warmth of your gentle Spirit . . . Be close to her . . . Be with her so she doesn't feel so alone . . . Please hear our prayer. Amen."

When he finished praying, he didn't take his hands off her head. The touch of her soft hair captured him. He stroked it slowly letting the strands flow between his fingers. She made no effort to move. When he opened his eyes and saw what he was doing he stopped. He placed his hands carefully on the sides of her head and raised it, then withdrew his hands slowly and stood up. She looked up at him. He reached down to her with open hands; she put her hands in his and he helped her stand up. She stood close to him, her face turned up to his.

"Thank you, Walter," she said softly. "Thank you for caring for me."

"You're welcome." He felt like he should say something more but couldn't find any words.

For a moment they stood silently looking into each other's eyes. Then she took his head between her hands and drew his face to hers. She kissed him on the lips, gently but firmly. Her mouth was open slightly. When she withdrew, she released his head slowly; he could feel her reluctance to let the moment end.

When her hands were no longer holding his head, he paused motionless and searched her eyes. He forced himself to back away and straighten up. He retrieved his jacket from what had been Bob's kitchen chair and spoke softly. "I better go now." He put the jacket on as they walked down the hall to the front door.

When they reached the door she said, "I know I shouldn't have done what I just did in the kitchen. My emotions are all over the place. I hope you understand. Bob always gave me something wonderful on my birthday. You just did today."

He answered quickly, "You don't need to apologize, Molly; I understand your feelings."

"I hope you'll come by again soon."

"I will; I'll call again some afternoon when Eddie and Jeannie are home. I need to stay in touch with them too."

She offered her hand. He extended his hand in a handshake. "God bless you, Molly."

"Thank you, he just did."

2. OPEN WOUNDS

It took longer to connect with sixteen-year-old Eddie and Jeannie, his thirteen-year-old sister. One afternoon when Molly wasn't home yet, Walter sat alone with them and tried to help them cope with the loss of their father. He didn't push pious palaver; he spoke form his heart. "I have no idea why this happened to your dad . . . I know how much it hurts to lose someone you love . . . it's okay to feel whatever you feel—to cry, to be angry . . .."

Tears ran down Jeannie's face; Eddie sat stoically silent. When Walter stood up to leave he felt like he hadn't been helpful to either of them. Jeannie held on to him and sobbed. Eddie looked at him and spoke in a voice purged of all emotion except anger. "Why do we pray? Your God just let my dad die. I will never forgive him."

Walter winced, "*your* God." The phrase pounded in his head like a deafening earworm. He thought but didn't say, "*My* God would never just let that happen and walk away." Somehow the thought seemed too trite to say out loud. But what response could he offer to this hurting sixteen-year-old who stared at him waiting for an answer? After pausing too long he shook his head. "I don't have a simple answer to your question, except to say that when your dad died, God cried."

Eddie turned away and hid his face in his hands.

After his dad was gone Eddie was adrift. He was bright enough to get by in school without much effort, but the old focus and motivation were gone. Except when he played basketball. He spent hours alone on the driveway shooting baskets through the hoop Bob had mounted on a backboard on the front of the garage several years before. With Bob gone there was no one to go one-on-one against him under the driveway hoop, but when he was out there where the two of them had spent so many hours together it was like he could somehow be with his dad again.

As a part-time coach at Schuylerkill Falls High School Walter worked closely with Eddie during basketball season. Even as a sophomore Eddie played well; he was fast. They both knew Eddie would never be a stand-out varsity player like the six-foot, three-inch minister was during his years at Schenectady's Mt. Pleasant High and Union College; at only five feet, eleven inches Eddie wasn't tall enough. But what he lacked in height he made up for in speed. He could really move the ball.

One afternoon in May as Walter drove down Grove Street, he noticed Eddie out in his driveway shooting baskets. He stopped, got out of his car and stood and watched. It was a warm, breezy spring day. Eddie kept shooting for a few minutes then made a quick pass to Walter. "Hi, Coach," he said with a grin when Walter reacted quickly and caught the ball.

Walter stared at the hoop on the front of the garage for a while and then spoke softly. "My brother and I used to go one-on-one against each other in front of our garage when I was your age. And then he was killed." He couldn't go on. His voice deserted him; tears welled up in his eyes. Finally, he got his voice back. "Can I join you?"

Eddie studied him for a moment, then nodded his head. "Yeah, I'd like that."

So it began, the two of them going one-on-one at the hoop in front of the garage. It was a bond made possible by reticence; they both knew what they couldn't talk about.

Over the years Eddie grew up and became Ed. Walter hoped that one day Ed would invite him to break the code of reticence. But it never happened; it was never the right time.

After high school Ed couldn't settle into anything. Molly pushed him to go to college. He tried it for a term and left. Books were not his forte; he thought with his hands. He bummed around for a while and then went to work as a mechanic at Butch Chichester's garage.

The job seemed a perfect match, but Ed was restless. One day he startled everyone with news that he had enlisted in the army. He explained that his dad had served in World War II so it seemed like something he should do. He was chosen to train as an army ranger; within six months he was in Vietnam.

Something happened to him in Nam that compounded his sadness. When he came back, he was not just sad, he was depressed.

Butch was glad to give him his old job back; none of the guys he'd hired while Ed was away were anywhere near as able. Ed seemed fine during the day at the garage, but after work and on weekends he came apart. The clinic at the VA hospital in Albany treated him for "chronic depression brought on by PTSD"—Post-Traumatic Stress Disorder. But the meds they gave him only compounded his addiction. He was arrested for Driving While Impaired twice in less than a year.

While Ed's driver's license was suspended, Walter sometimes drove him to clinic appointments. They talked—mostly about his struggle with alcohol and drugs, never about what happened in Nam. Except for one time when he said, "That memory torments me like a cat torturing a hopelessly wounded mouse."

It was nearly ten past two on that hot August Sunday morning when Walter parked his signature blue and silver Bronco on the street in front of the Grill. It occurred to him that some late-night partying Presbyterian might drive by and see it and wonder what their pastor was doing at the Schuylerkill Grill at just after two o'clock on a Sunday morning. He smiled at the possibility; they'd had seventeen years to get used to him.

He opened the restaurant door. Ed now awake sat on a stool at the far end of the bar; Jack stood behind the bar in front of the back counter that held bottles of liquor. They both looked glum.

Walter stopped at the end of the bar just inside the door and looked directly at Ed, "So, what's going on, Ed?"

Ed managed a slight smile. "Just the usual crap."

Walter eyed the tall blue bag leaning against Ed's stool. "Looks like more than the usual crap to me. Why don't you take out whatever you have in that bag and put it on the counter between us and we can talk about it?"

Ed raised a foot and set it on top of the bag and his grin broadened. "Nice try, Coach. We'll talk first, and then, maybe then, I'll give up what I've got in the bag."

"That's not good enough! Your buddy got me out of bed to come down here so you wouldn't have to use whatever you've got in that bag. Take it out and lay it on the bar and then we can talk." He was almost shouting. Adrenaline rushed through his body.

Ed stared at him. He knew that even at forty-eight the former Union College sports standout who faced him would be a formidable opponent. He smiled and cocked his head, "Well, maybe that's not the way I want to do it." He waited for Walter to respond.

The desperate look in Ed's eyes belied the bravado in his words. Walter sat down slowly on a bar stool. "What's going on, Ed?"

Ed shook his head back and forth and sighed. "I got to talk to someone, Coach. I've stuffed it down inside me too long. Maybe I need this bag to give me the courage to talk—like a kid's security blanket. I know what you think is in it, but you don't have to be worried for yourself or for him" — he tilted his head toward Jack. "Most of the time when I think about doing somebody in I think about myself. And I've thought about that a lot."

Walter looked straight into his eyes and shook his head no. "Don't do that, Ed, don't ever do that."

Ed didn't acknowledge him; he just went on. "You're supposed to be the big life coach, Mr. Macdonald. You tell people what to live for. What you say doesn't work for me. I have a horrible memory I can't live with.

"I was dumb! I didn't think about what it would mean to go to Nam when I joined the Army. But I didn't think through much of anything in those days. I just hung out.

"One day I walked into the army recruiting office in Albany. I had nothing else going and when the officer described all the benefits I could get by joining up for a few years, it seemed like a good deal. In some ways it was. I didn't have to figure out what to do with myself anymore; the army's a good place for people who aren't ready to think for themselves."

Walter shrugged his shoulders.

"I should have watched the news more before I signed up. I didn't think about Nam when I joined. After I was there it was too late not to think about it." He paused and shook his head back and forth.

"It's been three years since I came back—what's left of me; most of me never got away from that jungle." His voice faded away; he looked out the front window of the grill. A lone car drove past. After it was gone the street was stone quiet—lifeless.

"The choppers dropped us far ahead of the rest of the troops. We crept up to the top of a ridge overlooking a small village. The lieutenant told us the village was full of V-Cs, that the intelligence was solid, that there were lots of them hiding in the huts—and if we were quiet, we could take them by surprise. While we were setting up I thought it was strange that we could set up so close and nobody fired at us. But when you're a private you don't question a lieutenant.

"When we were ready the lieutenant nodded. We let go with everything we had—for probably ten minutes. When we stopped firing there was nothing: no noise, just dead silence. 'All right, sergeant,' he said, 'Take Hutchins, Peters and Farsacci and check it out down there. We'll cover you.' So we did."

He was breathing in short gasps, his eyes darting around the room like he was looking for hidden danger. "We checked every hut. There weren't any V-Cs." He shook his head back and forth slowly, "Just . . . just . . . kids . . . and women . . . and old men . . . what was left of them—with their eyes open, pleading . . . with me. But it was too late to plead; I couldn't do anything to help them." His voice dropped to a whisper, "I can't get away from those faces, Coach. I'm cursed with them. They're always with me. They follow me everywhere. They never forgive me!"

He stood up quickly, "I gotta get outta here." He raced across the dining room, dragging the blue bag behind him. The door to the men's room slammed shut. Walter and Jack could hear him retching. They looked at each other and then looked away. They had no words.

After a while he came out of the men's room, walking slowly, dragging the bag. He sat back down on his stool. For a while he was quiet. Then he looked straight at Walter. "Where was your God when I was killing all those innocent people, Coach? Was he on break? Why didn't he stop me? Maybe you know the answer? I don't. And I don't know what to do about it. Most of the time when I think about what I did I can't believe there is a God. And the rest of the time I'm afraid there might be—and if there is, what he'll do to me someday." He waited.

Walter leaned on the bar and shook his head.

Ed went on. "You don't know what doing evil is until you look it in the face. That's my life now, living every goddamn day with the memory of those faces. Nothing heals it. I'm sleepwalking in a nightmare I can't wake up from. I'm damned!

"So, tell me straight out, Coach, is there a God managing this game we play every day, like you say there is when you're in church? If there is, what's my next play? Or, maybe I've fouled out, and the game is over for me?"

For a while no one said anything. Then Walter spoke softly. "I hadn't a clue about any of this, Ed. You never talked about it when we were driving to the VA. Didn't the psych unit there help?"

"Nah, they treat addiction not memories."

Walter shook his head back and forth slowly and took a deep breath. "Nothing I say now is going to sound good enough to you, Ed." He looked at him intently. "It may sound like pious bullshit to you, but I believe that you'll find healing for that memory, that someday you'll remember it differently and there won't be as much pain. Yeah, I see that look in your eyes. But I never fed you a bad play when you were in a game. Right?"

"Right."

"Well, you're tired right now. Maybe all you can do is trust me one more time." He paused until Ed looked directly at him. "Can you trust me one more time?"

"Maybe."

"You need a time out, Ed. Let me give you a ride home. Maybe you're tired enough now to get some sleep. On summer

Sundays I'm done by eleven and free for the rest of the day. Why don't you come by for lunch and we can talk? Maybe if we talk, you can figure out what to do next. Okay?"

Ed didn't move or say anything for a few minutes. Then he stood up, sighed deeply and said, "Okay. You can just take me to the old house. My mom's away this weekend, so we won't wake up anybody. I can sleep in my old room and then in the morning walk back here and get my pickup." He reached down, picked up the long blue bag and slung it over his shoulder. He looked at Jack and then at Walter and grinned. "You guys are wondering what's in this bag, aren't you?"

"Yeah," Jack said with a smirk on his face, "I been wondering that for five hours!"

"I came in here to have a few drinks and hustle enough money to buy something stronger. Booze doesn't make the shit go away, but it's a start. When I get really down, I buy something on the street in Albany. It's no cure either, but it takes me away for a while." He looked toward the pool table at the back of the barroom and shook his head. "It was a stupid idea. I got too much reputation here; nobody in this town is gonna take me on in a game of eight-ball."

He grinned again. "Well, guys, the bag's full of dirty laundry, just dirty laundry. I was bluffing with it. I go to my mom's to do my laundry every weekend. I was threatening to shoot you guys with dirty laundry." He watched them look at him and then laughed out loud. "Dirty laundry can be lethal!" His laughter faded away and a sober look took its place. "Mine's damn near killed me—more than once."

3. ED'S DANCE

It was after one-thirty when Ed drove into the manse driveway in his pickup. Walter had about given up expecting him. He opened the door to the side porch as Ed walked up the steps.

"Sorry I'm late, Coach. The talk with you and Jack must have been good for me; I overslept. Then I had to wash the dirty laundry. And when that was done, I had to walk back to the grill and retrieve my truck." He saw the empty plates on the kitchen table. "Thanks for waiting lunch; you must be starved!"

"I am; preaching uses up lots of calories—especially after a short night's sleep!" He grinned.

Ed looked around the kitchen. "I haven't been in here since I got out of high school and stopped coming to youth group on Sunday nights." He glanced at the door into the dining room. "We used to lie all over each another on the floor in there and talk and eat pizza. Kids still do that?"

Walter nodded, "They do, and I still like to hear what they're wondering about. You want a sandwich? I do; my breakfast was a long time ago!"

"Mine too—yesterday! My mom's not home and I didn't feel like fixing anything."

"I figured she wasn't home because she always comes to the Sunday service when she is."

Ed tilted his head, a quizzical look on his face. "Sometimes she goes away for the weekend—I don't know where she goes or who she goes with; she's never said." He paused and grinned. "It's hard to think of your own mother as someone who could be doing something her church friends wouldn't approve of—even if you are." He held out his arms with turned-up hands and cocked his head to one side. "You've always been her confidant; maybe you know more than I know?" He watched Walter carefully.

Walter shook his head and shrugged his shoulders. "I don't."

Ed laughed. "And if you did, you wouldn't say; I knew that when I was sixteen. Anyway, I guess I don't have to be my mother's keeper." He watched Walter nod. "Right now, I'm starved."

"How about a ham sandwich and some iced tea?"

"Sounds good!" He paused, then said, "Damn it's hot, I'd really like a beer, but after what happened last night I probably shouldn't have one. I guess I better settle for a big glass of iced tea."

Walter laughed as he stood up. "It is a cold-beer kind of day and I'd love one too, but I'm meeting a bunch of high school kids for a pickup softball game in a couple of hours and it wouldn't do to have beer on my breath!" He took a loaf of bread out of the cupboard, opened the refrigerator and took out a plate of sliced ham, some mustard, a pitcher of iced tea and set them on the table.

After they made sandwiches and began to eat Ed made a face and said, "I'm really sorry about last night. I feel stupid about it today."

Walter sat back in his chair. "We all do stupid things, Ed, and the next day wish we hadn't."

"But what I do goes beyond stupid. Sometimes I get so far down I just can't get myself back up, and then I do something crazy—like threaten to rob the Grill. Thank God for friends like you and Jack. Care if I make another sandwich?"

"Help yourself."

"Saturdays I spend alone are the hardest. Butch closes the garage at noon and, except for the weekends when she's away, I go to my mom's and have lunch with her and do my laundry and then go back to my apartment over Smitty's store. I play my guitar and sing until nine or so and then drive to Albany and pick up Lauren when she gets off work." He stopped and tried to gauge Walter's reaction when he said, "Lauren." He couldn't tell.

"Playing the guitar helps; it was my dad's. Mom gave it to me the week after he died. You knew he played, didn't you?"

"I did. I heard him play; he was good. I'm glad you play it; it shouldn't sit idle."

"It's a '49 Southern Jumbo SJ, one of the best acoustics Gibson ever made. Playing it gives me solace—funny word for a mechanic to use, isn't it?"

"Maybe, but it fits. You're a guy with deep feelings."

He watched Walter's face for a moment, and then said, "Thanks." He took a breath. "I didn't sing at first—just played, mostly where nobody could hear me. My sister, Jeannie, sings—always has. She's really good. Years ago, when she was in college and she'd come home on breaks, I'd play and she'd sing—for hours. We even performed a couple of times at the coffee house the UU Church has in Albany. After a while I began to write my own songs—mostly about loss: losing your love, losing your dream, losing your way. About me.

"When I went to Nam, I left the guitar behind. After I came back it took a while, but one Saturday I picked it up and began to play again. Last spring, before I moved out on my own, on a weekend when Jeannie was home from med school for a day, I was singing in the basement, kind of lost in what I was singing, and when I looked up she was sitting on the steps. 'You're good,' she said. 'You need to share that.' I heard what she said, but I couldn't do it. Then one night, kind of on a dare to myself, I went to the open mike night in the back room at the Lark Tavern in Albany.

"I sang only two of my songs, but people seemed to like them. They didn't actually say anything to me, but they were quiet when I sang. That doesn't happen much when you perform in a bar. Johnny Millett happened to be there; he owns Downtown Johnny's. He walked over to me when I was packing up my guitar. I stood up and he held out his hand. I shook it and he said, 'I'm Johnny Millett, I like what you do. If you have Thursday nights open and want to play at Downtown Johnny's, they're yours. I pay $25 and all you want to eat and drink.' So, Thursday nights at Johnny's have been mine ever since. The money's not much, but the exposure is good." He stopped and looked directly at Walter, "I'm running on and on; I hope I'm not boring you."

Walter sat up and laughed under his breath as he raised his hand in a gesture of protest, "No, not at all; I want to hear more."

"You're curious about Lauren, aren't you; I can tell even though you tried not to look curious when I said her name." He grinned.

Walter nodded. "I am curious, but I figured you'd tell me about her when you were ready to."

"That's your way, isn't it Coach. You always cut the other person some slack."

Walter took a sip of iced tea and pondered the remark and then said, "I figure everybody has to play the game their way. I'm just a coach."

"Well, here's my way. Lauren's a waitress at Johnny's. The first night I saw her I knew she had more going for her than the girls you always find at a bar waiting for somebody to pick them up. When the waitresses get off, most of them sit and have a drink and hope some guy will notice them. When I finish playing, I eat something and talk to them, sometimes even buy them a drink. But that's it. I think some of them would like me to go home with them, but I don't. My mom said one time, 'If you go home with that kind of girl, you'll probably catch something.'" He laughed out loud. "Funny what you remember your mother saying isn't it?"

Walter smiled. "I got almost the exact same advice; my mother said, 'If you do something with a girl like that, you'll catch the itch.'"

Ed shook his head. "Lauren's not a 'girl like that;' she's different. That may sound corny, but she is. She's one of those women you just have to stare at whenever they're in the room. Every Thursday I'd catch myself staring at her while I sang. Once in a while she'd look at me, but that was it. Each Thursday when I'd get off, she'd be gone. Most nights she's done by ten because she waits table in the restaurant not the bar. Every Thursday I'd go home and lay awake and think about her—and lots of other nights too. You know what that's like?"

"I do. Once I had someone like that in my life."

"The song wrote itself. I called it 'Thursday Girl.' The first time I sang it in public was on a Thursday at the end of my last set. The restaurant got very quiet. It was busy that night and Lauren had worked late. She'd changed into her street clothes and was just coming out of the back room when I started to sing it. I'd waited to sing it until I knew it was about time for her to come out. She stood and listened. And so I sang to her. When I finished, she walked slowly over to the bar and sat down on a stool. I set my guitar on its stand and walked over and sat down next to her. I couldn't say anything; I just looked at her. Then she said, 'That song is about me, isn't it?' 'Yes,' I said, 'it is.' She looked at me, 'Would you like to come home with me?' And I said, 'Yes, Thursday Girl, I would like that a lot.' And so I did."

He took a deep breath. "Can I go on? I don't want you to be uncomfortable."

Walter looked at him gently. "I'm not, Ed—not at all."

"We made love that night—over and over and over again. It was like we'd searched a lifetime for each other and couldn't get enough. It was the most incredibly beautiful night of my life." He stopped and the two of them sat in the quiet. He sighed, "So, I spend every Thursday night with Lauren, sometimes other nights—even whole weekends when we can." He laughed out loud. "This is not the typical kind of story you share with your minister—or most anybody, for that matter."

"But it's beautiful, Ed."

He sighed. "I wish beautiful was all it is, but it's not. Lauren's married. His name is Gary Shanahan. He drives for North East Trucking as a long-haul trucker: Albany to Chicago, on to Omaha, Denver, Oakland, back to Chicago, home to Albany— that kind of trip, then a short trip just to Chicago and back in the alternate weeks. He's always gone on Thursdays.

"Lauren knows she's caught in one of those marriages made too soon. Gary seems okay with it, but it's not what she needs. She says it's a 'dead marriage.' She'd like to end it, but she's afraid to. Gary's never abused her, or anything like that—at least not yet, but she's afraid he might. Maybe it would be easier for her now if he had?"

Walter quickly shook his head. "No, Ed, abuse is never good."

"Yeah, I know that. One night when we were talking she said, 'I settled. We survive by not pushing. I have no idea what he does when he's away other than drive. He doesn't know what I do with you when he's not here. I don't know what would happen if he found out about you, but I'm afraid. He has a terrible temper. I've seen it.' She stopped and looked really scared and then said, 'There isn't any good way to tell him about you. I'm terrified of what he would do to me if it came out when I'm with him. He doesn't love me, but he's proud and he thinks I'm his property. He's never hurt me, but I've seen what he's like when he loses it. He smashes things. His fists are huge.'" He looked down at the floor. "She's trapped by what he might do."

He looked up at Walter. "She's risking a lot to be with me, isn't' she? I'm not sure whether what I'm doing with her is really okay or whether I'm just telling myself it's okay because I want so badly to keep her. Maybe I'm just making up what I want to hear? What do you think?"

"It would be better if she could make a clean break from Gary. You may be playing with fire. If it gets out of control, you could both get burned."

Ed nodded slowly. "I know we are, but even if she can't make a clean break, you understand, don't you, why I would keep on seeing her?"

"I do." He paused for a moment before he went on. "We both know what I'm supposed to tell you to do, so I don't need to say it out loud. Besides, if the truth be known, it's rarely that neat. Sometimes, the best we can do is dance on the edge between what we ought to do and what we need to do."

"That's me! I slipped and fell at the Grill last night because Gary's been home all this week. Been sick, or something—I don't know what. Since I've had Lauren I haven't bought a fix. When I feel like I'm gonna sink I hold on to her. But when I need her and can't get to her I go down. That's what happened last night." He paused and looked a little sheepish. "Probably I should feel guiltier than I am about what I'm doing with her, but if she hadn't come into my life when she did, I'd have gone down for the third time."

"If I was carrying around the memory of that horror that happened to you in Vietnam and Lauren came into my life, I would probably do the same with her as you are."

Ed looked out the window for a while and then back at Walter. "I really appreciate your honesty, Coach. It's the way you are; I don't know anybody who's more real than you are." He hesitated for a moment before he went on. "I wish I could say the same about your God. But your God seems like the old straight chair I have that belonged to my grandparents. I keep it around only because of the memories it holds; I never try to sit in it."

Walter winced. Only because of the memories! That's *all*? Ed was staring at him, waiting for him to say something. Here was finally a moment when Ed was open, and he should have something profound to say, but nothing came to him, and the right time he had longed for slipped away.

When Walter didn't say anything, Ed shrugged his shoulders and stood up. "I don't know if my game will have a happy ending, Coach. What the Thursday Girl gives me is how I'm hanging in for now. I just pray every day that I can have one more day with her." He grinned. "After what I just said about your God you wouldn't think I'd be a praying kind of guy, would you? Doesn't make sense, does it?"

"Doesn't have to, Ed. We don't pray because it makes sense; we pray because we hope it makes a difference."

Ed stood and looked at him for a moment. "Got it! Thanks for the breakfast, and for listening." He opened the door, stepped out onto the side porch, got into his truck, backed down the driveway, out into the street and drove away.

Walter shook his head as he watched Ed turn the corner onto Elm Street. "I need to have something better to offer than an old chair no one can sit in. A God who is only nostalgia is impotent."

4. MOLLY'S DANCE

On the Sunday after Labor Day the usually animated discussion with high school kids lying all over the old rug in Walter's large and mostly unfurnished dining room, challenging him with irreverent questions didn't take off. Everyone seemed to have the back-to-school blues. The meeting broke up early. Walter stood in the doorway and watched the group walking out his driveway—the guys punching each other and the girls taunting them. He liked these kids.

When he walked back into the dining room, he was surprised to find Kristen Klein picking up soda cans and paper plates and putting them into a plastic bag. She smiled awkwardly when she saw him. "I decided to help you clean up; it's not fair that we have all the fun and then leave you with a big mess." She watched his face carefully. "Maybe when I'm finished cleaning up you and I could sit and talk for **a** while?" She smiled cautiously and went back to picking up.

Kristen was smart, quick-witted, and could hold her own easily in a debate, but she was tall for a girl. She had what adults would describe as "a pleasant face." She was a fierce competitor on the gym floor—a major reason why the Schuylerkill Falls High School girls' basketball team was sure to be a contender for the state championship this year. But away from the gym Kristen never drew second looks.

Walter was gentle. "That's a really a nice offer, Kristen, but I was going to leave the mess to clean up later; before it gets late I have to check on an elderly parishioner who lives alone." He watched disappointment spread across her face. "It's starting to get dark; do you need a ride home? I can drop you off."

She sighed and shook her head. "No, that's all right, Mr. Macdonald; I'll be fine, I understand. I just thought you might need some extra help. We can talk another time."

"Thanks, Kristen; I'm sure we will."

She reached out and touched his arm as she walked past him. In that brief moment the teenager had become a woman.

He waited a few minutes after Kristen left and then walked out the manse side door and made his way alongside the old carriage house through the gap in the back fence, across the adjoining yard and up the steps onto the side porch of the house that was directly behind his manse. He reached up to the top of the frame over the window next to the door and found the key that unlocked the kitchen door. When he opened the door a grey, striped cat streaked inside, and Adele Simpson called out from the upstairs, "Is that you, Mr. Macdonald?"

He walked to the foot of the back stairs and called up the stairwell in a loud voice. "Yes, Miss Simpson, it is."

"Well, I'm fine and already to bed."

"That's good to hear, Miss Simpson. You're the early-to-bed one in our neighborhood. Did you have a good supper?"

"Marilyn fixed it before she left yesterday and put it in the refrigerator for me to reheat. Gertrude took me for a long ride after church service this morning and we had a wonderful Sunday dinner at the Paradise Restaurant in Bennington. So, I've had ample food today, thank you. More than an old woman needs!"

"Glad to hear it. And Marilyn will be back in the morning in time to fix your breakfast, right?"

"She will."

"I'm going along, then. Please call me if you need anything during the night."

"Thank you so much for checking on me, Mr. Macdonald. You're a wonderful pastor and much more of a good neighbor than I have a right to expect."

"I owe you a huge debt, Miss Simpson, for all the rhetorical coaching you've given me as a preacher. I don't think I'll live long enough to pay it off."

He heard her laughing. "Flattery shall get you everywhere with an old woman, Mr. Macdonald. Thank you for your care."

"You're very welcome; good night." He stepped out onto the porch, closed and locked the door and placed the key back in its hiding place. As he walked down the steps from the porch a refreshing west wind blew across his face. He stopped walking, turned toward the street and caught a glimpse of Molly Hutchins' house on the other side of the street. There were no lights on and her car was not in the driveway. She must be away; she always came to the Sunday service when she was in town on Sunday. He couldn't help but wonder where she was. He recalled the conversation with Ed the day after the confrontation at the Grill; he seemed evasive when he mentioned "her weekend away." It was like he didn't know where his mother was on her weekends away—or didn't want to say.

There had been no men in Molly's life since Bob died. "There'll never be another Bob—he was the love of my life." With that love gone forever she seemed resigned to (but now that he thought about it, he wasn't sure she was content with) living alone as a widow third grade teacher whose own children had grown up and moved on to live their own lives.

He gazed at the dark house silhouetted by the fading twilight and thought, "It's been too long since I've visited Molly; I'll call her this week and see if I can stop by sometime soon for a cup of coffee. Besides, she'll make a pie."

He turned away from the street and looked back toward his manse. "My life is full of women I can't touch."

Thursday afternoon at four-thirty he parked his Bronco under the basketball hoop in front of the garage attached to Molly's house. Molly saw him coming and opened the kitchen door as he walked up the steps and onto the side porch. Before she said anything he knew from the delicious aroma drifting out the door that she had baked a pie. "Smells wonderful, Molly."

She smiled. With her brown eyes and soft auburn hair showing only a few streaks of grey, at fifty-eight she was still beautiful. "Well, Walter, it's an apple pie. That was Bob's favorite, as you know. Whenever he knew I might bake a pie he always said, 'Molly, you can make any kind of pie that you want to as long as it's apple.'"

Walter saw the pain behind her smile. He looked into her eyes, "I miss him too—though I know it's nothing compared to what you feel." He watched a tear slip down her cheek. She let it flow. He wanted to hold her, but he didn't.

She looked at him and shook her head back and forth slowly. "After all these years I'm just as much in love with him. You're the only one I can still cry with and not think I should hide it." She stopped abruptly. "But enough of that! Please sit down. How about a piece of his favorite pie?"

"I would love one—even if I will have to add an extra mile to my early morning run tomorrow to repent!" He sat down in his usual chair at the kitchen table.

"If that's all the repentance you require, I wouldn't worry!"

"Well, there might be more, but I'm not going to confess it right now."

She laughed and cut a large piece of pie, set it in front of him, then poured a cup of coffee and handed it to him. "You take it black."

"I do; you always remember."

She smiled warmly. "Speaking of repentance, thanks for what you did for Ed the other night. I'm glad you stopped today so I can thank you."

"You're welcome; he just needed a friend and I was glad to be one."

She sighed and shook her head. "He slips and falls every once in a while. I worry about him—probably more than I should, but, sometimes, he feels fragile since he came back from Vietnam. Something horrible must have happened to him over there. He's never talked about it and, as much as I would like to help, I know I shouldn't pry. It feels to me like he has something he needs to confess but can't. Maybe you know more about it than I do?" She looked at Walter hopefully.

He spoke carefully. "Someday I think he will get by it and then I think he will tell you about it."

She accepted the block. "Well, at least he's met a nice young woman. When he came home to do his laundry on Saturday a month ago, he brought her along and we all had lunch. Her name is Lauren; she works at the restaurant where he plays on Thursdays. I could tell that he cares a lot about her; she's pretty and gentle and obviously devoted to him. I think he stays with her sometimes. I don't know much more than that; like I said, I don't pry. I think she's still married but stays on her own most of the time. Sometimes, I worry about what her husband could do if he finds out about her and Ed. He might feel he has property rights to her even if he doesn't love her." She shook her head and laughed. "People do things now that we couldn't have done when we were their age—but we need to remember it's the seventies not the fifties."

"And, sometimes, that's hard—even if you understand why."

Her laughter died away and a wistful look came into her eyes. "Actually, Ed doesn't have to tell me more about Lauren; the look he gets in his eyes when he talks about her tells me what I need to know. He's closed-mouthed about what matters to him. Like his dad was."

Walter nodded. "Bob didn't have much to say, but whenever he spoke it was worth listening." He watched her eyes. Her wistful look moved him from the present to the past.

"Do you remember the Thursday morning the spring after Bob died and I crashed and came home from school and you came to see me? We sat at this table. It was my birthday."

He didn't say anything.

"Walter, did I lose you?"

The sound of her voice catapulted him back into the present; she was obviously wondering why he was silent for so long. He realized he'd wandered off into a memory of lost time that touched something he both feared and longed for. He laughed defensively. "Sorry, for a moment I was back at that Thursday."

"Did you know that I had feelings of love for you then?" She saw the startled expression on his face. "Not at all like it was with Bob! But they were genuine. The kiss I gave you that day was an expression of gratitude, but it had some hunger mixed in. Looking back I realize how horribly mixed up and hurting I was, and that the crazy combination of grief and hunger for love lost made me want you to stay with me. Do you understand?"

He struggled to catch his breath. "I . . . had no idea you might be . . . that you might be having . . . feelings like that for me."

She feigned exasperation. "Oh, I know you didn't, Walter." She laughed. "I'm sorry; I shouldn't be so blunt, but that's my way now. You learn to be tough and talk tough when you become a widow. It's how you survive. I watched my mother do it; you've probably noticed it's happened to me."

She sat back in her chair and laughed louder. "Well, now that I've put it out in the open, I may as well go on." She noticed the concerned look was still on his face. "Don't look so worried, Walter; I'm not going to try anything today!"

He laughed nervously. "Well, that's a relief. You're a church member; it's against the rules!"

"Oh, Walter, you're always so on duty. Women fall in love with you all the time and you don't even notice. How can they help it? You're such a gorgeous man: a six-foot three-inch muscular hunk, with deep blue eyes and that fetching smile, and a full head of hair just beginning to grey with one unruly shock that refuses to stay in place. Women can't help but fantasize that there's something wild inside you and that just maybe they're the one to unleash it!"

His face began to color up and he shook his head in a gesture of disbelief. "I know that it sometimes happens with teenagers, but I don't let myself take them seriously. I assume they're just trying out their emotions. But I don't know of any women it's happened with."

"Well, they wouldn't just right out tell you! Besides we sober up and know it's hopeless. I could have loved you for years, but you would never have noticed. And I could never have pressed it—even though I knew you lost what everyone thinks was the love of your life when Mary Kerrigan moved away sixteen years ago and you didn't go with her. Everyone thinks you gave her up to stay here and serve God and us. With that kind of sacrifice and dedication staring me in the face, how could I press my own desires on you? You're like God, Walter; you give and give and give, and never expect anything in return."

He shook his head again. "If you hadn't said that out loud, I never, ever would have thought it." They sat quietly for a moment, then he looked at her. "Thank you, I'm touched."

"Well, sad to say, you're safe with me now. Not that I think you're necessarily celibate, just that you are . . . and always will be . . . 'the minister.' You're an all or nothing kind of man, Walter. It's all God for you; no woman has a chance."

He sat for a while and looked at the floor. When he looked up at her he said, "I suppose that's the way it seems to everyone. The truth is I just haven't found somebody I think could deal with both me and God without having it turn into a triangle. I hope someday I will." He paused again. "But to be completely honest, if I do, I'm not sure I would know how to make it work—how I could be faithful to two loves."

She nodded and looked at him. "That's what I've had to learn how to do."

He looked puzzled. "I don't know what you mean."

"I'm sure you don't, so I'll tell you." She sat back in her chair. "Even after the raw pain of losing Bob subsided, I thought that if I were to let myself love anyone else, I would somehow be unfaithful to him. So, the years went by and I settled into the life of Mrs. Hutchins, the widow third-grade schoolteacher. Ed and Jean graduated from high school and moved on with their lives. I taught school during the day, each evening got ready to teach school the next day, cleaned and did the laundry on Saturday and went to church on Sunday. For the first few years I had dinner with mom once a week—usually on Saturdays—and then she was gone.

"I thought that's the way it would be forever. Then Jean, my grown-up kid in the middle of her OB-GYN residency, helped me move on. A year ago last summer she was home for a visit and we were reminiscing about Bob—how incredible he was. I was looking out the window in the wistful way that had become a habit and she said, 'Mom'. . . . I turned and looked at her and she said very soberly, 'Mom, you're stuck. You're in love with a memory; a memory can't warm your bed on a cold night. You may never love again like you loved dad, but you could still love.' We sat together and cried."

She wiped a tear away with the back of her hand and sighed deeply. "Jean gave me a gift. I realized that day that all loves are not created equal. You love each one with whatever love you can give him—or her. Loving one person doesn't have to be at the expense of loving another—or the memory of another."

"I've never thought of it that way, but you're right—and it's beautiful."

"Thank you; I think it is too—and there's more. Is it all right to tell you more?" She stopped and searched his eyes.

He wasn't sure what she meant, but he wanted her to go on. He nodded and spoke softly, "It's all right."

She grinned. "That wasn't very convincing, Walter—but I'll take a chance. Besides, you're my priest, so it better be safe for me to make my confession to you."

He laughed. "It is; it really is safe."

She sat up in her chair and took a sip of coffee. "After Jean and I had that conversation, when I went back to school in the fall Frank Perelli began to stop by my classroom once or twice a week after the kids had left for the day. He doesn't coach in the fall, so he's done for the day when classes end." She paused, and then said, "You probably know Frank pretty well."

"I do; I've coached basketball and baseball with him for years. We've become good friends."

"Then you know how it is with his wife, Marsha—that she's suffered with Alzheimer's for years."

"I do. It's so sad. It came on when she was too young. It's really done her in; she's become abusive and very out of it."

She nodded. "It's been so hard for Frank. He cared for her at home as long as he could, but finally she became too much for him to take care of, even with caregivers coming in every day while he was at school. It nearly killed him to do it, but he had to give her care over to the professional caregivers at that convalescent center on the west side of Saratoga. She's been there almost eight years and he still goes to see her nearly every week. She doesn't even know him anymore, mostly just yells at him and tries to hit him, but he still sits with her and tries to be patient with her."

Walter sighed. "I know; I've gone there with him. It breaks your heart to watch them. I don't know how he keeps it up. His life is filled with emptiness."

Molly folded her arms in front of her and spoke hesitantly. "Walter, you can probably guess where this is going?" She laughed nervously. "Now that I'm up to talking about it I'm almost too afraid to go on, but for some reason I don't understand it's something I need to tell you." She stopped speaking and stared at him.

He wasn't sure what to say. Finally he said, "Molly, whatever it is you don't need to be afraid to talk about it."

She looked away and then back at him. "I know I don't, but I'm still nervous." She took a deep breath. "One day this past February it snowed so much overnight that school was closed. When I opened the refrigerator to get out some leftover soup to heat for lunch I saw a ham that had been in there for a couple of weeks and needed to be cooked. I bought it one day on my way home from school because I thought Ed would be home for dinner the next night, but he couldn't come. The ham was too big for me to eat by myself, so it just sat there. When

I looked at the date on it I thought, 'I need to cook this . . . I wonder if Frank would like to walk over though the snow and have dinner with me?'" She laughed nervously. "It took me forty-five minutes to get up enough courage to call him! But I did. He came over about five o'clock.

"I know you may find it hard to believe, but it was the first time I'd entertained a man at dinner since Bob died. That's sixteen years of aloneness! I'd thought about inviting someone a few times, but I could never bring myself to do it. It may sound strange to you, but all those years I felt like I would be betraying Bob if I invited another man to share my life."

She paused and looked through the doorway that led to the dining room. "Frank and I had a wonderful dinner together. We talked about all the crazy things that happened in our families when our kids were growing up—especially when they were teenagers. I hadn't laughed so much in years as I did that night. We sat at the table and talked from six until after ten.

"At ten-thirty we were sitting quietly and the parlor clock chimed once. Frank looked at it and said, 'It's getting late; as much as I don't want this evening to end, I guess I'd better be going.'" She took a quick breath. "I looked straight at him and whispered, 'Don't go.' He didn't.

"It was three in the morning when we woke up. We lay there and talked for a while; then he got dressed and kissed me one more time and let himself out and walked home." She sighed and paused. "After he left I wondered if I should have done what I did with him." She stopped and waited for Walter to say something.

For a minute he didn't say anything, then he asked gently, "How do you feel about it now?"

She spoke quickly. "Well, that's the only time we've done anything like that here! Schuylerkill Falls is a small town and you can't hide what might look scandalous very long. Some people love to dig dirt—even people in our church. They would be delighted to discover two schoolteachers having what looks like an affair. And I guess strictly speaking that's what we're having. Right?"

He nodded. "Strictly speaking . . . that's what most people would say it is."

"What about you? What does it seem like to you?"

For a moment he didn't respond. "I'm going to give that question back to you before I answer it. What does it seem like to you? That's what's most important."

She cocked her head to one side, folded her arms in front of her and laughed. "That's very clever, Walter—throwing my question back to me! You're ducking! But I'll let you get away with it this one time; I'll tell you first how it seems to me, then you have to tell me how it seems to you. Okay?"

"Okay."

She relaxed against the back of her chair. "A light went on inside my head that day Jean talked with me. I realized there's something practical about the way young people today deal with life. They realize that if you can't have it all, you can at least have something. I know I can't have it all with Frank; he will never stop loving Marsha. He will be faithful to her in the ways in which he can as long as she lives. I know she is still the love of his life and always will be. I know I'm not. And I know he will never be to me what Bob was. But I don't think what he's doing with me is taking away from his devotion to Marsha, any more than what I am doing with him is being disloyal to Bob. So, we're not naïve; we're not pretending. Now is not then; it's another now." She stopped suddenly and laughed. "I'm dumping; I hope that's all right."

"It's all right; I have a big dumpster."

She laughed. "I know you do. You're our minister; we all dump on you. I have no idea who you dump on." She saw him cringe, but she didn't give him a chance to respond; she just kept talking. "What Frank and I give to each other is a lot like what I suspect Lauren and Ed give to each other. What we give each other helps us both go on. Before Frank came into my life it was defined by tragedy. There were times when I was so overcome with grief that I was afraid that sometime I would drown in a sea of sadness. The best I could do most days was tread water; now I can swim.

"Frank and I meet one weekend a month at an inn in Middlebury. We give care and tenderness and strength to each other—and we have fun. We can go on with our lives in between because we know we will have another time together next month. We live in afterglow and anticipation.

"So, what's my answer to the question that you gave back to me? I try not to think of what we're doing as something we shouldn't be doing. I know that lots of people would condemn us, would say we're doing something immoral, even cruel. But they haven't been where Frank has been for years, having the person who used to be your lover screaming at you and hitting you—or where I have, feeling every day the emptiness that comes when the person who used to be your lover is ripped out of your life forever.

"I honestly don't think we're doing what we're doing at anyone's expense; it's a gift we give each other." She stopped speaking and searched his face and waited; when he didn't respond she continued in a softer voice. "Walter, I know I'm dancing a risky dance—that I'm doing something that could take me over the edge. I'm not asking you to approve or condone what I'm doing; I'm only asking you to understand. Do you understand?" She stopped and stared at him and waited.

He took a deep breath and let it out slowly. He spoke carefully. "My heart understands. But," he went on after a long pause, "there's more to consider than that—and it may catch up to you, Molly."

She nodded knowingly. "What your heart understands is enough for me right now; we can deal with the more another time."

He looked straight into her eyes. "We will—when you're ready." He paused for a moment. "But, that's not today, is it?"

She shook her head side to side. "No, it's not."

5. IN THE SHADOWS

It was almost four in the afternoon the following Thursday when Gary Shanahan parked his rig at the truck stop south of the I-80 exit east of Tinley Park. He was relieved to find an open slot and settle into it before the afternoon commuter traffic from Chicago clogged the interstate. He'd planned to fill his fuel tanks before he parked, but four o'clock was too late; he didn't want to risk taking time to fuel and not get a space where he could sleep for at least part of the night.

The stop in Tinley Park was the lone overnight on the short trip he made every two weeks. Early Wednesday he parked his old pickup at the North East Trucking garage in Albany where a tractor-trailer loaded mostly with bundles of packing boxes was waiting for him. He took the load from Albany to Appliance Park in Syracuse. Workers at the warehouse unloaded everything except the large cardboard packing containers marked "Samsung Washing Machine" with delivery labels for "South Chicago Appliance." They filled the trailer with crates of new GE washers and dryers, and he drove through the night to the South Chicago Appliance warehouse in Joliet, Illinois.

It was dusk when a knock on the window woke him up. The hookers were working the lot, but the woman who knocked on the passenger side window of his truck was no ordinary hooker. She was too well cared for. It was Lorna. He had checked in with her earlier in the day when she signed for the washers and dryers he delivered to the Joliet Warehouse. Lorna was the one who made everything go there. She was a real looker; every driver who came to the warehouse looked her over. But they knew better than to make a move on her. Jack who owned the warehouse also owned Lorna; she was his girl Friday. Sometimes she was his girl Friday, Saturday, and Sunday.

Gary looked out through the window, unlocked the door and pushed it open. Lorna struggled to lift her leg high enough to step up onto the high running board. Her short skirt rose to the tops of her legs. To anyone watching from a distance she looked the part. Gary reached down, took hold of her hand and pulled her up. She got in quickly and pulled the door shut. She raised her arms and held them in the cold air blowing out of the AC, "Jesus, what a hot night for September!"

"Yeah, glad for the AC; the noise is better'n the heat."

She took a large, fat envelope from the side pocket of her purse and a small one from inside it and handed both of them to him. The large one was sealed and taped; the flap was tucked into the top of the small one. Gary slid the large one into a hidden slit at the base of the back of the driver's seat. He opened the small one and counted five hundred-dollar bills. He unzipped one of the zippered pockets of the N.E.T. driver's jacket that was on the hook next to him and took out a roll of bills. He slid the rubber band off the roll, added the new bills and put the roll back inside the jacket pocket and zipped it up.

Lorna laughed when he crumpled up the small envelope and tossed it onto the floor. "How many times have we done this, Gary, and you've never even tried to touch me?"

"And won't. You're a marked woman, Lorna. You're more dangerous than jailbait."

She sighed and shrugged her shoulders.

"I'm no good with a long-haul woman anyway. I'm a one-overnight-is-enough kind of guy. I get home from a trip and I'm happy to see Lauren. We have a good time when she gets home from waitressing at Johnny's, but by lunchtime the next day I get antsy." He sighed. "She always wants to talk about stuff like when we'll get a house, and where it will be, and when we'll have kids, and how many. I have no idea when any of that will happen—whether it'll ever happen. By afternoon I can't wait for her to go to work. When she leaves I go to the sports bar down the street from our apartment. I have a few beers and a sandwich, play some foosball and watch a game. I hope she'll be asleep when I get home—and she usually is. I get up early and leave the next morning before she wakes up. I get back home in a week and we run the same routine."

"And that's it? That's what you want?" She looked incredulous.

He nodded. "It's enough; any more would be too much. She's my convenience." He grinned.

She shook her head back and forth. "You don't want a wife, Gary, you want a live-in hooker!"

He smiled. "Like you."

"You couldn't afford me; I'm too pricey for you."

"Yeah, I know. Besides, I'm savin' my money. I've almost got enough saved to buy my own truck. I been lookin' at used Freightliners. Eight more trips to your warehouse and I'll have enough for a down payment. Then I'll be an owner and get to keep the money that N.E.T. makes off me now." He reached over and patted the zippered pocket in his jacket. "My nest egg's all in there."

"You're not thinking of quitting?" She looked frightened.

"Yep, I got it all planned out."

"Have you said anything to anybody at N.E.T. about doing it?"

"Nope. They'd can me!"

"It'd be worse than that, Gary."

"How so?"

"Don't ever say anything to anybody that even hints you might quit. You can't quit this operation. Nobody close to it can. You know too much; you know what's in those fat envelopes, what it's for and where it goes and how it's connected with what's inside the washers in those cartons you haul from Albany to here every two weeks."

He shook his head back and forth. "Not really. As long as it won't blow up the trailer whatever's inside those cartons is none of my business. I suspect it's stuff I don't want to get into; you get into that stuff and it takes over your life." He grinned. "I'm Irish; beer and whiskey's enough for me. As to the fat envelopes I suspect there's money in them, but I've never opened one. They stay in that slot in the back of the seat. I park the truck and lock it when I get back to Albany. After I drop the key in the office whoever knows where the slot is gets the key, unlocks the truck and takes the envelope out. I don't know who gets them and I don't know what happens to them."

"But you know they exist and that's enough for them to be concerned about. If you quit, they'll take you out. It's as easy for them as erasing a mistake on a ledger. Nobody knows what happens to you; you're just gone." She paused for a couple of seconds and he thought he could see tears forming in her eyes. "That's the way it'll be with me when Jack's done with me. Our lives are written in pencil, Gary."

He shrugged his shoulders. "Yours, maybe, but not mine."

She stared at him and shook her head. "I gotta go. I've been here long enough to satisfy a customer. Help me get out." She roughed up her hair; the cab light went on when she opened the door. He held her hand while she stepped out onto the running board; he leaned out and let her down gently onto the pavement. She looked up at him, "Jack's people are worse than the Viet Cong, Gary, there's no escaping them. If they suspect you might jump ship, they'll go after you—and Lauren too if they think she knows about the stuff you bring here from Albany." She let go of his hand. "See you in two weeks."

6. THE LEGALIST

In his classes at Schuylerkill Falls Central High School George Morrison taught his students that the axioms of mathematics and the laws of physics were beyond questioning. In his Sunday school classes at the Schuylerkill Falls Presbyterian Church he taught the same students that true religion was founded on equally indisputable axioms of belief. George was governed by axioms; there was neither grace nor forgiveness in his world. On a hook by his desk a fly swatter hung ready to reprimand errant insects.

That George happened to walk from his classroom into the hall at four-thirty the previous Friday afternoon just as Kristen Klein came out of Coach Frank Perelli's office was an unfortunate coincidence. George stood still and stared as Kristen laughed and kissed Frank on the cheek.

Kristen was startled when she turned around and saw George in the hallway staring at her after Frank had gone back into his office. She smiled uneasily as she walked by him.

There was no question in George's mind that Kristen and Frank were guilty of something improper. Even though the coaches' office door was open when he walked down the hall three-quarters of an hour before and he could hear someone talking with Frank he concluded that something illicit must have taken place between Kristen and Frank—probably in the locker room that adjoined the coaches' office. Why else would she kiss him?

During the lunch period on Monday George shared his concern with Principal Jerry Ward. Jerry listened carefully. When George finished, he said, "George, you have no clear evidence that anything improper occurred; I think you may be jumping to conclusions. I know we discourage physical shows of affection between students and faculty as a matter of policy—and I'll remind Frank of that. Kristen came to see me early this morning before classes began and said she was concerned that you saw her kiss Frank on the cheek Friday afternoon. She said she had a personal problem and sought Frank out and that he listened to her and was very helpful. She said the kiss was simply a spontaneous gesture of thanks. Until there is clear evidence to the contrary, I suggest we consider it that. If there is anything more to discover, that will become apparent as time passes. In the meantime, I ask that you keep your suspicions to yourself."

George didn't respond; he just sat and looked out the window. When the bell rang he stood up and walked out of the principal's office.

After classes were finished for the day George called Walter Macdonald, his pastor, and made an appointment to meet with him late the following afternoon at the manse. As the two of them sat in Walter's study Walter listened carefully as George shared what he had seen happen between Kristen and Frank—and what he thought it implied.

"But you have no direct evidence that anything wrong occurred, George. Kristen could simply have been grateful."

George turned away and stared at the theology books in the bookcase on the other side of the room. When he turned back toward Walter he was frowning. "Perhaps she was, but there's something else that involves Frank Perelli and one of our church members that I think you should know about—and it may be pertinent.

"Last month Shirley and I went away to Middlebury for the weekend. On Saturday night after dinner, on our way back to our motel, as we drove past the Middlebury Inn, we saw Molly Hutchins and Frank holding hands and walking up the walkway to the inn's front door." He paused to be certain he had Walter's full attention. "I suspect they're having an affair, Walter—why else would they be entering an inn together that far away from home at eight-thirty in the evening?"

He paused and waited for Walter to respond. When Walter didn't speak, he continued. "That's why I'm suspicious of what Frank was doing with Kristen. If he will take liberties with one woman, he will do it with another. Probably you didn't know that something is going on between Frank and Molly. But as her pastor, I think you should know. If I were her pastor, I would confront her about it."

Walter took a deep breath and shook his head. He looked directly at George when he spoke. "I am her pastor, George, not her judge. As church elders our job is to help, not judge."

"But they're breaking the seventh commandment!"

"You have no direct evidence of that, George. What you consider evidence both for them and for Frank and Kristen is completely circumstantial—and I doubt that the two incidents are related. Besides, what two consenting adults may do is quite different from the possibility that an adult would take advantage of a minor."

As he continued, he searched in vain for any appearance of softening on George's face. "I can't believe Frank would make advances on a student, George—particularly in a place as public as the coaches' office. Two other coaches share that office; it has doors that open to the gym and the boy's locker room. At least one other coach would be around at that time of day; kids would be practicing in the gym.

"If I thought there was anything to be concerned about with Kristen, I would certainly follow up with Frank. Kristen is a student and not of age and he's her coach; it would be a criminal act. But I honestly don't think we have any evidence that would indicate anything other than a spontaneous show of gratitude."

He stared at George for a moment. "So far as Molly is concerned, do you recall the incident in John's Gospel when Jesus comes upon the Pharisees and a woman caught in the act of adultery and they are going to stone her because that's what the Law of Moses prescribes?"

"Of course, everyone knows that story; it's at the beginning of chapter eight."

"Then, as an elder of our church, I suggest you recall what Jesus told those elders. Do you remember what he said?"

"He said to the woman, '"Go and do not sin again."'"

"No, I mean what he said to the elders before that."

"He said, 'Let him who is without sin among you be the first to throw a stone at her.'"

"And then what happened?"

"They went away quietly beginning with the eldest."

"George, I suggest we leave the stones on the ground and like those chastened Pharisees in John's Gospel, go away quietly. Molly is a person of faith. She may be struggling right now to find the right way, but in time she will. Those of us who are part of her faith community need to help her walk on not put her down." He stood up; he was very tall. George glared at him and, without another word, stood up, walked out of the room and left through the front door of the manse.

As Walter watched him walk quickly to his car he thought, "George stands back from life and judges. He's afraid to participate himself. He won't dance." He sighed and shook his head. "I know that what I said won't stop him, but it may slow him down. He'll keep at it; he won't forgive Molly because if he did, he'd have to deal with her. She's all too aware that what she's doing with Frank is on the edge. She needs companions, not accusers. Given time she'll find her way. If she needs me to help her, she'll ask me. Someone's kitchen is no place for pulpit bullying."

He leaned back in his chair and gazed out the window at the church steeple next door. "George's God is like a cosmic police officer who sits just out of sight alongside the road of life. He enforces his commandments by running spiritual radar to catch violators, and then doles out quick and mean punishment. He never honors moral emergencies that would justify living in the fast lane even for a little while." He sighed and shook his head. "Who would want to be close to that kind of God? Not me." He laughed under his breath. "If George knew what I believe God is like, he'd probably have me arrested for speeding. But so would lots of church people."

He sat in the quiet for a while and then looked through the door that led into the dining room. "Maybe I shouldn't have put Kristen off so quickly when she wanted to help me clean up after the youth group meeting? But I wouldn't want to be found alone with her here in the house after dark; you never know when somebody like George will drop by."

He took a deep breath. "I wonder if Kristen has talked with her Aunt Katherine about what happened with George. She seems easier with Katherine right now than she is with her mother. Maybe I'll give Katherine a call and see if I can stop by talk with her on one of the days she's in town."

7. BLIND DATE

Walter's introduction to Dr. Katherine Klein happened in typical Dr. Erik Peterson fashion. During the coffee hour following the church service one Sunday in July Erik pulled him aside. "You may have heard that I'm taking on a partner in the fall. Her name is Katherine Klein and she has a special interest in OB-GYN. She's currently a doc at Saratoga Women's Care, the big OB-GYN practice in Saratoga Springs that her father started years ago. I turned sixty-four last year and I'm getting weary with the OB part of my practice—too much getting up in the middle of the night to wait around for babies to decide to make their appearance.

"So, beginning in September Katherine's going to be working with me two days a week. There's a nice furnished apartment above the office where she can stay overnight if she wants to. Becky and I invited her to have dinner with us Wednesday. We'd like her to meet you; you're a tad old for her, but you're the only eligible bachelor close to her age in Schuylerkill Falls. Can you come for dinner Wednesday?"

"Are you setting me up?"

He grinned. "Well, Walter, someone needs to; you're nearly fifty and languishing."

"Erik, I'm three years away from fifty; that's far from languishing!" He gave a friendly scowl and shook his head. "But I don't have a meeting Wednesday evening and I'll be delighted to join you. Even if I don't hit it off with the doctor, I know the food will be excellent!"

But he did hit it off with the doctor. She was bright, pretty and nearly tall enough to look him in the eye—which made her dark brown eyes, fair skin and authentically blond hair even more striking. After Becky and Erik introduced them and they were settled into comfortable chairs in the expanded area of Peterson's large kitchen drinking one of Erik's good reds Katherine said, "Well, tell me about you, Walter. Erik tells me you played basketball and baseball at Union College—and still do pretty well at both of them."

"I did play some—at Mt. Pleasant High in Schenectady, then at Union College, and I still coach both sports at the high school here, and, even though I'm not a Schuylerkill Falls graduate, I play with the old-timers in the annual benefit alumni-against-varsity basketball game every year."

Erik interrupted from the other end of the kitchen where he was making a salad, "Katherine, he's being too modest. Walter was named Most Valuable Player at Mt. Pleasant High School and at Union in his junior and senior years at both schools in both sports. He pitched not just one but *two* no-hitters at Union; nobody's ever done that but him. The autographed game balls sit on top of the desk in his study. He can still throw a mean fastball." Walter felt his face coloring as Erik continued, "Now, he should know about you, Katherine."

Becky walked past them carrying some dishes to the dining room. "Do the two of you feel like you're being interviewed on a talk show?" She glanced back toward the other side of the kitchen. "Erik, honey, lighten up!" She laughed.

Walter smiled, glanced toward Erik and shrugged his shoulders. "He won't; I found that out long ago; whenever Erik's around he takes charge."

Katherine nodded. "I know; I work with him. But he probably thinks you'd want to know that I played some basketball when I was in high school and then some six-on-six in college. But basketball lost out to the need for high grades. I needed to stay at the four-point level so I'd be sure to get into med school."

Erik interrupted again. "Another too-modest person! Her legitimately proud dad told me that she was MVP for two years at Saratoga High and led them to a state championship in her senior year. They gave her the game ball; I bet she still has it." He stood opposite them carrying a large bowl of salad. "I bet you can still put balls through the hoop with finesse, Katherine. Sometime, you ought to try going one-on-one on the basketball court against the local boys' basketball coach!"

Walter grinned, "Maybe we should! Are you game, doctor?"

"I am!"

Becky stood in the doorway to the dining room. "We interrupt this program for an important announcement. It's time for dinner!"

Dinner was delicious, as always. As they lingered over coffee, Erik took charge again. "You're sitting across from a Presbyterian minister, Katherine. He'd probably like to know about your unique religious background."

Becky interrupted quickly. "You really don't have to get into that, Katherine." She glanced toward Erik and scowled. "He's being pretty pushy."

Katherine sighed and shook her head back and forth. "It's characteristic of male doctors—as I'm sure you know. Actually, I don't mind because it would come out sooner or later and I'm really comfortable talking about it." She looked at Walter and tilted her head. "So, when Erik and Becky introduced us I'll bet you probably thought it was 'Kline,' spelled 'K-L-I-N-E'?"

Walter nodded, "You're right; I did."

"Well, it's 'Klein,' spelled 'K-L-E-I-N,' just like Kristen Klein who's in your high school youth group. She's my niece; my brother was her father."

"Well, that clears up a mystery! I've always thought Kristen doesn't look like a Klein." He stopped abruptly and laughed defensively. "I can't believe I said that; it was awkward, wasn't it?"

"It's all right; I'm used to it. Here's the story. I'm a hybrid: my mother is a Swedish Lutheran and my father is a German Jew. That makes me a Jewish Lutheran—now there's a combination for you! But I'm not just an ethnic hybrid, I became a religious hybrid too; my parents decided to expose me and my brothers to both faiths as we were growing up so we could make an 'informed choice' as adults. So, up through my teenage years I went to Sabbath services in Saratoga at the synagogue with my dad and to Sunday morning services at the Lutheran Church with my mom. I did a Bat Mitzvah when I was twelve and Lutheran confirmation when I was fourteen. To be honest, at times it was a little awkward—like I was committing religious bigamy, but like the infamous bigamist Mr. Pennypacker I decided not to tell each about the other—and nobody asked."

"So, which of the two did you choose?"

She shrugged her shoulders. "I guess you would say I've ended up eclectic: I chose what I think is the best of both. From what I suspect is your perspective, I think you would say I'm a marginal Jewish-Lutheran hybrid. But to be brutally honest, I've mostly shed the historical baggage: I've become a non-participating, very selective sometimes believer." She watched his face; she couldn't tell how he felt about what she said, so she decided to lighten things up. "Looking back I have to confess that the Jewish side almost won. The party at a Bat Mitzvah is a heck of lot more fun than the tame celebration that follows confirmation!"

He laughed. "I've never been to a Bat Mitzvah, but I've heard that Bar and Bat Mitzvah parties can be pretty raucous." He looked at the others at the table. "I think this conversation is on the verge of getting too serious for the present company (Erik nodded), but sometime I would like to talk about how you can keep up with even parts of two faiths. I have everything I can do to manage one!"

"Well, Walter, if you buy the wine, I'll answer the question."

"It's a deal."

But it was now October and they hadn't found a time to get together and have that conversation. She was consumed with getting established in a new practice and he was busy with fall start-up activity at the church. She came to the Sunday morning service once and stayed for the coffee hour afterward. A week later he saw her for a few minutes at Jim's market. Each time he wanted to set up a time when they could talk more, but he didn't want to ask her where someone might overhear.

The Thursday after George left in anger, he saw Erik before a committee meeting at the church and asked if he could share a personal telephone number for Katherine. Erik grinned and recited it from memory. "It's about time you called her, Walter. She's beginning to think you're not interested."

Walter gave him a quizzical look. "She actually said something that would make you think that?"

"She talks about it all the time."

"You're full of it, Erik!"

"You're a great ball player and preacher, Walter, but when it comes to women you need a coach, or you'll never get off the bench."

The committee meeting was unusually short; Walter was home at a quarter to nine. He walked through the kitchen into his study and punched in Katherine's number on the telephone. She answered on the second ring. "This is Dr. Klein."

"Hi, Katherine, this is Walter Macdonald."

"Walter! How are you?"

"I'm great; I just got home from a meeting I thought would last two hours and it lasted less than one!"

"That never happens to me."

Suddenly he felt awkward; he was slow to respond. "Well . . . I'm calling because . . . I wonder if we could get together sometime to . . ."

She interrupted, "I would enjoy that."

The tone in her voice relaxed him. ". . . for two reasons: the first is so we can compare calendars and set a time to drink the bottle of wine I promised to buy when we were at Erik and Becky's all the way back in July."

"That would be delightful."

"But there's something else I want to talk over with you before that—something pastoral. It involves your niece, Kristen."

"If you mean what happened with George Morrison, she's already told me; we had a long talk about it on Monday."

"That is what I mean. Maybe we could get together and talk sometime soon? I think I need to do some follow-up with George."

"Sounds like he's the one who needs to do some follow-up."

"I agree, but I still want to get together with you. I'd suggest meeting at the diner for breakfast or lunch, but I don't think it's the kind of thing we want to talk about in a public place."

"You're right; that wouldn't be smart—too many curious ears in the next booths. Here's an idea: I usually drive from Saratoga to here on Sunday evening and stay over because I begin seeing patients early on Mondays. Erik does our rounds at the hospital on Monday mornings so I'm free for breakfast. I stay in that nice apartment upstairs from the office, but there's still a big kitchen downstairs we could meet in. Could you walk over about seven? I'll bring some real bagels from the bagel shop in Saratoga. We'd have an hour to talk before I'd have to go to work. How's that sound?"

"Sounds like a plan. See you Monday at seven. I'll bring my date book and a wine list."

Monday morning just before seven he walked up the steps and onto the back porch of the large Victorian house Erik had converted into offices. When Katherine opened the door he could smell coffee. She held out her hand, "Walter, it's really nice to see you."

He took hold of her hand; it was warm. "I'm delighted that we could finally get together—even if this is kind of a work meeting." He looked around the room. "This is such a great, old kitchen. It's nice that he saved it when he and Becky moved to the farm and he transformed this house into offices; the wainscoting is magnificent."

"I really like this room. It's a place where we can escape to sip coffee between patients and when we break for lunch. I have a nice apartment upstairs—I'll show it to you sometime. Coffee and a bagel?" She passed the plate of bagels to him.

"Thank you; there's nothing like a real bagel-shop bagel." He chose one from the plate and took a bite. "Well, we don't have a lot of time so I guess we should get to the topic of the day."

She nodded.

"George Morrison is a member of my church—and, sometimes, not an easy one to deal with. A week ago Friday he happened to be coming out of his classroom into the hall when Kristen finished talking about a personal problem with Frank Perelli—he's one of the coaches at the high school."

"I know; Kristen told me."

"Apparently Kristen had something painful happen to her and she chose to talk it over with Frank. He's had lots of pain in his own life so I'm sure she sensed he could empathize with her. When she left Frank's office she kissed Frank on the cheek—I'm sure it was just a spontaneous show of gratitude. She didn't realize anyone was in the hall, but George happened to be there. He read things into the gesture that Kristen didn't intend. He thinks he has cause to be suspicious of Frank; I'm not free to talk about why, except to say that it doesn't involve Kristen. I know both Kristen and Frank pretty well and I doubt that anything improper went on between them that day or any other day, for that matter."

"It didn't. I hope you can find a way to make it clear to him that nothing questionable is going on between Kristen and Frank—because nothing is."

"I already have. George came to see me after school on Monday and I told him that casting suspicions he has no evidence for makes him the one who is out of line. I was *very* firm with him, but I doubt that what I said will stop him entirely." He paused and thought for a moment. "If you're comfortable doing it, maybe it would be smart to tell Erik what's going on. He's an elder in our church. If he knows what's happening and George begins to spread gossip, he might be able to hit him hard enough to get him stopped."

"That's a good idea. I'll check with Kristen to be sure she's okay with Erik knowing before I talk with him, but I'm sure she will be." She paused and reflected for a moment. "Probably it's important for you to know what happened to Kristen that got all of this started. After you called, I phoned her and asked her if I could share it with you and she said I could—that you would understand." She stood up. "Would you like more coffee before I get started?"

"Yes, and another bagel, if that's all right. I ran two miles this morning, half of it before dawn."

"That's impressive, but I knew you'd eat more than one before I knew about the run. That's why I brought six. Please have another one." She smiled, passed him the plate, filled their coffee cups and sat back down at the table.

"Two weeks ago Kristen was up in the attic at her house and came across a box filled with some newspaper clippings that describe the accident when her father was killed on the Northway on his way back from a meeting in Montreal. Did you know about that tragedy?"

He took a quick breath. "I did, and even though I should have connected the dots when we met at Erik's the other night and you spelled your last name, I didn't realize that Kristen's father was your brother. The aftermath of the accident must have been a horrible experience to live through."

She looked away but recovered quickly and nodded. "It was. It was very hard—still is." She paused, then went on. "When Kristen read the clippings she discovered that there was another woman in the car that day. Her name was Kimberly Thomaston. When Kristen's mother came home Kristen asked her who Kimberly Thomaston was, and my sister, Erin, told her the truth; her dad was having an affair."

He sat up and shook his head. "I didn't know about that."

She sighed. "Well, Walter, it happens even to the best people. Kristen's dad, my brother, Tom, was a brilliant microbiologist. Kimberly was one of his lab assistants and a doctoral candidate. They worked long hours together, often late into the night. It was a classic set-up—even to her name, Kimberly. No one knew Kimberly had spent three days with him in Montreal until the accident happened on their way home.

"Learning the truth about her dad devastated Kristen. The real dad she remembers from the time she was as a three-year-old has always been a hero to her. She built up a myth about him. The truth demolished her myth and she needed someone to talk with. She's never been close to Matt, her stepdad, so she chose Frank. He listened and held her while she sobbed. After she got it all out, he told her that her dad could still be her hero. He said even the greatest heroes have blemishes. We all have blemishes." She stopped and searched his eyes. "Don't we, Walter?"

He spoke softly. "Yes, we do—all of us."

"Kristen was still hurting when they finished talking, but she felt like she would be able to deal with the hurt. When she left Frank's office she turned around and spontaneously kissed him on the cheek. George Morrison happened to be in the hall and saw them. That's all that happened."

Walter took a deep breath and let it out slowly. "No wonder Kristen needed to talk with someone."

"Actually Kristen said she really wanted to talk with you about it before she went to Frank, but you said you couldn't when she asked you after a youth group meeting because you had to check on an elderly parishioner."

The comment cut into him like a bitter winter wind. "I did have to check on someone, but that could have waited. I should have been more sensitive to Kristen. I knew she was upset; I shouldn't have put her off."

She saw the pained expression on his face. "Don't be hard on yourself, Walter. We all make those choices. Kristen got what she needed from Frank; that's what matters." She looked at the clock on the wall. "It's ten minutes to eight; I should go out front and scan the charts of the patients I will see beginning at eight-thirty."

"Understand. One more question before I go. I still haven't come through with the bottle of wine I promised you. Are you here next Monday and Tuesday?"

"I am."

"After you finish with patients on Monday would you like to come to my house and relax over that bottle of wine and have dinner? I cook pretty well."

She laughed. "I'm sure you do. I'm on call next weekend which means Erik will take calls weeknights next week—so I won't have to worry that someone will need a doctor and I'll get paged. What can I bring?"

"You don't have to bring anything," (he paused) "but if you really want to contribute something, you could bring dessert. I cook quite well—like I said, but by all reports my baking is terrible."

"Well, the opposite is true for me, so we make a good pair. I'll get some tasty cheeses to add to the hors d'oeuvres and I'll make a chocolate cake for dessert." She stood up and held out her hand. "Thanks for caring about Kristen. See you next Monday at seven. When it comes to wine, I like anything that is red and dry."

He opened his eyes wide. "You're in luck: I've got two bottles of an excellent Haut Medoc on hand. When you arrive just walk down the drive and come in through the kitchen door. Only people who come for pastoral counseling use the front door—and that's not what I want to do when you come for dinner."

She looked at him soberly. "Walter, I hope we become friends, but I need to tell you that wine and conversation is all I do."

He nodded his head slowly and smiled as he stood up. "That's okay; wine and good conversation is what I had in mind."

8. OUT OF CONTROL

When he walked around the corner from Maple Street onto Church Street Walter noticed a car parked in front of the manse. As he walked past the car the woman sitting alone in the driver's seat turned her head away from him. He walked up the steps onto the side porch and through the kitchen into his study to check for messages on his answering machine. When he looked up from the machine his eye caught someone walking up the porch steps. He heard a gentle knocking on the kitchen door.

When he opened the door, he was startled. A mass of bruises covered the tear-stained face of the young woman who stood on the porch. Her lips were badly swollen. Both of her eyes were black; one was nearly swollen shut. Spots of dried blood were scattered through the hair on one side of her scalp.

She was asleep Sunday night when Gary came home to their apartment. He took off his shoes and walked quietly into the bathroom. When he was finished in the bathroom and came back into the living room to shut out the light, he noticed that his N.E.T. jacket was missing from the hook by the front door.

Panic shot through him. He walked quickly into the bedroom and rummaged through everything in the closet. It wasn't there. He ran into the kitchen and pulled all the clothes hanging on the hooks by the back door onto the floor. It wasn't there. Then he saw it hanging on a clothes hanger above the clothes dryer. It had been washed. He grabbed it, unzipped the zipper pocket, and pulled out the wad of bills and counted them. They were all there; they hadn't gotten wet.

Lauren had awakened and walked up behind him. He turned and scowled and held out the jacket, "Why did you wash this?"

"It was filthy. I don't think it's been washed for a year."

"Why didn't you tell me you were going to wash it?"

"You weren't home."

He shouted at her, "What's that supposed to mean?"

"Nothing. Please don't shout at me."

"But you saw the money."

"Yes. I was careful with it; it didn't get wet."

"You're not supposed to know about it. It's my secret."

"Well, I know about it now. We aren't supposed to keep secrets from each other."

Anger spread across his face. "Don't scold me about secrets. I know about your little secret."

"I don't know what you mean."

"What do you do on Thursdays, Lauren? Who do you spend the night with?"

She turned away and looked at the floor as she said, "His name is Ed."

"Well, I know about your secret nights with Ed. Tonight I ran into Tammy who works at Johnny's with you. I bought her enough drinks to loosen her mouth. He's fucking you, Lauren, isn't he?"

She spoke softly. "Ed doesn't fuck me, Gary; he makes love to me."

Her comment enraged him; he grabbed both her arms. "You're a bitch, Lauren Shanahan. You're just a bitch in heat!"

She winced and tried to pull away. "Gary, stop, you're hurting me!"

"Maybe that's what you need: a little discipline from your husband so you'll behave like a wife." He hit her cheek with his fist so hard that she fell on the floor.

She screamed, "Stop, Gary!" She pulled herself up and ran into the kitchen.

He ran after her and grabbed her and hit the other side of her face. "Now you'll have a black eye on that side that matches the one on the other side."

"You're a bastard, Gary Shanahan!" she screamed. She dragged her fingernails down the side of his face.

He reached up and felt blood. He grabbed her arm and screamed at her, "You cut me!" He threw her across the kitchen. Her head struck the side of the kitchen counter and she fell onto the floor. She didn't move. He stood for a minute and stared at her. "You'll come to; you won't die. I'm gonna get my stuff and get out of here. I've had too much of you. I have to take a truck west in the morning. That'll give you a week to come to your senses."

She spoke softly. "Are you Reverend Macdonald?"

"I am; you're hurt, please come in."

She walked through the door into the kitchen.

He pulled a chair away from the kitchen table and she sat down. "How can I help you?"

She looked at him carefully. "I'm Lauren Shanahan. Ed Hutchins is my friend. He's told me about you; maybe you can tell me how to find him? I've never been to where he works. I know it's somewhere here in Schuylerkill Falls and that he works for a man named Butch, but I don't know Butch's last name or the name of the garage. I need help." She began to cry.

Walter spoke softly. "I'll call Ed and he'll come here, and we'll get you some help. What happened, Lauren?" He waited for her to stop crying.

"Ed said you are the smartest and caringest person he knows—besides me." She smiled slightly. "He said a person can tell you anything—that you don't judge people, even though you're a minister."

"I just try to help." He paused and then said, "And I know who you are. You're the Thursday girl."

She looked straight at him, "Then you know that Ed and I are in love—and that I'm married to someone else."

Walter nodded.

"It's not a good marriage, Mr. Macdonald. It hasn't been for a long time. It's tolerable only because my husband, Gary, is a trucker and away most of the time.

"Gary's never asked what I do when he's away; I thought he probably didn't care. I've wanted out of the marriage for a long time; I just haven't had the courage to tell him. I've always been afraid of him. Late last night we had an argument. I found out something about him that he didn't want me to know. He got really angry and told me he'd learned about Ed. I should have known how he would react. He's proud and doesn't really love me anymore. He flew into a rage and screamed at me and beat me with his fists. He called me a bitch and threw me across the room. My head hit the kitchen counter and I was knocked out. When I came to, he was gone. My head hurts awful."

"That's terrible, Lauren; I'm so sorry. Have you seen a doctor?"

"No, I don't have money for that. The girl who lives next door woke up when she heard all the commotion. She came over after Gary left and tried to clean me up and wrapped some ice in a wash cloth so I could ice my head. I just want to find Ed. I want desperately to be with him, but I'm so afraid he'll want to kill Gary when he sees me." She began to cry again.

Walter looked out the window for a moment, then back at her. "I know Ed pretty well, Lauren. When he sees you and learns what your husband did to you, he'll be angry, but he'll get hold of himself. I can't honestly believe he could kill anybody—not after what he saw when he was in Vietnam.

"Right now I think the most important thing is to get you to a doctor. I know you think your injuries aren't serious, but that's a nasty wound on the side of your head. I don't mean to frighten you, but head injuries that aren't treated right away can have serious consequences. I know a doctor who will check you out and won't be concerned if you can't pay him. Will you see him? I know if I call him, he will see you right away."

She looked away for a while, then turned back and looked at him. She spoke softly, "What about Ed?"

"He works at the Front Street Garage for a man named Butch Chichester. I'll call him and tell him you're here and ask him to come over. Then I'll call the doctor and you and he can go to the doctor's. All right?"

She nodded. "All right."

He picked up the telephone and punched in the garage's number. "Butch, this is Walter Macdonald. I'd like to talk with Ed, please. Thanks." He paused. "Hi Ed, Lauren Shanahan is sitting here with me in my kitchen. She needs to see you right away . . . No, it's better that we don't talk about why on the phone . . . She's been hurt, but she's going to be all right. Please just come over." He listened for a moment and then hung up. "He'll be here in two minutes."

"Thank you; you need to be here when he sees me."

"I know. Now, I want to call the doctor's office. Will you go there?"

"If Ed will go with me."

"I'm sure he will; Dr. Peterson has been his doctor since he was a baby." He picked up the telephone and punched in the number for Erik's office. "Sue, this is Walter Macdonald. A young woman is sitting with me in my kitchen. She says her husband beat her during the night; she has lots of bruises on her face and a bad cut on the side of her head. I'm concerned that she could have serious injuries that aren't obvious. Would Erik have time to see her this morning?" He paused. "No, I know she could treat her, but I think this is someone Erik should see." He paused again. "Yes, we can do that. Her name is Lauren Sha-nahan; she's a friend of Ed Hutchins. Yes, they'll come to the side door and go into the kitchen and wait there. Thanks very much."

He hung up the telephone. "Dr. Peterson's receptionist said he will see you in a half-hour. His office is just two blocks from here. His receptionist suggested that you and Ed walk down the driveway and go in through the side door and wait in the kitchen so you won't have to sit with a lot of people in the waiting room. I'm sure Ed will take you." He looked out the window. "He's driving in right now."

Ed jumped out of his pick-up and ran up the steps and into the kitchen as Walter opened the door. He knelt down on the floor in front of Lauren and took hold of her hands. "Oh my God, Lauren, what happened? Were you in an accident?"

"No," she looked at the floor and then up at Ed. "I . . . told Gary about us late last night. I didn't think he would care, but he went crazy."

Ed shook his head back and forth and clenched his teeth. "He did this to you? I'll kill him! I'll find the bastard and I'll kill him! I know just how I'll do it."

Lauren took his head between her hands and looked straight at him. "No, Ed, no! Don't even think about going there. I want him out of my life—out of our life. He's gone. If you hurt him, that will bring him back—and I could lose you. We can have each other now. Don't mess it up, Ed, because you're angry."

He looked at her. "But I'm so angry, my beautiful Lauren." The tears ran down his face.

Walter interrupted. I'll go into the next room for a while so you can be alone. I'll come back in a few minutes when it's time for you to go and see Dr. Peterson. Lauren has an appointment, Ed. Can you take her? I'll call Butch and tell him you'll be away for at least an hour. All right?"

"Thanks, Coach."

Not quite ten minutes had passed when Walter heard a knock on the door to his study. Ed spoke when he opened it. "We're headed to the doctor's, now. We'll take Lauren's car. The keys are in my truck if you need to move it."

"That's fine, Ed. If I need to go somewhere, I'll pull the keys out and throw them under the seat."

An hour later Sue called from Erik's office. "Walter, this is Sue. Julie is finishing up with Lauren's wounds. You were wise to bring her here; she's been badly beaten. She has lots of bruises on her body and one of her cheek bones may be cracked, but Erik is most concerned about the wound on the side of her head. She says her head aches badly; Erik's worried that there may be some damage inside her skull. We put in a call to Dr. Marcellino; he's a neurosurgeon at Albany Med. Ed is going to take Lauren to the ER there; we called them, so they'll be ready for her when she gets there. It'll take a while for them to treat her; Erik is sure Dr. Marcellino will want to take x-rays. If they find something serious going on inside her head, they'll have to admit her. Ed is going to stay there with her and asked that you call Butch and tell him what's happening and that he probably won't be back for the rest of today—that he'll come in early and stay late tomorrow to catch up."

"I'll call Butch; I'm sure he'll understand."

"Lauren said she didn't notify the police. Did you call them?"

"No, I was waiting to hear from you."

"Well, we have to, as you know; there's little doubt that this is battery. It's a crime." She lost her composure for a minute. "It's a god-awful crime, Walter." She struggled to recover. "Sorry, sometimes this is tough job."

"I know; I was barely able to keep it together myself when Lauren told me what happened."

"Lauren gave us her address and told us that her husband's name is Gary. When we call the Albany PD, we'll tell them that she's headed for the ER at Albany Med and they'll send someone over to interview her. They'll check with the company her husband drives for to find out where he is and when he's due home from his trip. I'm sure they'll meet him and arrest him. Lauren said he'll be gone for a week, but Erik told her she needs to get a protection order right away—just in case. The police can take her husband to their apartment when he comes back so he can get whatever he needs to have to move out. If they suspect he might go after her again, they'll keep him under surveillance. Erik told her she shouldn't go back to her apartment alone until she can be sure it's safe for her to be there. Maybe you can help her find some place to stay for a while?"

"I can do that. Did she talk about Ed Hutchins?"

"Yeah, she's worried he'll go after her husband."

"Well, I honestly don't think he will. She talked straight with him and, as angry as he is, I think she got him to see that going after her husband would just make things worse for them.

When Ed comes back here to get his truck, I'll talk with him to be sure. Please tell Erik thanks for everything this morning."

"You're welcome, pastor. Anytime. It's what we're here for."

Walter was in the living room after supper watching the Yankees' game on television and reading a book when Ed came up the porch steps and knocked on the kitchen door. He walked quickly into the kitchen and opened it. "Come on in, Ed." He pulled out a chair from the kitchen table and Ed sat down opposite him. "How's Lauren?"

"I think she's going to be all right, Coach. They took a lot of pictures of every part of her, but all they found was a concussion where she hit her head on the counter when she fell. Dr. Marcellino said she has to stay quiet for a week—can't go to work or do anything active. She has to go back to see him a week from today, but he said she shouldn't have any permanent effects."

"You must be relieved."

Ed nodded. "I am; I'm very relieved." He took a deep breath. "They don't want her to stay alone—just in case, so I called my mom and she said Lauren can stay there. She can use Jeannie's old room. We drove there in her car and my mom is helping her get settled. I thought about inviting her to stay with me—I want to be with her all the time, but my place is too small and (he grinned) not fit for a woman to live in. It's a single guy's pad. I clean once a month whether it needs it or not—and this is the fourth week."

Walter shook his head. "Yeah, I know how that is; if it weren't for Avis who comes and cleans here every week, this place would look the same."

"Actually, I think Lauren would like to stay with me, but everything is too confused for her to decide something like that right now. When things calm down and she's feeling better she can decide whether she wants to move on from being my Thursday girl to being my everyday girl."

"Sounds like a plan. How about you? How are you? You seem easier than you were when you left this morning."

He looked away then back at Walter. "I'm some easier, but I still have moments when I'm almost out-of-control angry at Gary. I don't know if it would be safe for me to be in the same room with him." He looked at the floor, and then up at Walter. "I had lots of time to think while I was sitting in the ER waiting for them to finish with Lauren. I really want to make Gary pay for what he did to Lauren." He swallowed hard and shook his head. "But I know what people look like after you kill them. I never want to see that again." He paused. "I know I'm supposed to love my enemies, Coach, and I've learned to do that for those people who tried to kill me when I was in Nam. But I can't imagine how I'll ever be able to forgive that bastard for what he did to Lauren. That may not be good enough for you, but it's what I can do for now."

Walter reached out and touched him on the shoulder, "It's good enough for now, Ed."

Ed sat back in his chair. "When Lauren gets better, whatever she decides to do with me, she definitely has to stay away from Gary. I was in the room at ER when the detective talked with her. When he was almost finished, he asked her if she had noticed anything unusual about Gary recently, anything different. She thought for a while like she wasn't going to say anything and then said that when she was getting ready to do a load of laundry on Sunday, she saw his North East Trucking jacket hanging on a hook by the front door. He wears it all the time and it's been getting really dirty. She'd offered to wash it, but he always says, 'Nah, it doesn't need it.' She took it off the hook and was checking the pockets before she put it in the washer and felt something hard in the zipper pocket on the left side. When she unzipped it and reached inside, she pulled out a big wad of bills with a rubber band around them—all hundreds. She said, 'He must have thousands of dollars in that pocket. I don't know how he got all that money.'"

"What did the detective say then?"

"He didn't say anything; he just nodded like he knew something he didn't want to talk about. Then he looked at both of us and said under no circumstances should Lauren go back to her apartment unless the police are with her. And in the meantime, she shouldn't tell anybody about the money she found in Gary's jacket or where she's staying. And that she should let the police know when she's able to go back to work at Johnny's. He said he'd let Chief Haines of the police department here in Schuylerkill Falls know what's happened so he can keep an eye out for anything that might happen here. He didn't say what he was concerned about. That was it."

He sighed deeply. "Right now, Coach, I'm tired—really tired. I need to go home and try to get some sleep. I promised Butch I'd come in early tomorrow to catch up on the jobs I didn't finish today." He paused. "Thanks for all you did for us today." His eyes were moist. "Sometime, not right now because right now I'm too beat think about anything, but sometime I want to know how you can believe there's a God in charge when things happen like Lauren getting beat up and the horror of that day in Nam—because I don't get how." He shook his head back and forth and sighed deeply as he stood up.

Walter stood in front of him and said, "There'll be a time we can talk about that, Ed."

"Yeah, I know . . . sometime when I'm up to it."

Walter stood in the driveway and stared at the empty street after Ed drove away. "Some people would say that all this suffering is happening to him and Lauren because she's somebody else's wife, but I'm not one of them."

9. KATE'S DANCE

The following Monday evening just after seven o'clock Katherine Klein walked up Maple Street and around the corner onto Church Street. When she turned into the manse driveway, Jim from Jim's Market drove past in his delivery truck. He tooted his horn and waved; she waved back. Walter heard the toot and opened the kitchen door as she stepped up onto the porch. "Hi, Katherine, you look wonderful."

She smiled. "Thanks, I'm glad to be here; it was a long day in the office."

He shut the door behind her, set the bag she was carrying on the kitchen counter, helped her off with her coat and hung it on one of the hooks next to the door. He stood awkwardly across from her. "You can hug me, Walter. Tonight we're friends."

He laughed and hugged her carefully. "Did someone blow their horn at you out front?"

She nodded. "Jim from Jim's Market drove past just as I was walking into your driveway."

He grinned. "I should have warned you that living in a manse is like living in a fishbowl. Next to TV, minister-watching is the favorite form of entertainment in small towns. Yesterday when he cut the pork roast for me Jim said, 'That's a bit bigger than you usually buy, pastor.' 'You're right,' I said, 'it is.' You could tell he was dying for me to tell him who was going to help me eat the roast, but I didn't say anything more and he didn't feel like he could ask. He saw you headed across the street and into my driveway so now he knows. I'm sure he's already told three people. By tomorrow morning the whole town will know that you and I spent the evening together. I haven't produced anything worth watching for a while; they'll be delighted to have something to talk about. Actually, if you don't take it seriously, it's a fun game. I hope you're all right with it."

She shrugged her shoulders. "I am. Physicians have to play it too—just in different ways. What's more important right now is what I smell."

"It's the pork roast I got from Jim's." Suddenly he had a moment of panic; he looked solemn. "You do eat pork?"

She laughed. "The Scandinavian side of me does."

He let his breath out. "I'm relieved. I didn't think about your Jewish side when I was planning the menu." He grimaced. "What a faux pas that would have been! Well, nothing ventured, nothing gained—or something like that."

"Something like that. Actually, when I caught the aroma as I walked in I knew what was cooking. I bet you marinated the roast overnight before you cooked it?"

"You're right. How'd you guess?"

"By the aroma; I smelled the thyme right away. Let's see: salt, of course, probably one teaspoon for each pound the roast weighs, and using the same measure a quarter teaspoon of thyme for each pound, an eighth teaspoon of ground bay leaf and a pinch of allspice. Garlic is optional and I doubt that you used any because I can't smell it."

"You're amazing. You got every single ingredient in the marinade. How did you know?"

She looked sheepish. "I cheated. I saw the Julia Child cookbook on the shelf over there when you hung up my coat. That's her recipe for dry pork marinade. I always use it."

He laughed out loud. "That bodes well; we at least have ways of cooking in common. But enough cooking talk." He bowed and gestured toward the hallway. "While the roast rests in the warm oven, madam, I would like to invite you into my parlor where I have some ecumenical hors d'oeuvres set out and a bottle of Haut Medoc that has been breathing for a half-hour."

"Thank you, sir, that sounds delightful! And if you look in that bag, on top of the cake box you'll find a tray with some cheeses that I will contribute."

He smiled, "Cake box?"

"Yes, cake box. My research revealed that you have a weakness for chocolate cake."

"And you decided to exploit my weakness?"

She nodded. "Something like that."

They walked through the hallway and into the parlor.

She looked around the room. "This is *very* homey. I shouldn't tell you this, but I envisioned a single minister's manse would be like a monk's cell filled with overstuffed furniture. This isn't anything like that; it's beautiful. You have excellent taste."

"Thank you. The furnishing happened gradually—though I have to admit that my mother helped. One of the down sides of being a single man is a mother who imagines you can't survive without having a woman managing your home life." He threw up his hands. "But I've managed so far." He sat down beside her on the large sofa, lifted the wine bottle, filled both glasses just under half full and handed one to her.

They took a sip of wine. She held up her glass as she said, "This wine is superb!"

"Thank you, and if the evening gets long, I have another bottle! He leaned back against the pillow on one end of the sofa. "So, tell me, what was it like to grow up in a Jewish-Scandinavian family?"

She laughed. "It would take a very long time to answer that question—and some of it would be quite boring, so I'll just hit a couple of highlights. In a sentence it was a life between opposites. Scandinavians are droll and reticent; you learn to watch them closely and still most of the time you can only guess what they're thinking. The other side of the family are loud-talkers and in your face all the time—like my Jewish grandmother, my 'Bubbie.' Though it's been ten years since Martin and I split she's still not stopped telling me that I should have married him—'such a nice Jewish boy and a professor even,' she says, as she looks up at me from her chair, pointing her finger for emphasis. 'And you still haven't found anybody else, have you! You're not getting any younger, Katherine Esther.' Then she looks grave and nods. 'Remember Aunt Esther, your namesake—may she rest in peace; she passed up her opportunity and no one ever asked her again and she died when she was only ten years older than you are.' All of this spoken in a loud voice so the whole family will hear."

He made a face. "That must be awfully embarrassing."

"It was when I was younger but not now. I know my Bubbie can't help herself; it's just who she is."

"Well, it wouldn't be like that in my family. If my grandmother had any concerns about what I was doing or not doing, she would quietly tell my mother when they were alone; my mother would then quietly tell my father when they were alone; and, if he agreed, he would quietly tell me when he and I were alone."

"It sounds like Scots are sort of in between Jews and Swedes—at least you find out where you stand."

"Most of the time. Actually, I've been thinking about your Jewish grandmother ever since you mentioned her."

"My Jewish grandmother? Why?

"I don't mean to embarrass you, but you must know that you are very beautiful—I know the word is overworked, but you are 'striking.'" (She blushed.) "How *have* you managed to survive so many years without finding a man to make your life complete?"

She laughed. "Well, there's a simple answer: I'm just too tall for ninety percent of men."

"What about the other ten percent?"

She shook her head, "You think I should confess about my past just because you're a preacher?"

He grinned. "I do! But I'll make you an unpreacherly offer: if you confess tonight, I will."

She tilted her head and looked straight at him. "Do you think you can intimidate me?"

His voice softened. "No; I already know better than that."

"Then I agree to the deal; I'll even go first—*after* we eat."

Talk at dinner was fun. She shared some of the crazier experiences she had as an OB-GYN doctor; he told Schuylerkill Falls stories. After she finished her second slice of roast pork she sat back from the table. "I have never had better pork roast, Walter—never. And the mashed potatoes were like velvet. But I knew they would be that smooth when I watched you beat them hard before you added any milk and butter. You're a real find; you're strikingly handsome and you can cook. How have *you* managed to stay single all these years?"

He laughed and shook his head. "Tit for tat! Nice try with the question, but you agreed to go first."

"Your memory's too good!" She took a deep breath. "Well, I guess there's no way to avoid telling you about Martin, my first and only serious boyfriend. But when I'm done, you have to tell me about all the women who have come before me in your life."

"That won't take long!"

She watched him look at her. "You noticed the slip, didn't you?"

He nodded. "I did."

"Last time we were together I said, 'wine and conversation is all I do.'"

"I remember." He watched her carefully as he said, "You didn't say, 'Wine and conversation is all I want to do.'"

A sly grin spread across her face. "You're going to be more of a challenge than I anticipated."

He sat back in his chair and nodded slowly. "I hope so." They sat and watched each other. He broke the silence, "Before we begin our confessions that cake you brought is calling my name."

She laughed and stood up. "If you supply a knife, I'll cut it!" While he poured some coffee she cut one modest piece of cake for herself and one very large piece for him.

"It will take me about as much time to tell you about Martin Edelman as it will for you to eat that piece of cake."

"I doubt that, but if it takes longer, I will eat another piece of cake to sustain me!"

She gestured toward the cake. "You can have all you want." She paused and pondered for a while as he ate his piece of cake. Finally, she said, "It's hard to know how far back to start. Martin's and my parents were neighbors in Saratoga when he and I were growing up. Martin is very smart—as good in math and physics as I was in biology, and by the time we were juniors in high school he was almost as tall as I am—actually the tallest Jewish guy I've ever met. He was one of the few boys who could keep up with me in basketball.

"Everybody including us assumed that someday we would marry. Not that we ever felt a lot of passion for each other; marrying was more what we expected to happen than what we hungered for. After he went off to Harvard and I went off to Smith we had only occasional dates when our vacations coordinated. It was the same when he went on for his PhD at M.I.T. and I went to Med School at Columbia-Presbyterian.

"We both finished the long years of schooling the same spring; I got through my residency and he finished his post-doc. He got a tenure-track appointment at RPI in Troy and I got a job at a clinic in Albany and we moved into an apartment in an old house on Madison Avenue in Albany opposite the park.

"I think the fact that we just moved in together and didn't get married surprised everybody, but looking back I think we didn't get married because we both sensed it might not work for us for the long haul." She stopped talking and gave him a questioning look, "You aren't saying anything; am I boring you?"

He sat up quickly. "No, not at all! I want to know all about you."

"*All* about me? You better have that second piece of cake!"

"It's so good that I won't mind if it takes you so long to finish that I have to eat all of it."

She smiled. "I'm glad you like it." She paused and the smile left her face. "You can imagine how living together goes when both of you have new and demanding jobs; it's like dating. With me a first-year doc and him a first year prof we had hardly any free time to spend with each other. But the following spring we both had the three-day Memorial Day weekend off; I wasn't on call and he was finished with the term. Sunday was a beautiful spring day and we walked across the street and sat on a bench in the park.

"It's probably hard for you to believe, but that day was the first time Martin told me what he wanted me to be. He asked me how long I intended to practice medicine. The question surprised me; I told him 'at least thirty years.' He looked at me and scowled and said, 'I would like us to get married so we can have a family. I don't see how that can happen if you keep being a doctor.' Then it hit me: he wanted a nice Jewish girl at home who would have his babies and make his supper every day. I would be more of a habit than a passion."

"Really! After all the incredible commitment it took to become a physician, he expected you to give up practicing and be a stay-at-home mom? That's hard to believe."

She sighed and nodded. "It was. We had some hard conversations and tried to work it out, but we couldn't. At the end of June, he moved out. Within a year he had found his nice Jewish girl and they married and in three years she had two babies."

He looked at her gently and spoke carefully. "So, you lost the love of your life."

She looked away and didn't speak for a moment. Then she looked back and said softly, "No; that had already happened." She watched him closely; she could feel the warmth in his eyes as he looked at her. "I didn't expect to talk about this, Walter—it goes beyond the wine and conversation I imagined we'd have this evening; but for some reason I don't understand I want to tell you about it."

"And, perhaps, for the same reason, I want to hear about it."

"When I was chief resident at Columbia-Presbyterian I had an affair with a surgeon. He was as tall as you are (she paused), and almost as good-looking, in his late forties and kept a studio apartment in Manhattan where he stayed when he was on call. He had a home with a wife and family up in Westchester County, but he couldn't commute from there to the hospital quickly enough when he had to be on call. I met him when he was teaching a session on pelvic reconstructive surgery. After the session we happened to sit at the adjacent tables in the cafeteria at lunchtime. It may sound strange, even foolish, to you, but when I watched him that day, I knew I would love him."

She took a deep breath. "But he was married and fifteen years older than I was so I didn't think it would come to any-thing. It must have been nearly a month before I saw him again. It was late in the afternoon; I was sitting in the doctors' lounge having coffee. I was exhausted; I had just come off one of those twenty-hour marathons that residents suffer through. I heard him before I saw him. He stood next to the table and said, 'You look tired, Katherine.' I was startled that he noticed and that he remembered my name. I smiled weakly. 'I am.' He looked at me carefully and said, 'May I buy your dinner?'"

She stopped talking and searched his face. "Is it all right to tell you this, Walter? We hardly know each other."

He sat back in his chair and said, "It's really all right, Kath-erine; if you want to tell me, I want to hear. Sometimes, the right moments happen when we least expect them."

She watched his face carefully as she went on. "I'm sure you can guess what happened. We had dinner and I went with him to his apartment and we made love. It was incredible. I have never felt passion like I did when I was with him.

"For the next six months we spent at least two nights a month together. It was stupid, in a way, to keep doing it. I knew he was taking advantage of me and that he would never leave his wife for me, but I didn't care. Passion can be irrational when it's intense. The really dumb thing was that I got pregnant. You'd think two doctors would know how to avoid that, but as I just said, passion can be irrational." She looked away and then back at him. "I had an abortion, Walter. It wasn't hard to arrange. I didn't know what else to do; I couldn't have the baby. But there are still days when I'm sorry I did it—when I wonder what that child, my child, would have been like. It seemed like the only solution at the time, but actually it was a compromise that has haunted me ever since." She looked intently at him. "Do I need to make a confession? I was bad, wasn't I?"

For a moment he didn't say anything. "No, I wouldn't say that you were bad; doing something you later decide might have been wrong makes you human, not bad. Sometimes, the hardest forgiveness to give is the forgiveness you need to give yourself." He looked straight into her eyes. "It's time to do that. Regret doesn't have to be fatal."

Tears flowed out of her eyes and down her face. He reached out his hand across the table toward her. She took hold of his outstretched hand and said, "Thank you."

They sat together quietly for a while. Then she let go of his hand and sat up in her chair. "Of course, I didn't tell Kristen any of this the other day when she and I talked about her father's affair. I tried to help her understand that, sometimes, these things happen even to good and caring people." She smiled at him. "I've never told anyone about my affair with David. I guess I've just never found the right priest to hear my confession."

"I'm glad you told me about it. But I'm not your priest, Katherine, I'm your friend."

She reached out and touched his hand. "Sometimes, a friend is the best priest." She sat up and sighed deeply. "Anyway, that's how I lost the love of my life. It's been fifteen years now and I haven't found anyone who comes close to David. To be honest, I've stopped looking." Her voice lightened up, "Okay, Walter, you've heard my confession, now it's your turn, though I suspect you don't need a confessor to listen to your story."

He laughed, "Well, I just may."

She looked sideways at him and grinned. "Maybe there's more hidden in Walter Macdonald's past than anyone knows about?"

He laughed. "It's not anywhere near as interesting, or as traumatic, as what's hidden in yours. May I refill your wine glass before I start?"

"You can! Every time I take another sip I discover again how delicious this Haut Medoc is."

"I'm glad you like it; I've been saving it for a special occasion." He poured wine into her glass and then his own. He watched her look at him. "Our glasses are half full, Katherine."

"I know." She looked pensive.

He leaned back in his chair. "When I came here seventeen years ago, I was thirty and very sure of what I believed and not very sure of anything else. I met Mary Kerrigan at a barbecue that fall at Erik and Becky's farm. We were as she put it 'the only under-aged and unattached people' at the party. Everyone else was married and about as old as you and I are now.

"In the beginning I was more intrigued than smitten with her. I'd never been close to anyone like her before. She was smart and outspoken and, as I discovered soon, a disbeliever—someone who doesn't believe in God and knows what god and why. I think she was as intrigued as I; she'd never been close to a believer who could hold his own in a debate with her. So, we argued and fell in love.

"But we could never connect where it matters if you're a minister. In the beginning I was sure I'd find a way to deal with her disbelieving. When I was a student in seminary we had debates where one of us took the part of the skeptic, but the skeptics we imagined then were paper tigers; this woman was no paper tiger. She had a convincing response for every argument I knew and for lots I'd never thought of. The longer we were together the more it mattered to me to win her and win the argument. I thought I had to convince her to believe so she could fit into my life—and to protect my faith. And I couldn't." He looked at the floor.

She watched him carefully and waited, then said softly, "So, what happened?"

"It all came to head one spring day when we hiked into Erik's hunting camp. I'd been off to a minister's R and R week at my old seminary. While I was there I had several long conversations with a new Biblical studies prof who had originally been a biologist; I came home thinking I had gained the insights I needed to convince Mary to believe. I hadn't. She ably countered my new arguments. I knew then that I wasn't ever going to win, and that if I couldn't, there was no way she could fit into my life as a minister's wife. So, we split."

"But that wasn't the end, was it?"

"How did you guess?"

"Because there's too much passion in your voice."

"You're right; I didn't give up. Like you said, passion can make you irrational. After several weeks by chance we ended up at Eri Peterson's high school graduation party sitting at the same picnic table where we originally met. I told her I wanted one more chance with her—that if I went down, I wanted to go down fighting. She laughed and said I was a 'persistent fool.' I was."

"It was your heart talking."

He laughed. "It was. We met the next afternoon at her family's camp on Lake George. It was a beautiful summer day. We swam and flew around the bay in her grandfather's speedboat; we cooked steaks and drank wine—and tried one more time to connect. It went terribly. I was desperate and she knew it. Finally, she got exasperated with me. She said, 'I don't need to believe, Walter. Believers think everyone needs to believe in God. I don't; I'm happy the way I am.'"

He looked very sober. "She got me; I do think everyone needs to believe in God. I don't know what to say to someone who says they don't believe and that they're content." He stopped suddenly and looked at the floor. He looked up, reached across the table and took her hand. "I didn't think it would be this hard to talk about what came next."

She smiled gently. "Maybe you're not done with her?"

He sighed. "Maybe I'm not."

Neither of them spoke for a while. Then she broke the silence. "So, what happened?"

"Mary didn't say anything more for a minute. Then she said, 'We'll never find the answer by talking. Let's go swimming.' I protested that it was dark. She laughed and said, 'Dark is the best time.' So, we went swimming. And then we went skinny dipping. And then we made love and fell asleep."

He let go of her hand. "I woke up about two in the morning and wondered if anyone back at the parish might need me and not be able to find me. When I thought about that I couldn't stay; I left her sleeping and went home."

She looked stunned. "You just left her? My God, Walter, how could you do that?"

"I felt I had to go . . . and I knew that if I stayed the night with her, I would never come back here." He sighed deeply. "The next evening she stopped by. I saw her drive in and met her on the side porch. She handed me a bag, 'You forgot your bathing suit.' I made some stupid statement like, 'I wasn't planning on going swimming soon.' She didn't respond to what I said; she told me that she wasn't coming back to Schuylerkill Falls High in the fall, that she was going to Columbia to begin doctoral studies so she could teach in a college. Then she looked at me with those green eyes and pleaded, 'Come with me, Walter; please come with me.' In that moment I wanted her more than I ever wanted anything in my life." He stopped talking and shook his head side to side. "But I knew I couldn't go with her, and I told her I couldn't. She stood and stared at me and said, 'Such a loss, such a tragic loss.' Then she left. I never saw her again." Tears welled up in his eyes.

Katherine stood up, walked around the table, and sat down next to him and put her hand on his shoulder.

After a while he looked at her and managed a smile. "It's been sixteen years since she left and I've never really talked it through with anyone." He shook his head slightly. "I've been too much of a Scot; I've stuffed it and imagined it would go away . . . but it hasn't." He sighed. "I know if she'd stayed here, she would have eventually done me in. My God, I loved her."

She heard the pain in his voice. "I know; I can tell." For a moment she didn't say anything. "Everyone has a downside, Walter—sometimes, their downside is characteristics you couldn't tolerate over the long haul. When you're young and fall in love you either don't see the other one's downside, or you ignore what you couldn't tolerate over the long haul, but it finally does the relationship in. If you're lucky it happens sooner rather than later."

He sat up and wiped his eyes with his sleeve. "That's the way it was with Mary; it was her need to challenge, to confront anyone she didn't agree with about anything she thought was important. The problem was not that she couldn't believe; she couldn't keep still about it. That made her a misfit in the church world. The secret to getting along in a church is not what you say; it's what you don't say. You can be a complete atheist and you'll get along fine as long as you don't talk about it. Just keep quiet and help out at the ham supper and you'll get on fine. Mary couldn't keep quiet."

She reached out and touched his hand. "Walter, even when you know it won't work, forcing yourself to turn away from a lover is heart-rending. It's never all bad with someone; when you split you grieve for the good parts you lost."

For a while they sat together in the quiet. Then he looked up and said, "Thank you. I feel replenished and drained at the same time."

"You do look tired; probably it's time for me to go. But the next time I'm here I want to see the game balls that Erik said sit on the front of your desk—the ones they gave you after you pitched the no-hitters at Union."

"You don't have to wait until next time; you can see them right now." He stood up. She followed him through the doorway into his study. He picked up one of the baseballs that sat on his desk and handed it to her.

She held the ball in her hand and read, "'Mac Macdonald, no-hitter, Union College, 4/28/52.'" It was signed by members of the team. She handed the ball back to him. "You're impressive."

He smiled. "Thank you, but so are you. I want to know more about what you did on the UConn basketball team."

She nodded. "You will—next time. Right now I have a question. The inscription on the ball says, 'Mac' Macdonald. I've never heard anyone call you 'Mac.' What happened to Mac?"

He took a deep breath and let it out slowly. "I left him behind when I went to seminary."

She looked directly into his eyes. "What would it take to bring him back?"

He spoke softly, "I don't know. He watched her look at him for a while, then he asked, "What does the inscription say on the game ball they gave you at the state championship?"

She smiled. "It says, 'Kate Klein.'"

"Kate," he said quietly. "I like that name; it fits you." He paused and then asked, "What's happened to Kate Klein?" He waited for her to respond.

"She's . . . afraid to let someone kiss her."

They watched each other for a moment, then she whispered, "Kiss me, Mac."

He wrapped his arms around her and kissed her with gentle passion.

When their lips separated, he smiled and said, "I thought we agreed we would take it slow."

She nodded. "We did." She took a quick breath. "I'm afraid . . . but I want to take it."

He nodded in response as he said, "So do I." They stood wrapped in each other for a while; then he relaxed his arms from around her. "I'd like to walk you home."

She tilted her head and grinned. "You're not afraid some passerby will see us together and start a rumor?"

"No, I often walk around the village at night when I can't sleep and people see me, so they're used to me walking around at night. If they see you and me walking together, they'll talk but it won't rise to the level of a scandal. Besides, Jim saw you coming here earlier tonight, so the talking has already begun." He laughed.

They walked out the driveway and crossed over Church Street. As they walked along they held hands; it seemed easy and natural. A passing car's headlights shone on them just as they turned into Maple Avenue. After the car passed, she asked, "Did that car slow down so the driver could get a better look at us, or was it just my imagination?"

"No, it wasn't." He grinned at her. Like I said before, "It's what happens here."

When they reached the side door that led up to her apartment, she opened it and then turned and faced him; they stood for a moment and looked at each other. She smiled and said, "Can we kiss and just be friends—at least for a while?"

He nodded and drew her to him and kissed her.

"Thank you for a lovely evening."

"You're welcome; we'll do it again soon."

As he walked down the driveway toward the street he thought, "I heard what she said about being only friends, but I felt longing for more than friendship in her kiss." He laughed under his breath. "Or, maybe I just imagined she wants something I want?"

10. ALONE

He decided to take a long way home; he wasn't ready for the evening to end. He walked up Maple and across Church Street, and then turned left onto Grove Street. He walked past Molly Hutchins' house and Miss Simpson's—there were no lights on in either house. As he walked along in the darkness he pondered the conversation with Katherine. "She fell in love once and lost." He stopped walking and looked back toward School Street and said out loud, "So did I. We're both afraid."

He walked on to the end of Grove Street, turned left onto Main for a block and left again onto Church Street. When he walked up the porch steps and into the kitchen at the manse he, looked through the doorway that led to his study and noticed the message light blinking on his telephone answering machine. When he pushed the button he recognized the caller's voice right away. "Walter, this is Frank Perelli. I just got home from the hospital. Marsha had a massive stroke this afternoon—and an hour ago she died." His voice cracked. "I've really lost her now. Maybe you could give me a call when you get in? I know I should call a real priest, but you're the one I want."

He sat down in the desk chair and punched in Frank's number. Frank answered on the second ring. "It's Walter, Frank. I hardly know what to say . . . I'm so sorry about Marsha."

"Oh, God, Walter; I didn't think it would be this hard. I knew it was coming; the doctor told me weeks ago it could happen at any time. I thought I was ready. I'm not."

"Is someone with you, Frank?"

"Yeah, Andy and his wife, Susie, are here. They came down from Glens Falls this afternoon when I called them and told him about his mom. They're going to stay the night."

"I'm glad; you shouldn't be alone."

"I won't sleep anyway. There's so many things to think about."

"Maybe it would help to tell yourself that you'll do better with all of them in the daylight and with help from your kids and your friends." He paused. "You said on the phone message, 'You're the one I want.' Do you know what you want from me?"

"I'm not sure; that's the problem. Except for a couple of weddings and a funeral I haven't been in a Catholic Church for twenty years. A priest came by this afternoon just after Marsha had her stroke; I guess the hospital called him. He gave her last rites. It pissed me off at the time; I didn't think she was going to die. Now I'm glad he did, but he's gone, and I hardly know Father Nick, the new priest at St. Joe's. I thought maybe you could take over now. That's what I meant in the message."

Walter spoke carefully. "I don't think you should try to work everything out tonight, Frank. We can talk it through in the morning. But maybe it would help tonight to think about what Marsha would want. She stayed with her church all the way to the end. I've had lunch with Father Nick a couple of times; I know he's come by the nursing home pretty regularly and brought Marsha communion." He paused for a few seconds. "I want to be your friend and stand beside you, Frank, but I can't be the kind of priest that Marsha would want. I think she would want a Catholic priest."

For a while there was silence on the phone. "You're right, Walter. I'll call Father Nick in the morning; he'll know what to do. Thanks. I'm going to bed now and try to sleep."

Three days later Father Nick said a mass of Christian burial for Marsha Perelli at St. Joseph's Church. Walter read one of the lessons; Frank's children read the others. After the service Walter drove with the procession to St. Joseph's cemetery. He stood with the family and friends at the open grave as Father Nick read the words of committal and offered a final benediction. He raised his head and opened his eyes after the priest finished praying and saw a solitary figure standing by herself at the edge of the gathering. Molly Hutchins was alone.

11. THE PHILOSOPHER'S PIGEONS

An incident with the 1941 Lincoln Zephyr Dr. Woodrow Wilson Morton inherited from his father was actually what initiated Walter and Wilson's friendship. It happened on a Thursday morning in late June. Walter was up early working on his sermon. The writing went well; he finished the final draft just before 11:00. As he walked to the kitchen to reheat some coffee, Schuylerkill Falls Police Chief Pete Haines drove in the driveway. Walter's eye caught the thermometer as he walked past the kitchen window; it was already 85 degrees. He opened the screen door as Pete walked up onto the side porch. "Hi, Pete, I know it's already pretty warm, but it's never too warm for coffee. Can you come in and have a cup?"

"I'd love some, Reverend, but duty calls. I have an incident to tend to and it might be helpful if you come along. It involves one of your parishioners."

"Who?" Walter asked, with a show of concern.

"Dr. Morton."

"The retired professor? What in the world could he have done to warrant a visit from you?"

"Well, I'm not completely sure. The county dispatcher called and said she has a complaint from a neighbor that Dr. Morton is sitting in a chair in his backyard shooting at his barn with a shotgun." Pete grinned. "Does sound far-fetched, doesn't it?" Walter nodded in agreement. "But I have to check it out and I thought maybe you might like to go along. As you know, Dr. Morton can be difficult. Sometimes he has a bad night and doesn't sleep much and has a few nips. I decided to invite you along because he's your parishioner and you might provide a moderating influence. Want to come?"

"Sure," Walter said, laughing. "Whatever's going on, it can't be as bad as some of the calls you've taken me on."

It didn't take long to drive the three blocks down Church Street to Wilson's house. The sound of a gunshot behind the house greeted them as they stepped out of the police car. "Well, he's shootin' something," Pete said. They walked cautiously up the drive. Wilson sat in a lawn chair in the back yard, a 12-gauge shotgun stretched out across his lap.

"Dr. Morton!" Pete said. "What in the world are you doing?"

"I'm shooting pigeons."

"You can't shoot pigeons in the village. You can't shoot anything in the village. It's against the law."

"Then you do something about them. I'm tired of having the pigeons shit on my father's old car. Ever since that big windstorm blew the board loose underneath the soffit on the carriage barn the pigeons have gotten in. They've taken to roosting on the stringers. They shit all over the car; the pigeon shit will ruin the finish. Dad kept that 1941 Lincoln so spiffy it still looks brand new and I'm not about to let some goddamn (he looked directly at Walter)—sorry pastor—some goddamn pigeons spoil it now."

"I can sympathize with you, Dr. Morton, but don't you think shooting pigeons with a 12-gauge is overmuch?"

"Well, I'll get my .22 then."

"You can't get anything. It's against the law to shoot a gun within the village limits, and that's that! If you won't agree to stop, then you'll have to give all your guns to me for safekeeping."

Wilson gestured toward Walter. "Why'd you bring him along? He's a minister, not a policeman."

"Insurance," Pete said with a smile. "God's on his side; I've learned that, sometimes, he's better protection than a gun. Now, are you going to quit shooting, or are you going to give me your guns?"

"I'll make a deal with you, Chief. You agree to find somebody who'll close that hole below the soffit, and I'll agree to quit shooting the pigeons. I'd fix it myself, but I'm too old now to climb up that high on a ladder."

"I'm not," Walter said. "It's not much of a hole. I could fix it late this afternoon."

A big grin spread across Wilson's face. "I've heard you're handy, pastor. Most pastors I've known, my father included, are all thumbs, except for one finger they use to point at you when they're preaching. You fix that hole in the barn and I'll make an extra donation to the church. Inside the carriage barn there's a ladder that will get you up there."

Walter nodded. "Sounds like a good deal to me."

"Sounds good to me too," Pete said. "Now let me see you empty the shell out of the chamber of that shotgun."

Wilson emptied the chamber and held out his open hand with the shell in it toward Pete. "You want it?"

"No," Pete said. "Just wait for hunting season to use it— and not in the village."

Wilson grinned. "You'll hear one more loud bang this afternoon. It'll sound like a gunshot, but it won't be one. When Reverend Macdonald gets up on the ladder to fix the hole, just before he covers it I'm going to set off a big firecracker in the carriage barn to scare the pigeons out before he plugs the opening."

"You have firecrackers? They're against the law too."

"I'm going to set off only one. I'm saving the rest for the Fourth of July picnic I'll have with my brother's grandchildren at his camp on Sacandaga Lake. It'll be no concern of yours; that's out of your jurisdiction."

Pete shook his head. "And some people think police work is easy! Just one firecracker, Dr. Morton. If I hear more than that, I'll come back and confiscate all you've got."

The fact that they spend three years as students learning the intricacies of theology and then when they become pastors discover that no one in their congregation is interested in or able to discuss the intricacies of theology is a common source of frustration among ministers. Walter was delighted to find in Wilson Morton a friend who was eager to drink wine and talk theology late into the night.

Woodrow Wilson Morton was the prodigal son of Dr. Archibald Morton who served as pastor of the First Presbyterian Church of Schuylerkill Falls from 1930 to 1955. From their earliest years Wilson's older brother, Calvin, was the talented son his parents assumed would follow his father into the ministry. But Calvin had no taste for theology; after earning a degree in history and economics at Princeton, he returned to the village to begin a lifelong banking career at the Schuylerkill Falls Savings Bank.

With Calvin committed to banking Dr. Morton's hope that a son would assume his prophet's mantle rested on Wilson. At first it appeared that Wilson would embrace the calling, but that was not to be. Wilson went on from seminary to Columbia University where he completed a PhD in record time. After three years teaching religion at a small college in Virginia he joined the philosophy and religion department at Williams College where he taught for the next thirty-five years.

After Wilson's father and mother were both gone he spent summers and Christmas vacations in the home Abigail Pierson left to his minister father when she died. When Abigail's will was read leaving her house and Lincoln Zephyr automobile to her pastor a few in the village raised their eyebrows. As Wilson told Walter one evening while they sat at the chess board, "There was some talk—though, of course, no one ever said anything to me directly. Abigail was a beautiful woman—far prettier than my mother. My father visited her at least weekly; they obviously liked each other—if you know what I mean, but I doubt they ever did anything more than drink tea and talk. People didn't in those days. Her house was a godsend to my parents (don't take that literally); my dad lived in parsonages his whole working life and had no savings with which to buy a house or a fancy car. People got used to him driving around the village in that black 1941 Lincoln with its suicide rear doors. It's a great car. It still purrs when it runs and I love to drive it on nice days during the summer."

When Wilson moved back to Schuylerkill Falls fulltime in the summer of 1977, though he attended services occasionally, the status of his membership in the Presbyterian Church was a delicate matter for the church elders. There was a rumor that Wilson had become a closet Unitarian. The rumor was true—as was another, that Wilson was gay. Had he been a newcomer, some of the more conservative residents of Schuylerkill Falls would have shunned him. But in spite of his long absence from the village, Wilson enjoyed the pedigree of a native. So, locals were generous with him and classified him simply as "odd." Wilson helped them to accept him; he didn't flaunt either his theological or sexual orientation.

Just after four-thirty Walter returned to Wilson's house with his tools. He set the ladder against the side of the barn and climbed up to the loose board. Fortunately, nothing was split; it had just come loose. When he climbed back down the ladder to pick up his hammer and some nails he saw Wilson coming out of the house.

"You rap on the side of the building with your hammer when you're all set, Reverend. Keep your head away from the hole so you don't get a pigeon in the face when I set off a firecracker!"

Walter nodded. "Okay, Dr. Morton." He climbed up the ladder until he was just below the loose board. He rapped the side of the building with his hammer. After a few seconds there was a very loud report inside the carriage house. He saw two pigeons fly out the big front door. He was glad he had stayed below the opening; a pigeon flew out through the hole behind the loose board. He heard Wilson shut the big door.

"All clear!" Wilson shouted. "Plug her up."

He climbed back up opposite the loose board and nailed it down. When he climbed down to the ground, Wilson was standing at the bottom of the ladder. He looked contrite. "I'm really sorry to bother you with this."

"It's no bother, Dr. Morton. I'm glad to help out. Besides, it's more fun than sitting and drinking tea with some village gossip."

"I got something better than tea in there," he said, pointing to his house. "Make it myself. Best homemade red wine you'll ever drink. Ask Smitty, your organist, and he'll tell you nobody makes it better! Would you like a sip before you go? You'd get to enjoy good wine and get credit for a pastoral visit. I've even got some imported cheese. Doesn't get any better than that. Well, what do you say?"

Walter hesitated for a moment, then smiled. "Why not? I could stop for a while. I've got a meeting at seven, but if I get home by six, I'll have enough time to grab some leftovers for supper and still get to the meeting on time."

"Delightful. It will help me if you take the ladder down and put it inside the barn. I'll set out the wine and cheese while you do it."

In a few minutes they were sitting at Wilson's kitchen table. Walter took a sip of wine and nodded. "This wine is excellent. You could sell it!"

"That would ruin a good hobby and bring on the regulators. I'm happy with the hobby."

"Understand." He paused until Wilson looked directly at him. "I've wanted for a long time to have a chance to talk with you. I'm sure you already know a lot about me; ministers are public property in small towns." He watched Wilson nod. "I'm sure you know what that's like because you grew up with a minister father. But I know very little about you; this is the first time we've had a chance to talk face to face. And I'm sure the real Wilson Morton is much more interesting than the rumors."

"I doubt that, and, besides, if I get to talking, you may not be able to shut me up!

"I'll risk it—at least for one hour." He grinned.

"Well, I might just take a chance and treat you like as my pastor-confessor and then you can decide whether to risk reactivating my church membership. I'm sure this room is not bugged—though you never know to what depths Calvinists may stoop to smoke out a closet Unitarian in their midst." He watched Walter's smile broaden. "So, there, I said the word 'Unitarian,' and now you know that rumor's true; I'm a covert Unitarian. To be more accurate, I defaulted to Unitarianism.

"In college I slipped away from the Presbyterian Calvinism I inherited from my dad. I really didn't want to let go of the old faith, but I couldn't square so-called Biblical revelation with what science has revealed about humans and the earth and the universe. There are still moments when I think I might be able to hold on to both the old faith and contemporary science, but science and just plain common sense have pretty much overwhelmed what's left of it." He took a breath and looked wistful, then laughed. "But that tells you what I don't believe, not much about what I do believe."

"You're right."

"That's because I'm not sure myself! In what you would say are my best moments I teeter at the edge of the old faith. But Presbyterians don't have room for teeterers; they have a standard set of beliefs they have to at least pretend they believe. Unitarians don't have that problem; they can believe anything or nothing. That's their strength and their weakness. One doesn't have to pretend to be Unitarian—that's their real strength. But this unqualified acceptance is also a weakness; it makes Unitarians a kind of religious zoo."

Walter laughed and folded his arms in front of him, "I'm glad you said that, not me."

Wilson smiled. "Well, I did; in fact, you can even quote me on it if you want to! Actually, growing up in the Reverend Doctor Archibald Morton's household was good preparation for my later apostasy. Like they say, 'Takes a good Fundamentalist to make a good atheist; you know what you *don't* believe.'" His smile broadened, then faded . . . "but not what you do."

He stopped speaking and looked off into the distance for a moment. "My dad was an impeccable Calvinist in his head, but he had a soft heart. When people in the village struggled over the sickness or death of someone they loved who wasn't a Presbyterian believer, he would say, 'I'm sure God loves them and will take care of them.' No double predestination in those moments; in my father's heart there was no hell for anyone. That's a belief I'm glad I did inherit from him."

"He was a gentle and caring man, Dr. Morton. When people remember him they talk about how caring he was—never about his theology."

Wilson nodded his agreement. "That's how I remember him too. In spite of his Calvinism the God in his heart was more in charge than the God in the Bible. I think he knew even before I did that I'm gay. He never said that he knew, and I never made it obvious; being a PK, a preacher's kid, is tough enough. Being a gay PK is enough to put you under. Dad knew what it was like to be a preacher's kid on the schoolyard; he'd been one himself. And he was short, like I am. Short, gay and PK: that's three strikes against you. So, one time when I came home from school after I got beat up, after I stopped crying he said, 'Wilson, I'm going to show you what to do so that doesn't happen again.'

"And he did; he showed me how to make a fist, keeping my thumb on the outside and how to throw a really hard punch. 'When someone comes after you,' he said, 'hit 'em hard enough the first time to knock them down. Then you can turn the other cheek.' That ended my troubles on the playground. Bodybuilding and gymnastics during my teenage years headed off any would-be challengers in high school. I was too short for basketball but just the right size for gymnastics. I was a whiz on the horse and the parallel bars." He stood up and raised his hands toward the ceiling. "If the ceilings were higher in this house, I could still do a standing back flip!"

Walter tilted his head, a sly grin on his face. "I'd sure like to see you do one!" He shrugged his shoulders. "It's not that cold. Let's go outside and you can show me."

Wilson shook his head. "I saw that grin! You know damn well that I haven't done a back flip in years and I've had too much wine to test my skills right now. You'll have to wait for 'til one of Doc Peterson's parties when I can try a backflip off the diving board at his pool."

"Just let me know when and I'll be there to watch!"

"I will! But right now I want to go back to my dad. He knew he could never admit in public what he acted out with me. His Presbyterian colleagues would have drummed him out of the ministry. And that's so stupid! In spite of what bright people think is clear and convincing evidence that being gay is a matter of genes, those divines couldn't face reality.

"Lots of them still can't. That's the problem with people who don't look at Scripture critically. I know very well what Scripture says about gay people: 'condemn 'em, stone 'em, or, at least, shun 'em.' But those people who wrote the Bible were captives of the science of their times. So were the guys who wrote church doctrine in the sixteenth century.

"Why don't they update? Doctors don't hold the same beliefs now they held in Jesus' time or the sixteenth century—which everyone thinks is a good thing. None of us would want to be treated by a physician who practices medicine the way they did four hundred years ago. If the people who wrote scripture and church doctrine had known that it's your genes that make somebody like me gay, they would have thought differently about us. No one wants to stone you because you have green eyes."

Walter laughed carefully. "That's true; I never thought of it that way."

"You never had to think of it that way; you're a straight minister—though you're smarter and more open-minded than most I've met. It's true that you're almost fifty, but you're not married, and even though rumor is that you have a girlfriend, you still take a chance when you come here for dinner—even if I'm too old now for my sexual orientation to matter in any practical way." A somber look spread across his face. "You can be my pastor, Walter, but you'd risk all hell coming down on you if you were become my friend."

Walter looked at him intently. "But I've already decided I want to be your friend, Dr. Morton; I've already decided to risk."

Wilson looked away for a moment and then spoke to Walter in carefully measured words. "It's always riskier to care for someone than it is to condemn them. I'm a gay Zacchaeus; if you become a guest in my house some evening and eat dinner with me, you'll be acting too much like Jesus for your own good." He let the words settle for a while, then sat up and his voice brightened. "How about another piece of cheese and a refill in your wine glass?"

"Thanks for the offer, Dr. Morton, but it'll have to be another time. I have to drive home, and it wouldn't do to have my name broadcast on the police-band scanners as someone suspected of DWI."

"Oh, I forgot; you're the keeper of propriety in Schuylerkill Falls. God forbid that I be the one to spoil your public image. But sometime when you've got a whole evening to spend, walk on over and have some more vintage Morton red. You like beef burgundy?"

"I do."

"Mine's the best. You can ask Smitty about that; I make it for him once a month. I use a special cut of Black Angus that Jim cuts for me, and lots of my special brew. Takes all day to cook it. But that doesn't matter; most days I got nothing else to do—except read my books and shoot the goddamn pigeons. Just about any evening will work for me."

Walter grinned. "Thanks for the invitation, Dr. Morton. I would love to share some beef burgundy and more of your special homemade wine. I'll check my calendar when I get home and give you a call." He reached out his hand and Wilson shook it warmly.

Wilson held on to his hand and looked straight into his eyes. "I like you; you're a no bullshit kind of a guy. That's rare for a minister. Please call me 'Wilson,' Walter. I miss having somebody smart to argue with. Maybe you'd like to take that on?"

Walter nodded and smiled. "I would, Wilson. I'll give you a call soon." He let go of Wilson's hand, walked to side of the barn and picked up his tools and put them into the back of his Bronco. He stood for a moment and watched Wilson waving at his back door. It would be hard to be old and alone and lonely. He knew there would be times when Wilson would be difficult, but he liked him. He would enjoy having him as a friend.

12. WALTER'S DANCE

By late fall dinners and conversation with Wilson and, some-times, Smitty, the delightfully irreverent church organist, at Wilson's home had become regular occasions. On the last Monday in November the evening was still warm enough that Walter could walk the three blocks to Wilson's home wearing only a light jacket. When he mounted the steps onto the back porch he didn't have to knock; Wilson had seen him coming. A wonderful aroma greeted him as Wilson opened the door.

Wilson shook his hand warmly. "I see you didn't forget your assignment to bring cheesecake; I'll put it in the refriger-ator for safe keeping." He reached out and took the box Walter was carrying. "The only sad news of the night is that Smitty can't come. He called a little while ago to say that he came home from the store early this afternoon with one of those stomach things, so he's not up to beef burgundy. We'll miss him, but I'm sure he'll feel better by tomorrow."

"Sorry about Smitty, he always makes us laugh."

Wilson chuckled. "That's true but missing him could have one advantage. Did you ever notice that there's an inverse rela-tionship between the number of participants and the depth a conversation can reach? So, if the spirit moves—that should be your line—we'll see what kind of depths the two of us can plumb tonight." He gestured toward a chair at the kitchen table. "Have a seat while I mash the potatoes. I'll pour us some of my special wine to help you endure the wait. You're not in any hurry, are you?"

"No, not at all; I have the whole evening and there's nothing I have to do early tomorrow morning."

Wilson raised his fist in a gesture of triumph. "Good! By the time we finish eating and drinking and telling stories, you'll be saying, 'We've done enough damage to the world for one day.'" He poured red wine from an unmarked bottle into two large wine glasses, handed one to Walter, then raised his glass toward Walter's. "I offer a toast to both of us: To the keeper of philosophy, me, to the keeper of faith, you; may the best keeper win!"

"I'll drink to that!" He touched his glass to Wilson's and the sound of crystal reverberated through the room.

As usual Wilson's dinner was delicious. By the second glass of wine and the second helping of beef burgundy Walter was completely relaxed. Reluctantly, he refused a third helping of beef burgundy and potatoes. "Everything's so good, but I'm stuffed, Wilson; I need to take a break before I try to eat any of that cheesecake."

"Then we should pause, but only pause; it would be a tragedy not to eat cheesecake. I'll pour some coffee and cut a couple of pieces of cheesecake and set them back into the refrigerator so they stay cold until we're ready to eat them." He stood up. "Let's have cake and coffee in the living room. I've got wood laid for a fire in the fireplace. There's nothing better than a friendly fire on a crisp, fall evening. Why don't you put a match to the fire? The matches are in the tall tin on the small table by the bookcase."

In a few minutes they were settled into matching over-stuffed chairs facing a crackling fire. Walter took a sip of coffee.

"Who's the woman standing next to the Lincoln Zephyr car in that framed photo on the table where you keep the matches? Is that your mother?"

Wilson looked momentarily at the floor before he answered, "No, that's Abigail Pierson who left the car to my father."

"The one you said he used to drink tea with at least once a week?"

"Yeah, that's her. Like I said, even when she was sixty she was very pretty." He paused like he was hesitant to continue. "I found that photograph tucked away in a folder in the top drawer of his filing cabinet when I went through dad's papers after he died. There's an inscription on the back of it that says, 'Affectionately, Abigail.' I thought I should save it and display it in gratitude for the car."

He took a swallow of coffee and tilted his head sideway. "I can see the curious look on your face. Who knows if Abigail gave him anything besides the car? If she did, they took the secret with them to the grave." He sat back in his chair and grinned. "Besides, I know the picture irritates my banker brother, Calvin. He makes a point of looking at it and scowling whenever he comes to see me—which, thanks to your God, isn't often."

Walter laughed. "Sounds like there's still a bit of sibling rivalry."

Wilson nodded. "A little. Dad knew that if he gave the car to me, I would enjoy driving it, but that if he left it to Calvin, he would sell it and invest the money. I'm sure Calvin can't remember the last time he did something impractical. That's the way with Calvinists: they're afraid to enjoy." He stood up and put another log on the fire.

"Now, pastor, this is fun, but before the evening slips away entirely I want to talk about a question that's been bouncing around in my head ever since that day we first met, and I haven't had a chance to talk it over with you when we were alone. Do you ever think God might be up to something new and different, or are we just stuck with the nothing but the same old, same old God that's in the Bible? Seems unlikely to me that God would talk away for a thousand years like people in the Bible say he did, and then shut up completely for the next two thousand years. Don't you think God would at least keep talking to modify the shortsighted perceptions of him in the scripture?"

"I do. I think God still speaks."

"If that's so, when did you last hear him say something?"

Walter laughed. "You're a tough teacher, Wilson. Did you do this kind of grilling with your students?"

Wilson nodded. "I did. So, when did you last hear God say something?"

Walter sat back in his chair. "Okay, professor, I'll tell you. Not long ago I was confronted by a very narrow-minded person who believes someone in our church is committing a serious sin. This person doesn't know for sure, but thinks the circumstantial evidence is convincing. As the accuser talked I thought about the incident in John's Gospel when Jesus comes upon a woman who has been caught in the act of adultery and the Pharisees confront him with, 'Moses commanded us to stone such; what do you say?' You recall the scene?"

"I do. Jesus said something like, 'Let the person who is without sin be the first to throw a stone at her.' And the bastards all slunk away."

"You're right, they did. So, I looked straight at the accuser sitting opposite me and said, 'I suggest you leave the stones on the ground and go away quietly.' He wasn't happy with me, but he went away."

For a moment Wilson didn't say anything. Then he looked directly at Walter. "I like you, Walter Macdonald. I like what you're made of."

"Thanks, Wilson, I really appreciate the compliment, but I remembered the incident because I think it speaks to your question. I believe God spoke to me in that moment." He paused and watched Wilson watching him. He spoke slowly for emphasis. "I didn't hear a voice or come down from a mountain with tablets in my hands, but I definitely felt something moving in my heart as the words I spoke came into my head. I think there is still some kind of Power that moves among us. There are times when I'm sure I feel its presence."

Wilson looked pensive. "I would like to agree with you—which may be a surprise. The problem for me is coming up with a convincing description of that Something that you think speaks to you. A metaphor—and that's what I think you are using here—is credible only if it references something that seems real to us.

"In ancient cultures, even up through the Middle Ages, kings and emperors were like gods—often considered gods. Their speaking had incredible power. What people believed was God-speak in those earlier times was the most powerful phenomena they could conceive of. Think about it: God spoke and the universe was created! People believed that something akin to a personal cosmic power made it all happen. They didn't think there was literally a cosmic Being sitting on a throne somewhere in the heavens—it was a metaphor, but they believed the metaphor reflected something that really exists."

Walter sat up and crossed his arms in front of him. "You're right; their perception of God made sense within their ordinary, daily experience. It fit with the way they saw the earth and the heavens."

Wilson leaned forward. "Okay, so here's the problem: except for people who insist on holding onto a sentimental theology—and I know there are lots of them—the kind of anthropomorphic metaphors those old guys used to describe God are no longer convincing to people like me. But why should that be such a problem? If we know biblical perceptions of women and slavery and gay people were culturally conditioned, why can't we admit the same is true of biblical perceptions of God and update them?"

He stood up and gestured like he was lecturing. "Lords and kings are now mostly figureheads—like the British royals. In our time calling God 'King' or 'Lord' *demotes* God. It makes God a caricature, much too small to be big enough to be a convincing God in our universe. We can read the old texts that envision God as a potent cosmic talker and appreciate their power *then*, but that doesn't translate into *now*. We live in an age of science now, not an age of lords and kings. We need contemporary metaphors with everyday words that have the same convincing power now as the old ones did then. At best the old metaphors are quaint."

"Quaint?!!" Walter laughed under his breath. "We need more than quaint." He paused and took a sip of coffee. "A few weeks ago I had a long talk with a young man who went through a horrible experience in Vietnam that completely did in any possibility he could believe in God. He told me he has great respect for me personally and then said, 'I wish I could say the same about your God. But your God seems like the old straight chair I have that belonged to my grandparents. I keep it around only because of the memories it holds; I never try to sit in it.'"

Wilson looked straight at him. "He nailed you!"

"You're right, he did. I realized in that moment that I spend most of my time promoting ways of believing that were once part of most people's everyday experience, but, except when they're in church, aren't anymore. I knew I had to find a cosmic makeover for that old chair. A God who is only nostalgia is impotent."

"Have you found anything?"

Walter set his coffee cup on the small table next to his chair. "Maybe I have." He looked off into space for a while, then back at Wilson. "But to answer the question I need to tell a story."

Wilson stood up and walked toward the wood box. "Another story calls for another log on the fire—and maybe some more cheesecake?"

"Thanks, but I'm still too full."

"Well, if you're going to exercise self-control, I guess I'll have to. I'll put another couple of logs on the fire—in case you have a two-log story."

Walter grinned and settled back in his chair as Wilson put the logs on the fire. "Years ago I had a difficult and, looking back, I would even say 'traumatic,' relationship with a disbeliever. Her name is Mary Kerrigan; she teaches literature at Wellesley now. We fell in love when she lived here in Schuylerkill Falls, but we couldn't connect in ways that would matter to both of us in the long run and so we split. She challenged my convictions and my theology like no one ever has before or since—and I'm still grateful for that. I made a good defense, but I didn't win our debate and neither did she."

Wilson interrupted gently. "That must have been hard. Sometimes, the people we fall in love with don't suit us, but we still love them."

Walter raised his shoulders and tilted his head. "And, sometimes, they give us gifts that stay with us after they go out of our lives. That's what happened with Mary. After she left I had lots of time to think about what happened between us. I decided I wanted to know more about the world she represents. At first it was kind of like grief work, but it soon became much more than that. Mary had lent me her copy of Darwin's *Origins*; she left before I could give it back to her. I dug it out and reread it carefully. I also read some depth psychology, a little Freud but mostly Carl Jung. I called my old physics prof at Union College and he suggested some new physics texts for me to read. After I studied them—which took a while—I took an intro astronomy course at RPI. Now that was *really* challenging."

Wilson laughed. "You're brave!"

"Well, I passed, Wilson; it was a struggle, but I did. What I learned about us and the universe that surrounds us matters more than the grade I got. I still stand in awe whenever I think about it, that the universe is 13.8 *billion* years old and 91 billion light years across. Those are unimaginably big numbers. One light year is six *trillion* miles of distance—and the universe is ninety-one billion of those in diameter. In our Milky Way galaxy alone there are as many as 300 billion stars. And the whole thing is expanding at some incredible rate." He paused and shook his head. "Makes the six-day creation narrative in the Bible seem like a dated myth, doesn't it?"

Wilson raised his eyebrows. "It does! Creation has become cosmos; cosmology has displaced theology. Physicists are our priests, astrophysicists our high priests. They speak to us of forces, not spirits." He shrugged his shoulders. "Of course, none of us has actually seen any of the forces they talk about. But we trust their perceptions. We believe that what they describe is real—and that no Genesis-like God is required to explain any of it."

Walter sighed, sat back in his chair and folded his arms in front of him. "I know you're right, and that troubles me because I love the images in that six-day creation story in Genesis, like the Creator's Spirit brooding over the waters. For me the shift in belief represents a lot of loss. In the former time the old God is in charge. The creation is his creation. He rules everywhere. You can depend on that." He stopped speaking and looked at the floor for a while.

There was a lighter tone in his voice when he went on. "One week this summer the assigned scripture readings to base sermons on for the following Sunday included the book of Jonah as the Old Testament text to be used. As a kid Jonah and the whale was one of my favorite stories. God wants Jonah to go to Nineveh to preach to the Ninevites. But Jonah doesn't like the Ninevites, so he gets on a ship bound for Tarshish—which is in the opposite direction from Nineveh. As soon as the ship is on the open sea God makes a huge storm, and after drawing lots, the sailors figure out that Jonah's running away from God is what is causing the storm. Reluctantly they throw Jonah overboard and immediately the storm ceases. Jonah doesn't drown. God provides a big fish (kids always think of it as a whale) that swallows Jonah and then swims to the beach were Jonah boarded the ship to escape from God. But there's no escape. The big fish God sent to prevent Jonah from drowning throws him up on the beach so he can go to Nineveh and preach about God to the Ninevites.

"As I sat reading the Bible story, I went on a memory trip. When I was in fifth and sixth grade I had the best Sunday school teacher any kid could ever ask for. When she taught we didn't sit, bored to death, coloring pictures of Bible stories; we acted them out. We got up and moved; we turned the stories into games and plays.

"One winter this teacher helped us turn the Jonah story into a play. We designed a set to portray Jonah inside the whale. It was fun! He had a comfortable chair, a table with snacks on it, a reading lamp—one smart kid said it must have been a whale oil lamp; he even had a TV! When the whale brings Jonah back to beach where he started running away from God a TV reporter is there who interviews him and then broadcasts the story on the nightly news. In the conversation with the reporter Jonah explains that you can't run away from what God wants you to do. If you try to, God will find you."

"Sounds like a lot more fun than any Sunday school class I ever went to."

"That's why I can still remember what I learned. Of course, years later when I was a seminary student, I discovered that the Jonah story is probably not real history, just a story, but I still held onto Jonah's picture of God as someone who pays personal attention to us. I still want that to be true. But the more science I've studied the more I've struggled to hang on to this picture of God as a cosmic personality.

"I finally had to recognize that Isaac Newton's physics upset the Biblical God apple cart for good. Most of us now assume that the universe is a *natural* order governed by forces, not by spirits, let alone by some dominant spirit-like God. That realization has trickled down. It's what most people know is true, even those who wish it weren't. There's no way to get the apples back into the cart.

"So, I hit up against a dilemma. Do I give up my belief in a personal God, or do I ignore what I've learned about the nature of the universe and pretend that the old God is somehow up to doing God stuff in the universe as we now know it? For a long time I was just stuck between the old and the new. Then early one morning I realized that I have to do in this time what open-minded believers have always had to do in theirs: translate old perceptions of God shaped by old contexts into new perceptions shaped by a new context. You don't junk the old perceptions; you appreciate them for what they reveal—and then go on. God doesn't stand still so there's no reason we should have to."

"So, what have you found?"

Walter laughed nervously and shifted around in his chair. "I'll share it with you—though you have to promise not to laugh if I tell you where it came from."

Wilson grinned, "I promise."

"But let's take a break first; I'm ready for that piece of cheesecake you put in the refrigerator when I was too full to eat it."

"Good idea. Why don't you put a couple more pieces of wood on the fire while I get our cheesecake? More wine or more coffee?

"The wine is superb; I can't resist, but, please, just a half glass." He chuckled. "You really should bottle it for the market. The label could read, 'Wilson's Wonder Wine: It Will Lift Your Spirits.'"

Wilson shook his head. "Thanks, but philosophers make poor businessmen. I'll stick to 'For personal use only.'"

Walter placed two pieces of wood on the fire in the fireplace and stirred up the coals. Wilson returned with a tray holding two full glasses of wine and two pieces of cheesecake.

Wilson took a bite of cake. "Where'd you get this cheesecake? It's really good."

"At that German restaurant on the corner of State Street and Erie Boulevard in Schenectady. We should take a break from home cooking and go there for dinner sometime." He took a sip of wine and held out the glass toward Wilson. "This glass was full. Are you plying me with wine to loosen my tongue?"

"Whatever it takes; I've got a dozen more bottles in the cellar. So, let's cut to the chase. What did you find that I'm not supposed to laugh about?"

"I think God inspired me not long ago when I went to the movies!"

Wilson shrugged his shoulders. "I've never heard of God being at the movies, but I suppose God could go to the movies to make a point." He waited.

Walter leaned back in his chair. "Have you seen Star Wars?"

"I have; best film I've gone to in years!"

"What did you think about 'the Force' in the film?"

"It's an image that pulses with possibility."

"It does! —especially in the phrase 'the Force be with you.'" He paused and then looked intently at Wilson. "When I sat in the dark theater that night in May and Obi-Wan Kenobi said, 'May the Force be with you,' it was. The Force was inside of me and all around me. It lifted my soul off into the cosmos. I was there and here. I knew I was in the presence of God who is both there and here. I heard the music of the spheres." He paused and looked directly at Wilson. "I danced with God, Wilson. Does that sound crazy to you?"

Wilson shook his head slowly back and forth. "No, it doesn't sound crazy."

The two of them sat in the quiet for a while as the flickering light from the fireplace played all around them.

Walter broke the silence. "Envisioning God as some kind of superhuman figure was always egotistical, Wilson. Most of our metaphors for God were fashioned backwards—from our viewpoint, not from God's. We thought we were gazing through a window into heaven, but actually we were looking in a mirror.

"God was around a long time before humans came along; we're just a tiny blip at the end of the evolutionary chain. At the most we've been around a few paltry hundred thousand years. The stars and planets scattered across billions of light years, and bacteria and lizards and apes are our forebears. We're all inter-related links in the same cosmic chain. The same forces connect and energize everything in the universe; what happened light years away from us reaches across all space and time to touch us here and now.

"We need a perception of God that begins on God's side and that matches what we now know about how the creation works. God as 'Force' provides that; it recovers the potency that king and lord and spirit have lost. It pushes us beyond perceptions of God we have inherited without negating them. The old ways of thinking about God give us insights; they're just not the end-all some biblical literalists would like us to believe they are.

"I want to bring all of it together, the best of the old and the new, in one all-embracing reality. It's not a matter of choosing what was over against what is. It's not either/or; it's both-and. God is both Spirit and Force. Holy Force makes Holy Spirit seem potent again. Holy Force seems real now. It's plausible. It's not just a metaphor; it's God in up-to-date clothes."

He paused and leaned against the back of his chair and sighed. "Think of it, Wilson: God who was there when everything started is still creating the universe and is still alive in all of it. A caring Force ripples across thirteen billion years of space-time, and four billion years of earthly evolution to this night to touch us sitting together in this room. The Force that created the universe is here, right now. The Force is with us. I feel it. Can you feel it, Wilson? Does it seem real to you?"

He stared at Wilson, waiting for him to say something, but Wilson was silent. There was urgency in his voice when he went on. "Please tell me what you think, Wilson. Please help me. I'm trying hard to find my way."

Wilson sat silently for a while, then looked directly at him and spoke softly. "Sometimes, my friend, what touches us is more than we can understand."

For a while neither of them spoke. When the old grandfather's clock in the front hallway chimed eleven Walter took a deep breath and nodded. "You're right; it will always be that way." He stood up. "But at least now I know that however we describe whatever's out there, it's real."

A grave expression spread across Wilson's face. "Before you go, I have a secret I have to tell you about." He stood up, walked into the kitchen and returned with a baseball cap on his head. The cap had a big "B" on it. "I'm a Red Sox fan, Walter. They beat the Yankees yesterday. I listened to the game, and I rooted for Boston. I always root for Boston, even when they play the Yankees." He grinned, a very big grin. "Even if you pray for me, Walter, I won't repent."

"Well, the Yankees may never forgive you, but I will. I know I can't compete with your cooking, and I don't make my own wine, but I do make an excellent marinara sauce and I know my red wines well. I've been here and enjoyed your cooking several times; it's my turn to cook now. The next time we get together I'll provide pasta with homemade sauce and imported wine. And we can go on talking from where we left off tonight."

"Name your night, Walter. I've got lots of free nights. We just need to do it before the leftover cheesecake spoils."

"I'll call soon." He walked down the driveway toward the street. When he reached the end, a car drove by; the driver tooted its horn as its headlights shone on him. He waved.

Wilson watched the retreating car until all was silent darkness. He stood in the doorway and spoke softly. "I hope there is a caring Force with you, my friend. If you dare to dance in the open to praise the God you have discovered like King David in the Old Testament did to celebrate the God he discovered, you better keep your robe wrapped tightly around you."

13. DISAPPEARING ACT

The wind blew ruthlessly like it always does south of Lake Michigan in February. Gary Shanahan was glad to be settled down for the night in his warm truck cab. It was just quarter past six when he heard a knock on the passenger door. He grabbed his flashlight, scooted across the seat and shined the beam out through the closed window. It was Lorna. He opened the door and drew her up quickly into the cab. "Jeez, Lorna, this is no night to be out dressed like that!"

She grinned, "I know, but it's my work uniform."

"You're early; it's not even six-thirty; you usually don't show up until eight."

"I know." She gave him a bleak look.

He watched her for a minute. "You don't look good, babe. What's wrong?"

"Lots. Just after noon the runner came with the envelopes and I tucked them into my big purse and left the office early like I always do when I'm coming to see you. About three-thirty Jack called my apartment and told me not to go near the office and not to meet you—that someone would show up at my apartment after supper to pick up the envelopes.

"The Feds raided us this afternoon just as the delivery truck loaded with the stuff you brought from Albany was leaving.

They found the powder hidden in the cans inside the washers. Somehow they knew it was coming and would be out for delivery to the local pushers today." She looked straight at him and shook her head despondently. "I'm sure Jack thinks one of us was careless, maybe even tipped them off, and that's how they found out. Does anybody know about the money you carry around in your jacket pocket?"

"Just, Lauren, soon to be my ex, she's the only one, but she wouldn't rat on me." He gazed off into the distance for a moment. "If she has, it's the last time she'll rat on anybody."

"Maybe she wouldn't do it on purpose, but she might have accidently let it slip out. Anyway, we're done. And you don't get done and get out in this business." She was breathing quickly as she handed him a small envelope. "That's what I have for you tonight."

He looked at the large envelope protruding from the side pocket of her purse. "What you gonna do with that one?"

"I'm not going to leave it; in case somebody is watching I'm going to fold it over like this and put it right here in the zippered pocked of my purse. That way it will look like I left it with you. Jack told me to meet him at eight at the O'Hare Hilton; that usually means he wants me to go somewhere for a fun time with him. I don't think that's what he's planning for tonight."

"How you gonna get away? The guy Jack sent probably already showed up at your apartment and didn't find you. By now they're out lookin' for both of us." He glanced around the lighted parking lot.

"I'm going to disappear, Gary, and you better do the same. After I talked with Jack on the phone I made a quick trip to the bank and cleaned out my account." She took a bank envelope stuffed with bills out of her purse. "It's all here."

"My God, Lorna, there must be more in those two envelopes than there is in that wad in my jacket pocket."

"Not really, but it's enough. Between what I had in the bank and what's in the big envelope there's enough to get me far away from here and keep me for a long time. And when that money runs out, I'm sure I can find work wherever I go." She smiled. "There's always a demand for my kind of work."

"Where you gonna go?"

"You don't want to know and I'm not going to tell you. But you better get out of here—and quick. The truck you were going to buy with the money in your jacket pocket won't do you any good now. You may as well take the money out of it and leave the jacket here. You need to go somewhere where they won't find you. Because if they do, they'll do you in and anybody else they think might know what you've been bringing from Albany to here all these months." She gave him a very sober look. "They always do it the same way: just one shot to your head."

He answered quickly. "Let's go together."

She shook her head. "That would just make it easier for them. Two trails will make it harder than one. That way one of us might make it." She looked at him and sighed. "I like you Gary. I'm sorry we never got to do what we were supposed to be doing all those times I brought you the envelopes." She leaned over and kissed him on the cheek. "Good luck, Gary; I better go now." She opened the door.

He held her hand and let her down easy. When her feet reached the pavement, he didn't let go of her hand. She turned and looked up at him. He smiled at her, "If we both make it, I'll meet you here at that back booth by the kitchen in the restaurant on the Fourth of July—then we can go somewhere and do what we were supposed to be doing all those times we've met here."

She smiled. "My treat!"

He shut the door and watched her run across the parking lot and disappear around the corner of the restaurant. "Such a nice body," he said softly, "and she's got those envelopes in her purse. Maybe I shouldn't have let her go?" He pulled his heavy coat and overnight bag off the shelf behind the seat, took the wad of bills out of his N.E.T. jacket and stuffed them into the left lower zipper pocket of his heavy coat and zipped it up. He threw the N.E.T. jacket onto the shelf behind him, slid across the seat, unlocked the glove compartment, and removed the handgun that always traveled with him. He picked up a clip and inserted it into the gun and checked to be sure the safety was on. He slipped the handgun and an extra clip into the right lower zipper pocket of his heavy coat, put the coat on, slid back across the seat, opened the truck door, stepped out into the cold night wind, and ran toward the parking lot in front of the restaurant where Lorna always parked her fancy car.

At just after eight o'clock two DEA agents in a black suburban drove quickly in front of Gary's truck, parked, and shined their spotlight at the truck's windshield. They jumped out and jerked the cab doors open and searched the cab. It was empty except for Gary's N. E.T. jacket on the shelf behind the seat. They pulled the jacket off the shelf and checked the pockets. Nothing in them.

Just as they stepped back out of the truck a third agent walked up. "We found Lorna Keach in a car parked in front of the restaurant, sir."

"That's great!"

"Not really. She's lying across the front seat with a bullet hole in her forehead. There's a big manila envelope and a bank envelope on the seat next to her—both of them torn open and empty."

The next morning Walter was reheating the coffee left-over from breakfast when he saw Ed Hutchins in Butch's tow-truck drive into his driveway. Ed ran up the steps and onto the manse side porch. Walter let him in and shut the door quickly. "That's wind's wicked! The TV weather forecaster said it's blown all the way from Chicago to here."

Ed made a face, "Tell me about it. I just stood out in that wicked wind for a half-hour helping one of your neighbors get her car started."

"How about some hot coffee? It's already been reheated once, but it's still drinkable."

"That would taste good, thanks, but just a little. I can't stay long; I've got another car-won't-start call to make before I can go back to the garage and have some lunch."

Walter poured coffee into a cup and handed it to him. He took a sip and looked somber. "Lauren called me at the garage a little while ago. That detective from the Albany PD we met with when Gary beat her up last fall called her after I left for work this morning. Gary's disappeared. They found his N.E.T. truck parked at a truck stop south of Chicago last night. It was running, but he wasn't in it. The police watched it all night hoping he might come back, but he never did."

"What do they think happened to him?"

"They're not sure, but they're concerned. They found the hooker that usually visits him when he stops there. She's dead; somebody shot her in the head."

"Oh, good God, that's terrible!"

"Yeah—and it gets worse. The detective said the people who found the hooker are Drug Enforcement Agents. They've been watching Gary for months. They suspect he's involved in moving drugs and drug money. Yesterday they raided the warehouse south of Chicago he hauls appliances to every other week. They found drugs hidden in some of the washers he dropped off yesterday. They're sure he's been bringing drugs in the loads he takes there every other week and that he's being paid extra under the table for doing it. They think that's where the money came from that Lauren found in his N.E.T. jacket the day he beat her up. He probably got so upset because he knew it was drug money and didn't want anybody to know about it."

Walter looked away and then back at him. "I was afraid he might be into something like that." He shook his head side to side. "And now nobody knows where he is."

"That part really worries me. The detective told Lauren the DEAs aren't sure who shot the hooker—could be Gary or somebody from the mob. Either way, if Gary thinks Lauren's the one who ratted on him and got him into the fix he's in now, he could lose it—as we know, he has a history of that. If he does, there's no telling what he'll do if he gets close to Lauren. She got a protection order to keep him away from her while the divorce is getting finished, but that won't mean squat if he's upset." He paused. "But after today it'll be hard for him to find her."

"How's that?"

"On Saturday we're moving into the first-floor apartment in the yellow house that Brights redid up the street from you. I've stayed in Lauren's apartment in Albany for a while, but the commute from Albany to here is a pain and there are just too many bad memories for her in that place. So, she gave her notice at Johnny's and next week will start working breakfasts and lunches at the Grill here. The tips won't be as good, but with two of us paying the rent they won't need to be. Besides, when the weather warms, we can both walk to work. She can work at the Grill for a while, and if it's not what she wants, she can look for something at one of the restaurants in Saratoga."

Walter pursed his lips and let his breath out slowly. "Pretty scary, isn't it?"

Ed looked very sober. "Yeah, for all of us. Maybe you can use your influence with the Man upstairs and get him to look out for us—and while you're at it get the sun to shine Saturday when we move?" He grinned.

"I'll try, but you need to remember I'm in sales, not management."

Ed made a face. "I still think you have more influence than I do." He pushed his chair back and stood up. "The detective from Albany told us to be careful and report anything unusual right away. He said he'd let Chief Haines of the police department here know what's going on in case Gary somehow learns Lauren's here in the village and decides to come here looking for her." He took his heavy jacket off the hook by the door. "You better be careful, Coach. If Gary knows that Lauren came to see you after he beat her up and wants to find her and can't, he may think you know where she is. Gary's a big man—not quite as big as you are, but we know how vicious he can get. Maybe that hooker got the same kind of treatment that Lauren did?"

Walter nodded slowly. "Thanks for the heads-up; I'll keep my eyes open."

Ed zipped up his jacket and shrugged his shoulders. "Probably nothing'll happen. We just have to keep our fingers crossed and watch out." He paused and grinned. "Like I said, you can probably do something better than cross your fingers to influence whoever or whatever is in charge of what happens to us. I got to go now; it's nearly noon and I got to help one of your neighbors get her car going before I can go back to the garage and warm up and eat my lunch."

14. MOMENTS OF TRUTH

It was a cold and rainy day—not unusual for late March Monday in Upstate New York. With the exhausting schedule of Holy Week and Easter Sunday yesterday behind him Walter gave himself the gift of sleeping late. He spent the day reading and getting his trout fishing equipment ready for opening day while he listened to the Red Sox beat the Yankees in a spring training game.

The weather was better on Tuesday, still cool—overnight temperature in the thirties, but even before six o'clock it was clear that it would warm up. He was out running before the first rays of the sun struck the top of the church steeple. He followed his usual route: out to the end of Church Street, then on the Battenville Road to Petersons' farm, back to the village and along several village streets to the manse—about nine miles all together.

He approached Molly Hutchins's house on Grove Street just after seven-thirty as she was picking up the newspaper from her front porch. She called to him, "I'll bet you've run all the way out to Erik and Becky's and back."

He stopped at the end of her walkway. It took him a minute to catch his breath. "I have!" He motioned to the sky filling with bright sun. "It's a super day for a run."

She laughed. "I don't get up early and I don't run. At fifty-nine I'm not required to run; I walk, and I do it at the end of the day, not the beginning." She paused and then added, "Anybody making your breakfast today?"

He tilted his head and shrugged his shoulders. "The usual cook, me, I guess."

"It's school vacation week, so I haven't had mine. Do you have time for breakfast and some talk?"

"Sounds good—I have nothing scheduled until eleven, but I do need to go home and shower before I'm fit for company." He raised both his arms and made a face. "Would forty-five minutes from now work for you?"

"It would! See you at eight-thirty."

He pushed his chair back from the table. "That's the most breakfast I've had in ages. How did you make those incredible rolls in the time it took me to go home and shower? They taste just like the rolls your mother used to make."

"That's because they are the rolls my mother used to make. I bake big batches of them and put them in the freezer in case I have unexpected company—like you! Usually it's Ed and Lauren who show up unannounced—more often now that they live just a couple of blocks away. But I don't mind; I'm always glad to see them."

He watched her face as she spoke. "You really like Lauren, don't you?"

"I do! She's the best thing that's happened in Ed's life since he came back from Vietnam. She understands his hurt and isn't afraid of it. She stays close to him when it rears its ugly head. She's caring and very wise for someone as young as she is."

He nodded and took a sip of coffee. "I saw that wisdom the first time I met her—the day she came to the house after Gary beat her. When Ed saw how horribly hurt she was he was ready to go after Gary and do him in—and I couldn't blame him. But she held on to him and made him look at her and said, 'No, Ed, don't; that would just make things worse'—and it would have. She's smart and strong and tender."

"She's all of those! When she stayed with me while she was recovering we had lots of time to talk. I learned how she got to be the woman she is." She stopped speaking and waited. He didn't say anything. She laughed. "You want to know what she told me, don't you?"

He smiled and nodded. "Yes, I do, after eighteen years you can read me better than my mother."

She laughed again and shook her head. "Walter, I may be older than you, but not old enough to be your mother! And, as you already know, if there's anything I fantasized being with you, it wasn't being your mother!" She watched him shift around in his chair. "Anyway, I think Lauren would be okay with you knowing. Want some more coffee before I start?"

"Thanks, I do; yours is the best."

"I call it 'Bob's coffee;' it's a special blend he (she hesitated for an instant) insisted on having." She paused and her eyes looked wistful. She sighed and shook her head slightly. He watched her carefully. "I see you looking at me."

"This is tit for tat: I've known you long enough to recognize that look; something that matters is happening inside you."

She laughed. "I almost said 'insists' instead of 'insisted,' as if he was still here."

He watched her look at the empty chair.

She sat up straight. "Okay, enough of that; now about Lauren. Lauren grew up living in a duplex in Menands north of Albany. Her father worked construction from spring through fall, and then was unemployed and spent most of his time at the local tavern during the winter. Her mother cleaned houses all year-round. Lauren pretty much had to take care of herself as far back as she can remember. She went to a neighbor's after school when she was young, then became a latchkey kid when she was in fifth grade. By the time she was in junior high she was making supper every day and keeping the house clean. She started busing and waiting tables at a neighborhood coffee shop when she was fifteen."

"Sounds like a tough life for a kid growing up."

"It was—and once she was old enough to get away, there wasn't anything to hold her at home. Her soon to be ex-husband, Gary, is the older brother of one of her high school girlfriends. They met by chance when Lauren was at the friend's house one Saturday night for a sleep-over. He's six years older than she is. She didn't exactly fall for him—she realizes now that she married him right after she graduated from high school as much to get away from home as because she wanted to be his wife. At the time she fantasized that he would give her a better life than her parents had. The trucking job he had seemed like a good job: it lasted year-round, and, while most of the time when he wasn't on a trip he was off with one of his buddies who races cars, at least he didn't spend all of his time off at a local tavern and come home drunk.

"Besides, she thought she'd soon be a mom with babies to love. But the babies never came. She doesn't know why; they never had the money to get tested to figure out why. So, their lives settled into a rut: she waiting table and he driving truck and at the races or the garage working on his friend's stock car whenever he wasn't on a trip. It wasn't bad, but it wasn't good— just dull normal. In the beginning she tried to get him to spend more time with her, but nothing worked. So, she gave up; like her mother she decided that what she had was all she could have.

"Until Ed came into her life. That Thursday night he sang to her, the woman inside she thought was dead came alive again. For a long time she thought she was tasting forbidden fruit with Ed—sometimes she still wonders whether she is. But after Gary beat her, she knew there was no way she could go back to him." She paused and looked at Walter. "You don't think she should, do you?"

He answered quickly and emphatically. "No, never. She's probably connecting two things that aren't really connected. After Gary beat her, she has the right to get away from him. The life she and Ed have is a different chapter. I hope they find their way together—they seem to be really good for each other, but whether and how they do it is theirs to discover."

She sighed and said, "That's a typical Walter response. You don't judge people, Walter; you don't even lecture us!"

He laughed. "That's not my job." He reflected for a moment. "I used to think it was. When I began as the minister here I thought I was supposed to be the expert on God—that I was called to be the preacher who told people what God is like and how God wants us to live. I proclaimed. When I'm in the pulpit I still do that; when I'm there I'm commissioned to consult the Scriptures and tell people how God wants us to live.

"But when I'm in someone's kitchen, I'm the same ordinary human that everyone else is. Life is tough all the time for lots of people—and has its tough moments for the rest of us. My job as a pastor is to help people through the tough times, and to let them know that God wants to help them too. I like Ed's word for me; he calls me 'Coach.' A coach is someone who knows how to help people play the game, and I hope I've learned how to do that. Sometimes I think that the way someone is playing the game is wrong and have to tell them I think it's wrong. But unless what they are doing is harming someone else, I have to wait for a time when they can hear it. Sometimes it takes a while, but with encouragement, and, sometimes, some 'coaching,' most people eventually find their way."

"Like me?"

He laughed. "That's a leading comment if I ever heard one! So, are you going to tell me now why you invited me here for breakfast?"

A serious look came onto her face and she nodded gently. "Yes, I am. I'm one of those who need your non-judgmental coaching."

He looked at the kitchen clock. "If you need me to, I can stay as long as another hour."

"You must think I have a lot to confess!" She laughed nervously. "Well, I do, so I better refill your coffee cup."

"Thanks."

She sat back down and looked directly at him. "A month ago Frank and I went out to dinner for the first time since Marsha died. We went to a small out-of-the-way restaurant in Glens Falls. When he called the previous week to invite me I was relieved to hear from him. We hadn't seen each other alone or even said more than 'Hi' to each other for weeks.

"The dinner was pretty awkward—none of the relaxed feelings, or fun and easy conversation like we used to have when we went away together. We talked mostly about how his kids are struggling to deal with losing their mom. He told me he wanted to get back together with me and have fun times like we used to but didn't know how to do it. He was sure his kids would be hurt and angry if he were to tell them about us—about our relationship when their mom was slipping away."

He spoke gently. "Finding out could be really hard for them. They would surely see it as—to use your word—an 'affair' and would likely be hurt, maybe angry."

"Well, this past Saturday night I had a chance to see how difficult it's going to be. When Frank and I were out to dinner we decided that the only way we could know how his kids would react to me was to have them meet me. He invited me to his house for supper Saturday as 'a friend from school.' His children and grandchildren were there."

"How did it go?"

She looked somber and shook her head back and forth. "It was *very* difficult. I felt like a fifth wheel the whole evening. I tried to help his daughters-in-law get the meal ready, but they know where everything is in Frank's kitchen and how the family likes their food—and I don't know any of that. I didn't know that Marsha always made the mashed potatoes using the water they're cooked in, not with milk and butter, because his cholesterol is high, or that one of his daughters-in-law is vegetarian so there have to be extra vegetables cooked for her. I didn't know that his six-year-old grandson, Andy junior, hates peas; he started to cry when I put them on his plate because the family has a rule that you have to eat everything on your plate."

She paused and sighed. "The whole evening was like that. When we were having dessert Frank talked about me and described how much he respects what I do at the school, he reached out and almost touched my hand. He caught himself before he actually did it, but I saw Andy's wife, Susie, staring at me. Actually, they all kept staring at me the whole evening. I'm sure they suspect what's gone on between their dad and me. Now I wonder even with time if they could ever accept Frank and me together. If the purpose of the evening was to test the waters, it didn't turn out very promising." She stopped and looked at the floor, then up at Walter.

He watched her for a while and then said, "I'm sorry it was so hard. Maybe it was just too soon?"

"I appreciate your kindness, but I think there's more than just timing to deal with. During those years when Marsha was sick Frank moved on emotionally. He cared deeply for her, but at some point he knew he was going to lose her and would have to build a life after that. Maybe he was wrong to do what he did with me while she was still alive, but he was burned out and needed someone to care for him.

"His kids weren't sitting with Marsha week after week watching her lose it and become an angry woman who lashed out uncontrollably at her husband. I know they knew it was the disease warping her mind, but they couldn't feel his suffering the way I did. He lost the woman who had been his wife and lover for years before those kids came into the picture. After she died their memories were of the family like it was when they were growing up. They're still trying to live back there.

"It's different for us here. Jean and Ed lived here for years after their father died; they got used to us as a family without him. They've moved on with their lives and, as much as they and I miss him, they want to help me move on with mine.

"Frank's kids haven't moved on. And they may not be able to in the same way that Ed and Jean had to. They didn't have to finish their growing up without their mom. When I sat there I thought, 'they'll always be her kids; they will always see me as an interloper in their family.'" She watched his face and waited for him to say something.

"If you're right, what are you going to do?"

She sat up and looked straight at him and said loudly, "First, I'm going to yell at *you*! You knew that what Frank and I were doing was over the edge, that probably it wouldn't work in the long run, but you didn't tell me that it wouldn't. You didn't tell me that sometime I would have to back off—that what we were doing would never fly with the rest of his family. Why didn't you tell me to cool it?"

"Would you have done it before you knew you had to?"

She laughed nervously. "No, probably not; but you should have told me anyway. That's your job."

"No, I don't think so. We talked about that earlier. Some of our church members would like an old-fashioned preacher who is stern and inflexible, but that's not who I am, and this time is the wrong time for that kind of minister. It's not my job to rub your nose in what you already know could be wrong before you're ready to do something about it. If I start doing that with people, they'll turn me off; I will never have conversations like you and I are having now. I can't start from where someone should be, only from where they are. If I lay on them what I think they should be before they're ready to hear it, I will just frustrate them or, worse, make them hopeless."

She sat back in her chair and nodded.

"My job is to hang in with you until you're ready to hear what I think you need to hear. You began to get ready to hear what we're talking about now the day of Marsha's funeral when we were at the cemetery and you stood at the edge of the mourners apart from everyone else. I could tell what you were feeling then; you were beginning to hear the message I knew you needed to hear."

She sighed again. "You're right. When I stood there by myself and looked at Frank and his children standing at their mother's grave, I realized that they're a family and I'm not part of that family. Nothing Frank and I did all those months we went away together made me part of his family. Marsha's illness was so costly to Frank that he sought me out to give him love and care—and I did. That may not have been right, but it did help him survive. I understand the reason we did what we did, but I know that doesn't excuse it. The reason is different from the excuse."

He nodded. "That's hard to admit, but it's true."

"Things are different now. For Frank the reason we did what we did then is gone. If we go on together, it will have to be different; it will have to include our families. I think Ed and Jean will be all right with it, but I know that it will not be easy for Frank's kids. When they learn about the relationship Frank and I had before their mother died—and they will surely learn about it, they will be angry. And I understand that. But then is not now. I can be patient, but the time will come when I will have to say to them, 'I love your father and I want to love you too. Please forgive me for any hurt I may have caused you. Please give me a chance to love you!'" She stopped abruptly and waited for him to say something.

He spoke softly. "And if they won't forgive you and give you a chance?"

She looked at him with determination filling her eyes. "If they won't forgive me and give me a chance, then I will have to let them have their father to themselves—but only for a while. We can only play the hand we've been dealt, Walter. I know I'm not perfect, but neither is life fair. So, I will hope for forgiveness and carry on. That's what I can do."

He spoke gently. "Your head has caught up with your heart." He watched a tear trickle down her cheek.

"You've been waiting for that to happen, haven't you?" He nodded. "Why are you so patient with me, Walter?"

"Because being patient *is* my job." He laughed.

"Then you will have to keep doing it because I always listen first with my heart even when I know it might cost me; it's my nature."

"It's all of our nature, even if we don't believe it is. Sometimes, though, your head has to overrule what your heart hears."

She hesitated before she answered. "And there will be times when it can't." She watched his face; there was gentleness in his eyes. "Do you think I'm wicked?"

He laughed as he answered. "A little."

She sat up and laughed defensively. "What do you mean 'a little'?"

He answered carefully. "Very little of what we do in life is completely selfless; most of the time what we do is a mixture—we're both giving something and getting something. That's what I mean."

She thought for a moment and then said, "So, what should I do, Coach?"

"What you've been doing: pay attention to the mixture. You're human, not perfect."

They sat quietly for a while. When she spoke, he could tell that she had moved on. "Can I ask you a personal question?"

"After all you've shared with me, I can hardly say no!"

"Does your heart ever overrule your head?"

He twitched around in his chair. "I guess it must, sometimes. Why do you ask?"

"I was just thinking: in the church world there are fathers and mothers and sisters and brothers, but there are no lovers. You're nobody's lover, Walter. I think you should be someone's lover; you're too good to waste."

He smiled awkwardly. "First, I have to find someone who wants to be my lover."

"Rumor has it that you already have." She saw the look of surprise on his face and laughed. "This is getting too close for comfort, isn't it; you'd like to leave now, wouldn't you? But I'm not going to let you; I have something to say to you and I think you may be ready to hear it."

He folded his arms in front of him. "I already got your message."

"Only part of it; there's more."

He relaxed his arms, leaned forward and smiled cautiously. "Okay, 'pastor,' I'm ready. What's the more?"

"It's about loving and being loved, Walter—not just my right to have love but also yours. People in our congregation act like you're married to them; they want to keep you all to themselves. They're like Frank's children who can't let their father have another lover. They're like kids who can't imagine their parents having sex. You have the same right to love another person as the rest of us do—even if some church members can't bear to think of you doing it.

"You're in a bind with the congregation that's not much different from mine with Frank. His children need to grow up and recognize that their father has the right to have a life of his own that may not include them. People in our church need to do the same. As long as they think of you as their spiritual parent, they won't feel like they have to grow up and take responsibility for their own faith. I think lots of them are just being childish, Walter. They want a pastor who will be their mommy or daddy."

He was sitting up straight in his chair. "Really?"

"Yes, really. I was a childish church member until I lost Bob and had to grow up and have it out with God and move on with my life. That took a few years. But the day after that first night Frank stayed here with me, I made a decision that I'm not going to spend the rest of my life as a grieving widow. I'll keep my memories, but I'm moving on with my life.

"I'm not going to give up loving Frank. It may take a while, but his kids need to let him move on with his life—and I want to be part of that life. I want to love them too, but I can't do that if their grieving deteriorates into childish nostalgia that pretends they can keep on living with their father like they did when their mother was alive and vital. That wouldn't be fair to them or to me, and I really don't think it's what Marsha would want anyway."

He nodded. "Marsha, before illness did her in, was too much of a person for that. It's not what she would want for him or them—or you. If you give them some time, I think that's what her grown-up kids will ultimately realize."

"I so want to love them, Walter, and I want them to love me—at least to accept me. If they'll have me, I want to fill in for the grandmother their kids have lost."

"I hope they'll let you."

"So do I." She paused and took a deep breath. "Loving one person doesn't have to be at the expense of loving another, Walter. That's the way Frank's kids see it now, but if he gives in to them, they will never grow enough to give their dad a chance to have another life." She paused and looked directly at him. "It's the same way for you, Walter."

"Why do you say that?"

"That shepherd and sheep image that pastors use for themselves and their congregations keeps church members as perpetual children who don't have to grow up. It lets us off the hook. You don't have to be a surrogate God, Walter. When you take your robe off, you're just another guy who has the same right to be as human as the rest of us. To be a faithful minister doesn't mean you have to choose between having faith and making love. You also are human, not perfect."

He squirmed in his chair. "What if I'm content with my uncomplicated life?"

"Are you?" She looked directly at him and spoke sharply. "Don't try to duck! Am I to believe you never long to have someone to love and share your bed?"

He laughed nervously. "You're prying."

"I know I am, but it's for your good. You've done it to me for seventeen years; I'm just returning the favor. Self-denial isn't always holy, Walter. Sometimes, it's sickness. Sometimes, it's suffering we impose upon ourselves and then imagine it's godliness." She waited until he looked at her. "So, do you never long for someone to love and share your bed?"

He sat for a few minutes and avoided her gaze. Finally, he sat back and looked at her and sighed. "I do. For months after Mary Kerrigan left I woke up at night longing for her. My head knew she and I would never have made it, but my heart wouldn't stop longing for her." He stopped talking for a moment and stared at her. "So, I closed my heart to passion. I'm still afraid to let it hear what it heard with Mary. I'm afraid to risk losing that kind of love again; it hurts too much." He reflected for a moment and then said, "My head has overruled that part of my heart for so long that I think it's atrophied. It's become deaf."

He watched her nod. Tears trickled out of her eyes as she whispered, "I know; O dear God, I know how that is." She looked into his eyes. "You don't have to hide them, Walter; I see the tears pressing to come out of your eyes. You deserve them." She reached across the table and touched the back of his hand. "You can't live fully without risking being hurt. Life is full of gifts and hurts; you can't have the gifts without risking the hurts." She smiled gently. "You said that once in a sermon."

He smiled carefully. "I don't expect my sermons to be preached back at me."

She sighed and waited before she went on. "I may have pried too much, but I care about you. All loves are not the same, Walter. You can never replace the love of your life, but there can be other loves besides the love of your life. I don't love Frank like I loved Bob; Frank is not Bob. You may never love someone else the way you loved Mary Kerrigan, but you can love again. If you loved once, you can love again." She leaned toward him and waited until he looked directly at her. "I want you to love again. I want you to have that richness in your life."

They gazed at each other for a while. Then he turned his hand over and took her hand in his and said, "Thanks for the gift. I hope I can wear it."

"You're welcome. I hope it fits."

"When the right time comes, I hope I'm brave enough to try it on." For a few moments they sat together in quiet. Then he let go of her hand and sighed deeply and said, "It's hard to move away from moments like we've just shared, but I guess I need to. I have to go home now and put on a tie to get ready for my next appointment." He stood up. "Thanks for breakfast—and all the rest."

She stayed seated. "I know you need to go, but why do you think you need to change clothes? You look fine to me the way you are."

He shook his head and said, "For some people it's important to dress ministerially."

She stood up and gave him a sober look. "That may be true for some ministers, Walter, but you're fine the way you are. You don't need to dress up in a minister costume to be convincing."

"Thanks for the compliment!"

She walked around the table and stood close to him and said, "You can hug me before you go. Now that we're both in love with someone else we won't risk doing something that's unethical."

He wrapped his arms around her and hugged her and then kissed her on the forehead. She looked up at him and touched the side of his face with her hand and said, "Thanks, Coach—for everything."

15. LOVE CHILD

After he left Molly's house Walter walked along Grove Street until he reached Miss Simpson's driveway. He walked up her driveway, along the side of her garage, through the gap in the back fence, past the manse carriage house, and across the manse driveway. As he mounted the side porch steps he glanced toward the street and was relieved to see that no car was parked in front of the manse. When he entered the kitchen and looked through the doorway into his study he saw the message light button blinking on the answering machine on his desk. He pushed the button.

"Good morning, Walter, this is George Morrison. Something has come up that I have to deal with right away, so I need to postpone our appointment for this morning. I still hope to attend the education committee meeting at the church this evening. If you can stay a few minutes after that meeting, perhaps we can talk then or at least decide when to reschedule our appointment."

Walter shrugged his shoulders. "He sounds upset; I wonder what happened. I guess I'll have to wait 'til tonight to find out."

The machine continued with a second message. This time it was Katherine's voice. "Hi, Mac, it's Kate. I'm between patients and hoped I'd catch you, but obviously I missed you. Kristen came to see me last night and shared something that I want to talk over with you. If you come in sometime during the morning and hear this message and you're free at lunchtime, maybe you could stop by? I'll have only about forty-five minutes, but that should give us enough time to eat and talk. I made soup last night and there's enough to share. If you can get here by a little after twelve, please call the office and let Sue know. In case I'm running behind with patients I'll leave the side door unlocked so you can come in and go upstairs. I know you're coming Friday night for dinner, but this is something I'd rather talk about before then. Hope it works. Love you, Mac. See you soon."

He stood staring at the machine, wishing he could talk to her right then. "I hope she's all right." He looked at his watch; it was eleven thirty. He called Katherine's office and asked Sue to let Katherine know he would meet her at five past twelve.

When he reached the top of the stairs and knocked on the upstairs apartment door there was no response. He opened the door slowly and said, "Kate? It's Mac." No answer. He let himself in. The rich aroma of soup keeping warm in the crock pot filled the room; the kitchen table was set with two places. He washed his hands at the kitchen sink and sat down in the chair that had become his. He was barely seated when he heard her running up the stairs. He stood up as she burst through the door, a broad smile across her face, "Mac, I was so afraid you were off somewhere and wouldn't be able to get here!" She threw her arms around him and hugged him.

He tilted his head back and looked into her eyes. "Well, my love, here I am both for a chance to see you and have some of that soup. You look delicious and (he gazed toward the crock pot) it smells delicious."

She smiled. "Thanks." She almost touched his cheek and then pulled her hand back. "I need to wash up before I touch you. Lots of kids with runny noses today. I don't want to give you whatever's going around."

He shrugged his shoulders. "To have you touch me, I'll risk it."

She laughed. "If you catch the runny nose, you'll wish you hadn't. Why don't you put some soup in our bowls?"

He sighed and shrugged his shoulders. "Rejected again." He filled the soup bowls while she washed her hands vigorously at the kitchen sink. He ate a spoonful of soup as soon as she sat down. "This soup is fantastic; you are the champion soup-maker."

"Thanks."

"This is fun, but I know we don't have much time, so maybe you want to get going right way with what you said you wanted to talk about in the message you left this morning. I hope nothing's wrong."

She set her soup spoon on her bread plate and looked straight at him. "Kristen is pregnant."

He took a deep breath and let it out slowly. "Oh, no, not really! That's hard to believe. You're sure?"

She sighed and nodded. "I'm sure. She came to see Erik the day before yesterday. He's continued to be her doctor—as you know I don't like to take on family members as patients. She came over last night and we talked a long time. I saw Erik early this morning and he said she's missed two periods and there's no doubt a child is growing inside her."

"I'm blown away. She must know who the father is."

"She does, but she didn't tell me, and I didn't press her. He knows she may be pregnant; they've sweated about it for weeks. By now I'm sure she's told him it's for real. It's really their issue to deal with. She's just turned eighteen and she said he's eighteen which means that both of them are of age and have the right to make their own decisions about the future." She paused. "Maybe you have some idea who the father is?"

He looked pensive. "I'm pretty sure I know, but probably I should wait to say until she tells us."

"That will happen soon. When she left here she said she hopes he will agree to come with her to see you so you can help them decide what to do. I'm really glad they want to talk with you."

"It'll be hard, but so am I. What's happening in the meantime?"

"Kristen said they had already agreed they would tell their parents if Erik confirmed she's going to have a baby. I encouraged her to go ahead and tell them right away. As tough as it is to share that kind of news, there won't ever be an easier time."

He nodded. "You're right."

"Kristen thinks that for now you, Erik, I and the parents are all the people who need to know what's happened. Actually, they could decide not to let anyone else know; it's a first pregnancy and Erik thinks she's barely three months along, so even if she decides to keep the baby, she won't show much between now and graduation."

He looked surprised. "Do you think she might not keep the baby?"

She stopped eating and sat back in her chair. "That's another reason I wanted to see you right away. Her first response when Erik told her he's sure she's pregnant was to ask him how difficult it would be to make arrangements to terminate her pregnancy. She wondered if that wouldn't be the simplest way out of everything. Erik answered her question carefully. He told her she could decide to terminate the pregnancy—she's of age and not married so it's legally her decision, but he suggested she not decide right away. He said once you have an abortion there's no way to undo it." She paused and sighed. "Then he suggested she talk with me—not only as a doctor, but also as a woman—before she makes a decision."

He spoke carefully. "Does Erik know what you decided to do when you discovered you were pregnant years ago?"

"No, he doesn't."

"Do you think it would be helpful to tell Kristen what you did?"

She paused and took a breath. "I thought about telling her but decided not to—at least not right away—because she came to see me, in part, as a doctor. As a physician it would be inappropriate to intrude my personal experience into any conversation about her situation. Besides, I know I'm kind of a mentor to her; knowing what I did might encourage her to do the same thing. That wouldn't be right; it needs to be unbiased decision she and the baby's father make."

He nodded. "True."

She sighed deeply. "You know I couldn't be impartial, Mac—which is what a physician is supposed to be with a patient. Anyway, as we sat and talked the awful reality of the solution Kristen was contemplating hit her. I honestly don't think she could consent to an abortion."

He looked pensive for a moment and then said, "I don't think she could either."

She looked off into the distance. "As I listened to Kristen struggling over whether to have an abortion, I couldn't stop thinking about how she might feel when she's forty-six and it's too late to think about having a child." She turned away for a moment and then turned back and looked at him. "But even as her aunt, Walter, I shouldn't use my personal experience to make her think about how she might feel about the abortion when she's my age and looking back."

He watched her face as he spoke. "This isn't about Kristen anymore; it's about you, isn't it?"

She nodded. "After Kristen left what we talked about threw me in a way I hadn't anticipated. I woke up in the middle of the night and couldn't get back to sleep. I kept thinking about what my life might have been like if I'd kept that child I conceived with David—what that kid and I might have had together. I felt so alone in the dark; I cried for a long time. I wish you had been here to hold me, Mac." She looked away; in the sunlight reflected on her face he could see tears welling up in her eyes.

He stood up, walked around the table, knelt down and put his arms around her and held her.

After a while he sat back on his heels. She looked at him and managed a smile. "Thanks." Her eye caught the clock on the wall. "Now, I have to stop crying and fix my face so I can go downstairs and begin seeing patients in less than ten minutes."

"I know you need to go downstairs and be the doctor, but I think you could use some healing yourself. Maybe I can help with that—when there's time."

She spoke softly. "I want you to."

He placed his hands gently on the sides of her face and looked into her eyes. "In the meantime, if you cry again in the middle of the night, I want you to call me so I can come and be with you."

She forced a smile. "I will." She reached out and touched his cheek. "We're doing what we said we wouldn't, aren't we, Mac? We're falling more and more in love—and we both know we're not going to turn back."

He nodded. "And I hope you feel it's as right as I do because I want to keep going." He glanced at the clock. "You're down to five minutes now. We'll have to wait 'til Friday to talk more."

"Friday seems too far away."

"I know; it does to me too, but right now I know I have to go along so you can get ready for the next runny nose. Besides, there's an old woman in my congregation who's dying to spend an hour with me this afternoon."

She laughed. "That's all right—as long as she's old."

He leaned toward her and kissed her.

16. THE LEGALIST RECONSIDERS

The education committee meeting didn't last long, partly because George Morrison was uncharacteristically quiet. When the meeting adjourned everyone except George left quickly, glad for the found time. George remained in his chair while Walter walked down the hall with the other committee members to the outside door. When he came back into the church parlor he found George still seated. George looked very sober as he spoke. "If you're not too tired, Walter, I'd like to have the conversation we missed this morning."

Walter sat down in a comfortable chair opposite him. "Fine, George, it's not late; let's do it."

George looked directly at him. "I want to speak with you in my role as an elected ruling elder in our congregation. One of the responsibilities of that office is to pay attention to the minister's beliefs and life. As we both know your beliefs are, sometimes, too liberal in my view. We've talked about some of those differences before."

"Yes, we have."

"But recently something more serious has come to my attention."

Walter shifted his position in his chair. "What's that, George?"

"Your relationship with Wilson Morton."

Walter looked puzzled. "I'm not sure what you mean; Wilson's a parishioner and I'm his pastor."

"To begin with I don't think Wilson is a member in good standing of our church. The status of his membership in the church has never been clarified since he retired from teaching and returned to Schuylerkill Falls. While I know that he was confirmed as a young man by Dr. Morton, his father, in all the years he was away from the village he never once contributed or participated in worship in our congregation. As you know, our congregation's by-laws provide that a member who neither contributes nor participates in worship for five years can be dropped from the active role. To my knowledge that's been true of Dr. Morton for more than two decades."

Walter tilted his head and raised his shoulders. "But George, you know that dropping someone as an active member requires an action by the full board of elders. The board would have to act formally and inform Wilson of their action in writing, and then he would have to state in writing whether he accepted their action before they could place him on the inactive member list—and to my knowledge in his case none of that has happened."

George took a deep breath. "Well, be that as it may, there is something else about your relationship with Dr. Morton that I think the elders need to review."

Walter sat up in his chair. "And what is that?"

"If we assume that Dr. Morton is still a member, then, of course, you have every right to visit him in the course of carrying out the duties of your ministerial office. But several times recently you have been seen leaving Dr. Morton's home late at night. That concerns me and I think it should be a concern of our church. Dr. Morton does not seem to me to be the kind of person that a minister should have as a friend."

Walter shook his head in a gesture of disbelief. "Why?"

"You know the answer to that question. Dr. Morton is a suspected homosexual. If he is, in fact, a homosexual man, he is living in sin and is unfit to be a church member. If you are seen regularly leaving his house late at night, people will suspect that you also might be a homosexual." He paused for emphasis. "The circumstances of your personal life could support that view: you are not married to a woman and except for a brief relationship with a schoolteacher many years ago, you have never been in a continuous relationship with a woman."

Walter could feel anger mounting inside himself. He spoke in a controlled voice. "Have you spoken to the other elders on the session about this? Am I under surveillance?"

"Of course not, out of consideration for you and our church I decided to share my concerns with you before I share them with any of the other elders."

For a few moments Walter didn't respond; anger seethed inside of him and threatened to erupt in whatever he might say. When he regained control, he responded carefully. "For the record I am not a gay man, George; I have no inclination in that direction at all. However, Wilson Morton is not only a member of our church, he is my friend—and a good friend, at that. Wilson is a brilliant and ethical man who so far as I know has always lived a responsible life. Whether he is or is not gay is his to say. I know well that some texts in the Bible state clearly that being homosexual is sinful, and that some people of faith have no doubts about that. I respect them, but I am not one of them. I think modern genetics already offers clear evidence that sexual orientation may have genetic roots. If that's so, one does not choose to be gay or straight; it's in the genes. The biblical writers did not have access to that information."

George sat up in his chair, "But . . ."

"Please hear me out, George; I listened carefully to you, now I'll be grateful if you do the same." George sat back in his chair. "Like you I believe the Bible is inspired, but I also believe it reflects the culture of those who wrote it. They had no more access to modern genetics than they did to modern physics and paleontology. Modern science has demonstrated that the creation was not completed in six days as the Bible says, it took billions of years. The Bible is theologically accurate about the creation of the universe, but not about the scientific details of creation. You teach science and you know that is so; I doubt that you teach the biblical version of creation as scientifically valid in your science classes. If you did, you would lose your job, right?"

George answered quietly. "That is true."

"Well, George, as science has corrected the Bible's description of the details of creation, in time it may also correct the Bible's view of homosexuality. If the biblical writers had been aware of modern genetics, I doubt that they would have viewed being homosexual as they did. I think their concern was promiscuity, not sexual orientation. I think they viewed, and that many people still view, gay persons as inherently promiscuous, but there's no hard evidence that promiscuity is more common among gay persons than it is among straight persons. No matter how we may view homosexuality, George, I am very clear what Jesus would do with Wilson,"—he paused until George looked at him and then spoke directly to him— "he would go to his house and eat dinners with him, regardless of how many Pharisees would speak ill of him for doing it."

He waited for George to say something, but he looked away in silence. Walter smiled and spoke gently when George looked back at him. "Besides, George, if God can use a Zoroastrian king in the Old Testament to rescue the Hebrew people, and a Samaritan who was a member of a despised minority to model devoted care in the New Testament, then I think it's quite possible that God could offer words of wisdom through a man who lives in our village and might be gay."

George took out his handkerchief and blew his nose. "I can see that you and I will not come to agreement in this matter. I concede that the Bible's physics is naïve in the matter of creation. In spite of that evidence, I am not ready to concede that scriptural condemnation of homosexuality is also wrong. Morality is different from science. Scripture is very clear that homosexuality, adultery and fornication are all sins. I think our young people need to hear that message very clearly from you both in what you say—and in what you do. They need to learn from their minister how God expects them to act. They may not like God, but they have to respect God." He shifted around in his chair. "Modern liberal perspectives on sexual behavior are dangerous when the young people in our church and community see you condone them."

"I'm not sure what you are implying."

George scowled as he spoke. "Since I asked to meet with you to share my concerns about Dr. Morton something has come up that makes our meeting even more urgent. Your lax approach to sexual morality may have affected my own family. You may or may not be aware that Kristen Klein is pregnant and that my son, Marshall, is the father of her child. They both have had extensive contact with you as members of our church's high school youth group."

Walter shook his head. "I did know that Kristen is expecting; I didn't know that Marshall is the child's father. That must be difficult news for you and Shirley to hear."

George folded his arms in front of him and looked stern. "It's more than difficult. It violates everything I have tried to inculcate in my children. Marshall and Kristen met with us yesterday and told us about their situation. They have not decided what to do—whether to be open about her pregnancy, when to marry, even whether to keep the child. Shirley and I agreed not to share their news with anyone except you. While they may be able to keep the pregnancy secret for a while, it will ultimately become known. Personally, I think they should marry, and not just because of shame associated with conceiving a child out of wedlock. Kristen is considering whether to abort the child. That is a completely unacceptable solution; killing an unborn child is a far worse sin than conceiving one out of wedlock."

Walter spoke carefully. "I really want to be sensitive to your beliefs, George. Personally, I could not agree to an abortion were I in a similar situation. It feels like a horrible solution to me. But not everyone feels the same in the matter. Kristen is eighteen years-old and unmarried. By law whether to keep the child is her decision . . ."

George interrupted in a loud voice, "Not by God's law; abortion is murder!"

"I know that's your view, George but not everyone shares it—not even all sincere Christians."

"But . . ."

"Please let me finish, George. I know Kristen and Marshall quite well; they're ethical and caring persons. Though I can't be sure, in the end I think they will decide both to marry and to have their baby. I think our role now is to stand with them and support them and help them move on with their lives in the best way possible. The challenge now is not how we are going to justify what Marshall and Kristen did to a sometimes too-judgmental community. The bigger challenge is how we are going to support them so they can prepare themselves for a sound future as adults and, at the same time, provide a nurturing home for their child."

George spoke softly. "That's pretty much what Shirley said to me after Marshall and Kristen left last night."

"I'm glad to hear that. I know you hold deep convictions you believe Marshall has violated, but I think what you need most to focus on now is how you're going to be a good father to Marshall and the woman who, if all goes as we now expect, will be his wife, and how you will be a good grandfather to the child, God willing, they will bring into this world in a few months from now."

Walter stood up; his expression had softened. "You're going to be a grandfather, George; this child will be your grandchild. God sees you as a grandfather—that's the big picture. God speaks in our hearts, as well as our heads. I will pray that you can hear God in your heart."

George sat motionless for a while. Then he stood up and walked slowly out of the room. Walter heard the outside door at the end of the hall shut softly.

17. FASTBALL

After George left, Walter shut out the lights in the parlor and the hallway and locked the outside door of the church. He walked along the sidewalk, past the front of the manse and into the driveway. He didn't notice the black pick-up truck parked just below the corner where Elm Street intersected with Church Street.

When he passed by the study window that faced the driveway, he could see the light blinking on the telephone answering machine on his desk. He walked into the kitchen, through the open doorway into his study and pressed the blinking button.

"Hi Coach; it's Ed. I'm down here at the garage; Butch and I are working on Butch's antique Cadillac. Lauren just called and said a detective from Albany called her a few minutes ago. He said Gary's locked pickup disappeared from the space where it's been parked at North East Trucking ever since he went missing that day the narcotics agents tried to pick him up at the truck stop south of Chicago. The police think that he's got it, or it was stolen—most likely that he has it. The detective said he'd let Chief Haines here know that Gary is on the loose and might show up around here; he told Lauren we need to keep our eyes open and be careful. Lauren's going over to my mom's; we don't think she should be alone at our apartment—and probably that it wouldn't be smart for us to stay at our place tonight. Please give me a call at the garage when you get in so I know you got this message. Thanks."

Walter heard a man's voice behind him. "All right, pastor, turn around slowly." Walter turned around carefully and saw a figure in the shadow behind the open door that led to the kitchen. "I figured with the light blinking you'd go right to that answering machine and wouldn't notice me here behind this door." He was holding a gun and it was pointed at Walter.

"You don't have to guess who picked up that truck; I did. I decided it was time to quit running. My money's gone and I'm tired of hiding. I figure the people who got Lorna are gonna catch up to me soon, so I decided to pay some debts before they do. The bitch that ratted on me and her lover are first on the list. The message on that machine tells me that probably you know where I can find them. Maybe you and I can cut a deal? You help me find them and I'll let you go when I'm done with them."

As the breeze outside blew through the branches of a tree the light from the streetlight in front of the manse flickered on the gun. Walter's heart was pounding, but he tried to sound calm as he spoke. "So, Mr. Shanahan, how do I know you'll keep your part of any deal I agree to?"

"You don't, but then you don't have much choice, do you?"

Walter thought, "I have no idea what I can do; I have to keep you talking while I try to figure out something." He spoke again in the same steady voice, "So, what's the deal?"

"Well, pastor, nice to hear that you're a reasonable man. It's no big deal for you. You get to be my chauffer and drive me to wherever the bitch and her live-in boyfriend are. We'll take your car because by now the police are looking for my pick-up. When we catch up to the lovers you can watch what happens to bitches who rat on their husbands and guys who steal them."

"And then?"

"Then I'll give you a little something to occupy you while I borrow your car. It won't be anything serious, just something to slow you down long enough for me to be on my way. Don't worry about your car; I won't wreck it. I'll just leave it somewhere where it will take them a while to find it."

"But that's no sure getaway for you. The police will figure out that you took my car; they'll catch up to you before you're ten miles away."

He laughed. "I'd rather have them catch me than the guys who caught Lorna. If those guys catch me, they'll do me in the same way they did her. You know about Lorna?"

"I do. Sounds horrible."

"I hear they always do it that way—two holes in your head: one in the forehead where the bullet goes in and another in the back of your head where it comes out. They say you never feel it, but who knows for sure? No one ever has a chance to say."

As Walter heard the last sentence the back of his pitching hand brushed against the no-hitter game ball sitting on the desk behind him. At the same moment, a voice came through the door leading to the dark front hallway: "Don't bother with him, Gary; I'm the one you want. I'm the lover."

Gary turned quickly and pointed his gun toward the darkness and spoke sarcastically. "Well, I think there'll be a slight change in plans. I'll tend to the lover first and then we'll go look for the bitch."

With the gun aimed toward the hall door the back of Gary's right hand faced Walter. He grasped the game ball firmly and with all of his strength threw it at the back of Gary's hand. The throw didn't have the best form, but it was a dead-center strike. Out of the corner of his eye Gary noticed some movement as the baseball left Walter's hand, but not in time to react; the ball travelling like a streaking missile hit the back of his hand and knocked the gun away. The gun bounced off the bookcase and ricocheted into the center of the room.

Gary grabbed his hand in pain and shouted, "You bastard, you broke my hand!" He eyed the gun on the floor and started toward it, but Walter lunged toward him and tackled him before he could reach it. Ed bolted through the door and snatched up the gun. With one hand writhing in pain Gary was no match for the minister; Walter rolled him over onto his stomach and pulled his hands behind him. *"Be careful!"* Gary screamed, *"You're hurting my hand."*

Ed stood six feet away holding the gun. "Okay, Coach, you can relax. I've got him covered." He cocked his head to one side as he spoke, "I don't think you'll try anything, will you, Mr. Shanahan? But if you do, after what you did to Lauren, I would love to have an excuse to repay you."

"That won't be necessary." Schuylerville Falls Police Chief Pete Haines came through the doorway from the kitchen. "You keep Mr. Shanahan covered for a minute and I'll clip these cuffs on him to be sure he'll stay put; then you can put the gun down." Without touching Gary's injured hand, he leaned over and placed handcuffs on his wrists.

Ed laughed and shook his head. "It worked, Chief, just like you said it would." He removed the ammunition clip from the revolver and placed the gun and the clip on Walter's desk. He looked at Gary. "If you'd given me a reason to use that gun, you son of a bitch, I would've—even if I did regret it afterwards."

Gary grimaced, "Just get me somewhere where they can fix my hand; it's killin' me."

Pete spoke calmly, "We'll do that, Mr. Shanahan. I'm sure your hand hurts, but you should be grateful that it's just your hand that's killing you. If the preacher hadn't knocked that gun out of your hand with a fastball, you'd have more to worry about than your hand." He motioned to Walter. "You can relax, pastor; I'll take care of him now."

Walter sat back on his heels. "Where'd you guys come from? How'd you know what was going on?"

Pete shrugged his shoulders. "I keep an eye on things in the village; it's my job. When I saw a strange truck parked too close to the corner on Elm (he gestured with his head toward the window that faced the intersection with Elm Street) with nobody in it just the keys, I parked behind it and ran a check on it. Sure enough Mr. Shanahan's name came up. I figured he might be seeking some advice from a local minister. Just then Ed knocked on the window of my cruiser. He said he'd left you a phone message earlier in the evening and hadn't heard back from you, so we decided to leave my cruiser parked in the dark behind Mr. Shanahan's truck and check up on you to be sure you were all right.

"When we walked across the street and onto the sidewalk and looked through your front windows, we could see what was going on in here. Ed said your front door is always unlocked so we decided he'd sneak in there while I made my way quietly through the side door into your kitchen. He'd wait until he was sure I was inside and then say something from the dark hall to distract Mr. Shanahan so I could hold my gun on him from behind." He laughed. "We hadn't figured the fastball into our plans. That was amazing pitch, pastor—more sidearm than over the top but right on the mark!"

Walter shook his head. "I knew I'd get only one throw and that it better be a strike."

Pete turned toward the handcuffed figure on the floor. "You're under arrest, Mr. Shanahan. I radioed the dispatcher to send a couple of sheriff's deputies for backup. I told her to have them come in quietly in case we needed to surprise you. She said they're both pretty far away, but they'll be here soon. They'll read you your rights and give you a ride to the county jail in Salem. The jail staff'll see that you get some medical attention for your hand. We'll get Butch Chichester to tow your truck somewhere for safekeeping."

He gazed out the window. "Looks like it's still quiet on the street, pastor; I guess none of your neighbors have noticed the commotion in here. Maybe they think you're just having a late-night counseling session. If we keep it that way, you'll get a good night's sleep. The three of us can walk Mr. Shanahan out your front door, and deposit him in the screened-in back seat of my cruiser for safekeeping until the sheriffs arrive. In the morning I'm sure the federal prosecutor's office in Albany will be in touch with both of you to get formal statements. Hauling drugs from Albany to Chicago is a federal offense." He looked down at Gary sitting on the floor. "Now, Mr. Shanahan, I hope you're going to be cooperative."

"I know my rights; I'm not doin' or sayin' nothin'. Just get me somewhere where they can fix my hand; it hurts like hell."

"The sheriffs'll take care of that." He gestured toward Ed. "After we get Mr. Shanahan stowed in the back seat of the cruiser, I'll give you an evidence bag and a glove so you don't get any more of your fingerprints on that gun and you can come back and put the gun and clip in the bag. We'll send it along with the deputies for safekeeping." He placed a hand on Walter's shoulder. "I bet those first few minutes when you were alone with him staring at his gun were pretty scary."

Walter nodded and looked very sober. "They were."

Pete grinned. "You're quite a guy, Reverend; I'm glad we're on the same side."

After the sheriff's deputies drove away with Gary and Pete went on his way, Walter and Ed walked back across Church Street. When they reached the side porch of the manse Ed shrugged his shoulders. "I guess there's nothing more for me to do here, so if you're going to be all right, I'll walk on over to my old house and pick up Lauren." He looked carefully at Walter. "You gonna be all right, coach?"

"Yeah, I think so—once I get some sleep; all of sudden I'm very tired."

"Me too." Ed eyed him carefully. "If you're sure you're okay, I'll go along."

Walter reached out and touched Ed's shoulder. "Thanks for the rescue. I don't know if I'd still be here if you and Pete hadn't showed up when you did."

"Well, we were all lucky." He paused and tilted his head. "Or, maybe your God keeps an eye out for you and we got the benefit of that?"

Walter laughed. "I think he keeps an eye out for all of us, Ed—but I was still scared."

Ed shrugged his shoulders. "See you around."

Walter went inside and walked through the kitchen into his study. He saw the game ball resting on the floor next to his bookcase. He picked it up and caressed it with his hands. He spoke out loud to himself. "Ed's right; that was a lucky pitch. Or, maybe it was more than that?" He placed the ball back in its resting place on the front of his desk, shut off all the lights in the downstairs except for the lamp on his desk that he always left on, and walked up the stairway from the kitchen to the upstairs hall. He took a long shower and went to bed.

As tired as he was, he couldn't sleep. In the dark silence the terror he'd subdued when Gary faced him with the gun came back and overwhelmed him. He started to shake. He kept telling himself that he was all right now—that there was no reason to be scared, but he couldn't stop shaking.

When he first heard it, he thought he was imagining her voice. "Mac, where are you? Tell me where you are!"

He sat up in bed.

"If you're asleep, Mac, wake up and tell me how to get to you."

He jumped from his bed, ran to the top of the stairwell leading down to the kitchen and switched on the stairway light. He saw her at the bottom of the stairs. "Kate!"

She bolted up the stairs and threw her arms around him and kissed him over and over. "Oh, my God, Mac, he could have killed you." She held him and sobbed. When her sobs subsided, she looked up at his tear-stained face.

"How'd you know what happened, Kate? Who told you?"

She wiped her eyes with the back of her hand and smiled. "When Ed Hutchins got home and told Molly about it, she called my office number and told the answering service it was an emergency, that something had happened to you and that she had to reach me. The service called me, and I called her back. She told me about Gary holding the gun on you. She said I needed to go to you—that you needed someone to share your bed tonight and that I was that someone. And that's who I'm going to be."

He looked into her eyes and gently stroked her hair. "You in my bed tonight? Am I dreaming?"

She laughed. "No, you're not, but don't let your dream get out of control; I didn't come here to make love with you tonight. The first time we do that I want it to be at the end of a happy evening. I came here tonight to lie down next to you and hold you so you can feel me and smell me until that awful scene with Gary Shanahan goes away from you and you can go to sleep. We'll bundle like they used to. In the morning before it starts to get light I'll go home and change and drive to the hospital to make rounds."

He touched the side of her face. "I love you, Kate; I want you."

"Then get back in your bed!"

It was still dark outside when he awakened and saw her standing next to the bed, outlined by light filtering in from the hallway.

She smiled and leaned over and kissed him. "You slept hard; will you be okay now?"

"I think so." He sounded tentative.

"Well, it's a quarter past three. I better go home before some nosey church member notices my car in your driveway and thinks I spent the night with you."

"I don't care who knows or what they think."

"You will in the daylight. Call me tomorrow evening. Erik and I will have worked out the call schedule for the coming week by then and we can set a time to get together for some fun. In the meantime, don't push yourself today, and call me if you can't sleep tonight—even if it's the middle of the night."

As she started to walk away he leaned over and took hold of her hand and stopped her. "I already know I'll have trouble sleeping."

She smiled. "Call me tomorrow."

18. THE DAY AFTER

At ten o'clock the next morning Ed and Walter met with the federal prosecutor and gave their statements. After the prosecutor briefed them about what they could and could not say to the media they appeared at a media/press conference, then had a leisurely lunch at a restaurant in Troy and drove back to the manse.

When they were parked in the driveway Walter reached out to open the door, then hesitated and turned toward Ed. "Maybe I could entice you to stop for a few minutes before you go back to work? A parishioner I visited a couple of days ago gave me some great-tasting molasses cookies."

Ed grinned. "I love molasses cookies and Butch told me I could take the whole day off if I need to. Maybe I can use your phone and give Lauren a call and she can update my mom? I'm sure they're wondering how it went with the prosecutor this morning."

"Help yourself; you can use the phone on the desk in my study." They walked inside and he turned on the burner under the coffeepot and sat down at the kitchen table while Ed made his phone call.

A few minutes later they sat quietly drinking coffee. Ed interrupted the quiet. "When we started talking with those newspaper and TV reporters, I thought they were making too much out of what happened last night, but then all of sudden it hit me how close we came to disaster."

Walter grimaced and nodded.

Ed took a sip of coffee and a bite of cookie. He stared at the floor for a while and then looked up at Walter. "Do you think your God helped you throw that strike last night, or was it just a good pitch by a good pitcher?"

Walter shrugged his shoulders. "Maybe both. Why do you ask?"

"Because if I'd tried, I'd have missed and we'd probably both be dead!"

"But it was a strike, and we're not."

"And I think we're not, Coach, mostly because you're a good pitcher. I think for it to work you have to be a good pitcher to begin with—and I'm not."

Walter cocked his head. "So, you think God can build on something you're already good at and make it better, but can't make you good at something you're not good at to begin with?"

"Something like that." Neither of them spoke for a while, then Ed said, "I just had another funny thought."

"What's that?"

"If there's a God, I don't think he takes any better care of you than he does of the rest of us."

Walter laughed. "What would make you think he would?"

"Because he'd see you as more essential. You're the coach; the rest of us are just team members. Teams come and go, but coaches stay. Seems like God would be more concerned to keep you safe, but evidently the crap is just as likely to come down on you as on the rest of us. That doesn't make sense to me. Good coffee, by the way—a lot better than the stuff we reheat all day at the garage!"

"Thanks, it does taste good." He didn't say anything more for a while, then said, "I think in spite of what God can do, there's crap everywhere—I don't know why or how to justify it in a world that's supposed to be run by God—but it's there: from earthquakes to tsunamis, from wars to a guy pointing a gun at you in your own house." He paused and looked directly at Ed. "Sometimes, you're the guy who makes a horrible mistake he never would have made if he'd known ahead of time what was going to happen. I don't think God puts the blame on you when that happens."

Ed didn't say anything in response. The noisy second hand struggling around the face of the old kitchen clock was the only sound in the room. Finally, he broke the quiet. "Last night when I held the gun on Gary I thought about that day in Nam. I wanted to shoot him, even though I knew that afterwards I would realize it was a horrible mistake." He grinned. "But your God got in the middle of it and he wouldn't let me."

Walter laughed. "So, maybe you've got just as much faith as I do?"

Ed returned the laughter. "I don't know about that." He cocked his head to one side, "So, did you pray for help when Gary was pointing his gun at you?"

"I did; I was scared."

"What did you say?"

He grinned. "I didn't use any special words—just the usual, 'Show me the next play, God.'"

"And he did! It was a fastball."

"Yeah, it was a fastball—and some Force from God was behind it. Most of the time it's something like that. I had a seminary prof who reminded us that we're told to pray, 'Deliver us from evil,' not, 'Save us from evil.' There's a difference. One way or another, sooner or later we get delivered, but the world is full of crap and there's no way even God can make certain we escape all of it. 'Shit happens,' as they say, and, sometimes, it comes down on us. There's no guarantee we'll escape all of it."

Ed set his elbow on the table and leaned on his upturned hand. "Do you think I'll ever be able to forget what I did that day in Nam?"

"No, but I think you're already beginning to remember it differently."

"How's that?"

"You're starting to remember it as forgiven." He looked at Ed carefully. "God forgave you a long time ago, Ed; you just didn't get it."

"I still don't." He paused and smiled. "But right now I can feel something trying to get through!"

"That's progress!"

He stood up. "I should go back to work, Coach. Life goes on—even the day after somebody could have killed you."

Walter nodded and watched his eyes. "Go ahead if you need to, but you can stay longer if you want to."

Ed turned away and started toward the door, then stopped and turned back. His eyes were filled with tears; he wiped them with his sleeve. "Sorry about the tears, Coach, but I used to hug my dad at moments like this. My God I miss him." He hesitated and then continued, "I know you would hug me if I asked you—even if it wouldn't be the same." A smile spread across his face. "But it would be something!"

Walter stood up and walked over to him and opened his arms and hugged him.

19. WILSON'S WALTZ

After Ed drove out of the driveway Walter's eye caught the kitchen clock; it was nearly four-thirty. He turned toward the doorway that led into his study and noticed the light blinking on his answering machine. He walked to his desk and pushed the play button. "Hi Mac, it's me. One of my patients has gone into labor so I'm off to the hospital. It's a first baby for her so I'm sure I'll be there for the night. When we talked before I left early this morning, I forgot that Erik and Becky are going away for a long weekend starting Friday so I'll be on call right through Monday night. Maybe we can do something some evening next week? Even if we talk in between I don't want to wait all the way until next Friday to see you. Call and leave me a message. I miss you. Last night was wonderful. I hope you're doing all right today. I'll call you tomorrow. Love you!"

"Damn it, Kate! That's almost a week! I don't know whether I'll survive that long without seeing you." He looked quickly at his desk calendar. "Whew! At least Tuesday and Friday next week are both free." He punched in Kate's home number and left a message. He blew her a kiss.

As he started to get up, he glanced at the partly finished page of the sermon manuscript in his old typewriter. Usually by this time in the week he had an entire first draft finished.

He didn't have to leave to go to Wilson's house for dinner for more than an hour; maybe he could make up for some of the lost time. "No, Walter," he told himself as he straightened up, "You're too tired to work on it. If you try to work on it now, tomorrow morning you'll decide that anything you produced isn't good enough and you'll end up throwing it out. Besides, if you're going to stay awake for dinner and keep up with Wilson, you need a nap. You have time to sleep for an hour and still catch the news at six to see what they say about last night's standoff and walk to Wilson's house in time for supper at seven." He nodded decisively. "Good advice, if do say so myself!" He walked across the hall and into the parlor and stretched out on the extra-long sofa and quickly fell asleep.

He awoke with a start and looked at his watch. It was six-thirty; he'd missed seeing himself on the news. "Rats," he thought as he sat up, "but it's all right; whatever they ran at six they'll probably run again at eleven. I'll catch it then—if I can stay awake. Anyway, I'm sure somebody taped it."

Just before seven o'clock he walked up Wilson's driveway and knocked on his back door. Wilson opened the door, smiling broadly and bowing as he spoke, "Behold a hero graces my humble threshold!"

Walter laughed awkwardly. "You watched the news, didn't you?"

Wilson nodded. "You're not only amazing for a preacher; you're just plain amazing. If some guy faced me with a gun like that guy held one on you, I'd have loaded my pants. How'd you keep your cool?"

"I'm not sure I did. Maybe I just drew on all those times I faced guys with a baseball bat threatening to knock my best pitch over the fence? You somehow have to strike them out."

"No credit to God for the strike out?"

He grinned. "God doesn't need credit for strikeouts."

Wilson cocked his head to one side. "Clever! But let's postpone any further exposition until after we consume some beef bourguignon." He gestured toward a Dutch oven sitting on the stove. "I put a half cup of cognac and a whole bottle of imported Cotes du Rhone in that pot and it's been done and resting for a half-hour." He handed Walter a bottle of wine. "So, kindly apply the corkscrew to this bottle of my home brew and I'll put the warmed slices of sourdough into the breadbasket. If you bring the wine, I'll bring the bread and bourguignon to the table—and we can eat. I've been smelling that fancy stew for hours and I'm *very* hungry."

The dinner surpassed even Wilson's high standards. When Walter finished a very large second helping, he pushed his chair back from the table. "As usual when you're the cook I overate, Wilson. I hope there's not some rich homemade dessert."

"No, I don't bake, as you know, so I can offer only a piece of the usual cheesecake I bought at that fancy bakery in Williamstown when I was over there to have lunch with an old faculty friend the beginning of the week."

Walter took a deep breath. "A modest piece of the 'usual cheesecake' will be more than enough, but I need to wait for space to open up in my stomach."

"We can pause long enough for that. How about some more wine?"

"Okay, but only an inch or so in the bottom of my glass."

He held out his glass and Wilson filled it two-thirds full. He looked at the glass and then at Wilson. "That's the biggest inch I've ever seen."

Wilson chuckled. "I'm sure you can handle it. Besides you're walking tonight so you can have as much as you want."

He set the almost empty wine bottle on the table and sat back in his chair. "Now that we've taken in enough food and wine to nourish our bodies—that's as close to sacramental talk as I get—maybe you're up for some head work?"

Walter sounded a little uncertain when he spoke. "Last night was a very long night and I don't know how long I'll last, but (he shrugged his shoulders) I always get energized when you're on the other side of the table, so let's see what I can do!"

"Good, let's get right to it while you're still wide awake! Remember that probing conversation we had the night we had supper right before the holidays? It was the night Smitty had the flu and you tried out a theological update on me; you likened God's Spirit to the Force in Star Wars."

"I do; it was the first time I'd shared the idea with anyone."

"Well, you got me thinking. That metaphor's been stuck playing over and over inside my head like a 'brainworm' ever since. Have you gone any further with it?"

"Only a little. I used 'Force' in a sermon once and I thought I did a good job of explaining why I was using it, but afterward I wondered if I'd made a mistake. Most people looked either puzzled or uneasy; some of the more conservative members even scowled. But when you think about it that's not surprising; most people who go to church services regularly don't see any need to use different language or contemporary metaphors to refer to God. They come to the service Sunday after Sunday because they want more of the same because that's what nurtures them. They expect me to reassure them that the old ways of describing God are still valid and the old familiar words are all we need to talk about God. When I don't hold to what's familiar, I think it scares them. Something different is not what they want."

Wilson sighed. "That's because something different is not what they're used to getting in a church service. It's all scripted and very controlled and I suspect they're content with that. When I was growing up, I remember only a few times when there was something different." He laughed. "When I was in high school there was an old lawyer who sometimes came to the Sunday morning service. He was very smart and very outspoken. Looking back, I can see that he was actually a free thinker, but he came to church anyway because that's what all the lawyers and bankers in town did in those days.

"But this guy stood out from the crowd. Once in a while when my dad was in the middle of his sermon he would stand up and interrupt and disagree with what dad had just said. He'd explain why he thought differently on the subject. Dad was up to the challenge and, sometimes, the two them would go at it for quite a while—like a verbal tennis match. I thought their debates were fun, but most people obviously didn't. They didn't try to do anything to get the old man to stop talking—church people don't voice any disagreements they may have straight out—they just squirmed around in their seats, whispering their disapproval to one another. Actually, I don't think any of them paid any attention to the substance of the old man's arguments. But the whole scene sure supports your point that something new and different in church is definitely not what regular churchgoers want."

He stretched out his arms in a gesture of openness. "So, maybe you should begin trying out your new perceptions of God on me; people like me are the ones who need to see some kind of evidence that makes God seem real now. I have lots of friends who used to be Presbyterians or something similar who have written off church believing like I have as just an antique curiosity. 'Get with it!' is what we want to say to the church. 'Who cares what people who wrote the Bible two or three thousand years ago thought God is like? They thought the earth was flat too. Now everybody knows the earth is not flat, and that most of the rest of their other primitive perceptions were wrong as well—like their Great Grandfather in heaven.'"

Walter was about to respond, but he noticed the look of self-confident irreverence had faded from Wilson's face.

Wilson settled against the back of his chair, took a deep breath and shook his head. "But don't let my Wilsonian sarcasm fool you, Walter. In the end it's not all fun and games for me. Even though some of my friends may be smug disbelievers, I'm not. Science gives you a viewpoint but not a home. If the truth be known, some, maybe lots of, people like me who've bolted from the old faith feel like we've ended up out in the cold, dark universe by ourselves. When you have a Heavenly Father who is King of the universe you belong to a cosmic family. There's a place for you in the cosmos. I don't have a cosmic home I can go back to. There's no one waiting to welcome me home."

Walter spoke gently. "That sounds so sad, Wilson."

"It is sad! There are times—more than I care to admit—when I feel like the proverbial Prodigal Son who would like to go home to the Father's house. But I can't; there's no Father waiting to welcome me back. The father-like God I thought was real has turned out to be a fiction. And as much as I sometimes long to have a cosmic home, I can't pretend to believe in a cosmic father-like God to keep one."

He looked off into the distance for a while. "My father had a younger brother named Ernest. I loved to spend time with 'Uncle Ernie;' he was fun, and he was real. In spite of six years between them my father and Uncle Ernie were very close. Dad was Uncle Ernie's mentor; Ernie followed dad to Princeton and then to Eastminster Seminary and into pastoral ministry. He was a superb pastor and we all thought he would minister into his old age like dad did. But that wasn't to be; one sad day we learned that Uncle Ernie had pancreatic cancer. That disease almost always progresses quickly, as you know. We all prayed fervently that Uncle Ernie would recover, but he lived only four months.

"The funeral was in Glens Falls late in the morning on a hot August day. After the reception we drove home to the manse here. In the early evening dad went out to tend his garden—he kept a beautiful garden in what is now your backyard. He was filled with grief; I wanted to be helpful to him, but I didn't know how. So, I just stood on your side porch in the quiet and watched. After a while he began to sing the old hymn, 'In the Garden.' When he got to the refrain he sang only the first two lines:

> He walks with me and he talks with me,
>
> And he tells me I am his own.

He stopped singing and I watched him wipe his eyes with his handkerchief. He nodded and said, 'Ernie is God's own; we all are—forever.' He walked back to the house and saw me standing on the side porch. When he reached the top of the steps, he placed his hand on my shoulder and looked at me and said, 'It's all right, Wilson; I'm all right now.'"

He paused and then looked directly at Walter. "My father's faith gave him a cosmic home. There was a time when I could find that kind of comfort from his kind of faith but not now— not anymore. I've assumed for years that there's no chance I'll find a God somewhere in the dark void because like Emily Dickinson says in one of her poems there's no God to find."

He tilted his head and raised his shoulders, a quizzical look on his face and a quizzical tone in his voice. "But maybe the *kind* of God I've been looking for is the problem? Maybe the picture I've had of God as some kind of superhuman Lord is skewed? It makes God far too small, far too narrow. That evening last fall when I listened to you talk about the Force was the first time since I dumped that childhood picture of God that I've thought there *could* be some kind of Godlike reality in the cosmic darkness."

Walter nodded.

Wilson spoke quickly. "But that glimpse wasn't enough for me to suspend my disbelief; I need to hear more. I need to know more about the nature of that Force, especially where it comes from, before I can believe it exists. Have you found that kind of convincing evidence?"

"I hope I have."

Wilson stood up quickly. "If what you've found convinces you, I want to hear about it right now. Why don't we take a break and have a piece of cheesecake and some coffee, and see if that gives us enough of a recharge to keep going? What do you say?"

Walter stood up. "Let's do it! But I can't cross my legs any longer. Maybe you can fix the cheesecake and coffee recharge while I use your facility?"

"My 'facility?'" Wilson laughed boisterously. "When you get to my age you would have scoped out the premises and located the nearest quote 'facility' long before now. There's a small one tucked under the front stairs, off my office. Just go through that door behind you; once you're inside the office the bathroom is through a small door on your left. The light switch is inside on the left wall. I'll get us some coffee and cheesecake while you're in the bathroom."

"Sounds good." He walked into the office and through a doorway into what he hoped was the bathroom. He felt along the wall on the left until he found the light switch. When the light came on he could see he was in the right room, but the room was so small he could barely close the door. There was a small sink and mirror on his right; the toilet was straight ahead under the stairs. When he tried to approach the toilet, his forehead hit the sloping ceiling. To get close enough to the toilet he had to bend his knees, arch his back and turn his head sideways—in a sort-of squatting, head-cocked to one side swan dive. He caught a glimpse of his profile in the mirror and laughed out loud. He was glad no one could see him.

When he sat back down at the dining room table, he found a large piece of cheesecake on a plate in front of him. "I hope you found the light switch." Wilson grinned. "Doing it in the dark is risky business."

Walter hesitated, "I did," he began to laugh, "but I almost had to ask if you had another bathroom I could use."

Wilson cocked his head, a puzzled look on his face. "Why? And what was so funny? I heard you laughing in there."

"That facility with its sloping ceiling was not designed to accommodate six-foot, three-inch guys." He stood up and assumed the pose he had seen in the mirror.

Wilson laughed out loud, shaking his head. "I didn't think of that, but now that I see it, the image is hilarious!"

"I'm glad you don't have a security camera in there. You could blackmail me with the images!"

Wilson nodded and grinned. "You never know what even a marginal Unitarian might do to discredit a Calvinist."

Walter shook his head. "Well, my friend, I guess we've milked all the levity out of that scene we can." He finished his last bite of cheesecake, took a sip of coffee, and pushed his chair back from the table. "Your elegant food and drink have again compromised my vow to eat modestly; tomorrow I will have to go back to being careful."

Wilson shrugged his shoulders and tilted his head. "As the scripture says, 'Let tomorrow take care of tomorrow.' Sufficient for this day is the cheesecake thereof!"

Walter relaxed against the back of his chair. "You were right about taking a break to recharge. The comic relief has revitalized my circulation and enough caffeine has reached my brain to give me a burst of energy. So, let's go back to the question you asked before we took a break."

"And see if you, the resident theologian, can come up with some encouraging words for an uneasy skeptic like me."

"That'll be a challenge, but I'll try!" He measured his words carefully. "To put it in a single sentence, I think there's convincing evidence for an actual caring Force with a capital "F" that pulses through the universe. I think this Force represents a different kind of reality from the forces that physicists talk about. It's not mechanical like the force of gravity that holds things in place. It's *relational.* That's why no one can prove it scientifically. And that's also probably why people have for so long imagined it as something super-personal—like a king or a lord was in the old days.

"But just because you can't prove something scientifically doesn't mean it's not real. Science has its limits. To say that there is no scientific evidence for something is not to say that there can't be any kind of evidence for it. Right?"

Wilson answered quickly. "Right! Just because you can't measure something objectively or impersonally doesn't mean it's not real. Our friendship is a good example. It flows like a force that touches and connects something deep within both of us. We know it's real, we can tell other people about it, but no one apart from us can experience its fullness. But we know it's not only real, but that it's powerful; we can both feel the 'force' of it—to use your word."

Walter got up and stood at the back of his chair. "Okay, we're in sync on that. Ready to take it a step further?"

"I am, professor, we're in your classroom, and I'm paying attention."

Walter chuckled. "Good! Then, let's go on. Nearly everyone agrees there's some kind of elusive reality within us; scientists usually refer to it as 'consciousness,' but most people think of it as their soul. Unlike something hard science can prove exists, this soul, or whatever we choose to call it, is a reality we can know only by experience—when we experience it in ourselves and when we sense it in others. When I feel your presence, I think I'm being touched by your soul. I feel that presence even when I'm not with you physically. I'm sure it's the same for you. There's a powerful relational soul force we sense as friends both when we're together and when we're apart." He paused and stared at Wilson. "Are you still with me?"

Wilson folded his arms in front of him, a half-hidden smile on his face. "I am, but as you know, I don't convince easily. I want to hear more."

Walter leaned forward. "Okay, here's the more. I think there's a similar Soul Force that radiates from a source at the heart of the universe. It's like the force we feel flowing between us as friends. If we open ourselves to this caring cosmic Soul Force, we can feel its presence like we feel the presence of a friend's soul. It's just as real. It's a Force that comes from a cosmic Soul. When we feel its presence, we're being touched by God's soul. Its powerful caring touch can be just as impacting as any mechanical force physicists describe. I've felt it deep in my bones."

He paused until Wilson looked directly at him. "The universe is not just vast and cold and dark, Wilson; it has a Soul. That Soul is God, not the flat-earth God of antiquity, but God for real now." He stopped speaking and watched Wilson's face. "So, what do you think, Wilson? Am I onto something?"

Wilson nodded his head slowly. "Maybe, I need to think about it all for a while."

"Take your time. There won't be a quiz until the next class."

"Good!"

He walked around and sat down in his chair. "I know that what I'm proposing won't fly with some people, but maybe it might with people like you and me who are not defensive and want to find common ground. It takes mutual respect to find common ground and a dose of humility—like when we first talked about the Force last fall and you said, 'Sometimes, what touches us is more than we can understand.'"

Wilson laughed. "You remember something I said four months ago? I'm honored!"

"It's worth remembering, Wilson. Mature believers know they always live on the edge. Right? Anyone who says they have snared it all protesteth too much."

"Or, is just plain arrogant!"

Walter smiled and nodded. "Speaking of arrogance, when I arrived tonight and we talked about the pitch that knocked the gun out of Gary Shanahan's hand you wondered, 'No credit to God for the strikeout?' I put you off with what may have seemed like a flip response. I didn't mean to be arrogant."

Wilson raised his eyebrows. "Even if you were, it's okay. A little arrogance among friends is all right." He grinned. "To be real, I knew you weren't being arrogant, just that you weren't ready to say more. Well . . . ?"

"It was a team effort, Wilson. I threw that pitch with pitching skill I developed over many years of practice, but the Holy Force of God that permeates the universe was in it too. I threw the ball, but the Force was with me. I felt it. It's always ready to be with us and empower us, to join with us: Force touching force, Spirit touching spirit, Soul touching soul. It's potent and it's positive. It's what old-time believers thought happens when they said, 'God bless you.' They knew something real happened; it wasn't just a figure of speech. They believed in a creation energized by spirits. We live in a creation energized by forces. We know they're everywhere, all around us. The Holy Force of God is one of them. It was with me that night I faced Gary." He paused and then said softly, "You don't have to go back home to find God, Wilson; the Force is in your far country."

They sat together in the late evening quiet for a while, then Walter stood up and took a deep breath. "I see your old grandfather's clock is about to chime eleven and I really need to head home and get some sleep. This has been such a great evening; I hate to see it end."

Wilson sat still in his chair and stared toward the windows that faced his driveway. Finally, he looked at Walter with steady eyes and spoke cautiously. "Late last Tuesday evening I took a walk like I often do to relax before I turn in for the night. When I came back up my driveway I stopped for a few minutes and looked up at the sky. The air was crisp, and it was completely clear, and the stars were so brilliant I felt like I could reach up and touch them. I just stood there mesmerized for a while. A fresh, warm breeze began to blow. I felt like it wanted to pick me up in its arms and draw me up among the stars. I so wanted to go with it. For a few moments—I don't know how long—with arms outstretched, head laid back and face tilted upward toward the heavens I danced. And suddenly it felt like someone or something danced with me. I waltzed with the stars." He paused and laughed under his breath. "I'm sure if anyone had driven by and seen me, they would have thought I've gone around the bend, but I didn't care.

"Until tonight when I listened to you talk about a cosmic Soul Force, I hadn't thought much about what that experience might mean beyond the exhilarating feelings it gave me. But now I wonder if it was something more than just the beauty of the creation that touched me. I wonder if it was that Soul Force you think pulses throughout the universe." He shrugged his shoulders and smiled. "I want it to be."

"Well, my friend, 'Sometimes, what touches us is more than we can understand.'"

20. FACE-OFF

At four-thirty the following Monday afternoon George Morrison walked down the stairs from the second floor of the Schuylerkill Falls Central School building and started down the long hall that ran the length of the building. When he passed Molly Hutchins' third-grade classroom her door was open and the lights were still on. She glanced up as he walked by and called after him, "Good night, George."

He stopped, turned back and looked through the doorway into her classroom. She was hanging students' artwork on the wall opposite the windows. He sounded awkward when he spoke. "Working kind of late, aren't you, Molly?"

"I am; parent-teacher conferences for the early grades are tonight. I always like to show parents what great artists their kids are." She laughed. "As you can see, some are more talented than others."

He stepped into the room and stood opposite the drawings. "I'm no judge of art, but I think this one is really good."

"Yes, she is a good artist—and what will probably matter more to you when she begins your classes seven years from now, she's equally good in math."

George smiled and nodded. "Well, I best be going." He held up a large envelope. "I have a bunch of exams to grade tonight and I'd like to get some of them done before supper." He started to walk away.

Molly spoke hesitantly. "How is Marshall holding up?"

George stopped abruptly and looked surprised; he answered carefully. "Marshall? Marshall's all right. Why do you ask?"

She smiled and spoke gently, "You know why I ask."

George frowned. "Who told you about Marshall and Kristen? We all agreed that we wouldn't tell anyone."

"Why don't you close the door, George, and come in and sit down for a few minutes?"

He closed the door to the hall and sat down slowly in one of the adult chairs she had placed next to her desk in anticipation of parents' visits.

"Kristen told me what's happened to them. She often stops after school and we talk. We've been doing it since I had her in third grade. That was a hard year for her. Actually, it's never been easy for her at home; there's a lot of tension in that house. It was particularly bad the year she was in third grade, but it's never easy."

"So, Kristen talks with you about her personal life?"

Molly nodded. "She does, but she's not the only one. Other former students do as well. I live alone and my kids are grown up and on their own so probably I have more time for them than most teachers do. Kristen's eighteen now and a woman, so we talk about what women talk about when they're trying to find their way. It's not easy to be a young woman in this time." She could see the scowl George was trying to hide.

"So, you've become her confessor. Do you think that's appropriate?"

"All right, George, let's get right to it. You don't think it's appropriate for me to talk over personal things with Kristen not only as a teacher, but also because there are things I do in my life that you don't approve of."

He pursed his lips before he spoke. "Well, now that you've said it, yes, there are, but I would never discuss that kind of thing with Marshall."

"I'm glad; Kristen and Marshall have enough to deal with without wondering about me."

"So, Marshall has been talking with you, as well?"

"He stopped by just once."

"Did he talk with you about her illegitimate pregnancy?"

"He did."

"And what did you advise him to do?"

She answered carefully. "Ordinarily, the tone of your voice would put me off and I would respond that it's none of your business, but in this instance I think it is better to tell you what I said to him. I advised your son to treat Kristen the way Joseph treated Mary when he found out she was pregnant with Jesus."

"But that child was conceived by the Holy Spirit, Molly. It's hardly the same!"

"All children are conceived by the Holy Spirit, George; they have souls."

"I don't think it's appropriate to mix church doctrine into this conversation."

"For Mary and Joseph the Virgin Birth was an experience, not a doctrine. I may not know church history as well as you do, but I suspect most doctrines began as someone's experience with God. Maybe it's important to recall the experience when we cite the doctrine?"

"Mary was uniquely impregnated by the Holy Spirit. I don't think her and Joseph's relationship has any bearing on what Marshall and Kristen have done. I know we live in a time of lax morals, but we are Christians and the Bible explicitly forbids unmarried sex. I raised my son to honor the Word of God; his failure to do that with Kristen reflects on both of us."

"I think that's true, but maybe not in the way you are thinking."

"I don't know what you mean."

"Could it be that Kristen and Marshall stepped over the line because they found comfort in each other that neither has found elsewhere in their lives?"

"But even if that's true, it's no excuse; it doesn't alter the fact that according to scripture what they did is wrong."

"Probably not. But I think scripture is much more than a rulebook, George; it describes a God who understands human frailty and forgives those who falter. I agree that what they have done reflects on you as well as them. I think it challenges you in ways you don't expect to be challenged. Jesus spent most of his time forgiving people who faltered. Marshall and Kristen faltered. If we are to follow Jesus' example, then my question to you is how are you going to forgive your son and the woman he loves—because forgiving them seems to me to be the godly thing to do?"

"That sounds too easy!"

She shook her head. "I don't think so, George. Real forgiving is not easy. You have to care more about people than you do about whatever wrong they did."

"That still doesn't excuse what they did."

"No, it doesn't. It changes how they can remember it—as forgiven, and that changed memory can help them move on with their lives. 'Forgive us as we forgive…' the prayer says. I think we show the quality of our faith not so much by the scripture we can recite as by the way we deal with those who sin—especially those we love. Life is not just a matter of doing good or bad; it's the art of the possible. You have to live with the hand you've been dealt." She watched his face for a while when he didn't respond. He kept looking away from her. "Do you know much about the hand that Kristen was dealt?"

He faced her and spoke softly. "No, I don't inquire into my students' personal lives. Kristen's a good student, does 'A' work in math, and from what I hear in the rest of her subjects, as well. I know she's a good athlete. She's unusually tall for a girl—which I'm sure helps with basketball, but she has a pleasant smile, always a pleasant smile. I don't know much more than that; her family doesn't attend our church, even though she is active in our church youth group." He shrugged his shoulders. "That's all I know."

"Then let me fill you in a little. Do you know that her real father was killed in a tragic accident when she was only four years old?"

He nodded. "I did know that."

"Kristen's mother married Matthew Ellis three years after Kristen's father was killed. To put it gently, Kristen has never been close to Matt. It's always been obvious to her that her stepfather wanted Kristen's mother and that Kristen was baggage he had to accept to have her. For her part, I think Kristen's mother has always felt like she needed to encourage Kristen to care for Matt even though she knew that he didn't have much love for this child of another marriage. Until your son, Marshall, came into Kristen's life and gave her unconditional love and warmth she never felt deeply loved and cared for by anyone."

She watched his face carefully as she spoke. "I don't want to be hurtful to you, George, but Kristen told me that Marshall has some of the same feelings about his home that she's had about hers. She said he's always felt that your love for him depends on meeting your standards and living according to your convictions. He's never been sure you would keep caring for him if he failed to measure up. Marshall and Kristen found in each other the unconditional love neither had found in their families. They're young and they were awkward in the way they cared for each other—as young people often are—and she's ended up pregnant."

George was quiet for a while and then spoke softly. "I am sorry to learn how my son feels about me. But he wants me to excuse what he has done with Kristen and I can't. I have to be faithful to my God no matter what that may cost me."

She folded her hands in front of her and sat back in her chair. "My husband, Bob, who was the love of my life, died suddenly early in the morning seventeen years ago last month. He was your predecessor upstairs; he taught math to high school students. When he lay in his bed in the hospital I prayed as fervently as anyone has ever prayed that he wouldn't die. But our God let him die anyway. I have lived with that God-given emptiness in my life ever since. No one softened that emptiness until on a whim I invited Frank Perelli to have dinner at my house one snowy night last year. We sat at the table and talked for three hours after we finished eating. About ten-thirty Frank said, 'It's getting late; I should be going,' and I said, 'Don't go.' He didn't leave until three in the morning. We both knew even as we did it that most people would consider that what we were doing is wrong, but we did it anyway, that night and some other nights—because the emptiness in our lives had become unbearable." She paused until he looked directly at her. "Have you ever experienced that kind of emptiness, George?"

He didn't answer right away. Finally, he said, "No."

She was silent long enough to let his "no" settle in, then she went on. "Sometimes we stray from the straight and narrow because we're desperate. Can you imagine yourself doing that?"

"No."

She looked directly at him. "Maybe I can help." She took a deep breath. "When you go home tonight Shirley will greet you at the door with a smile, and, perhaps, a kiss. Right?"

"Yes, she will; she always does."

"You will smell food cooking while you relax and enjoy watching and listening to your family. When you sit at the table and eat you will tell them about your day, and they will tell you about theirs. There will be stories and, I hope, some laughter. After supper you will grade the rest of the exams in that envelope and maybe watch a TV program or read for a while. Then you will go to bed and feel next to you the warmth of someone who loves you. Right?"

She watched him nod and then continued, "My day will not end that way. I will stay here in this classroom through the supper hour and beginning at six o'clock parents will come by to talk with me about how their children are getting along in third grade. I will listen carefully to each one and suggest what they can do at home to help their kids succeed. When the last parent leaves, I will turn out the lights and shut the door and go home. When I get there, I'll turn up the thermostat—no use to keep an empty house warm all day. I'll reheat some leftover stew and eat it in silence. Unless I turn on the television there will be no noise in the house —and I won't turn it on because I hate the prattle that comes from the screen. No one will ask me about my day, and no one will be there for me to ask about theirs. After I wash up the dishes, I'll take my book upstairs and get into bed and read and hope I can settle down before too long and go to sleep." She paused and looked directly at him. "This is what's it's like for me every day. Can you imagine why I would want warmth from a friend in my life—that I might even sin to have it?"

He looked at her with fear in his eyes and said softly, "I would like to."

She smiled. "Thank you."

He stood up slowly and picked up the envelope full of exams from her desk. For a moment he didn't move; then he looked at her and said, "You're welcome," and walked through the doorway into the hall.

21. OPENINGS

Walter was standing in the Schuylerkill Creek fishing for trout as the sun came up Tuesday morning. After two hours with no luck he gave up, drove home, ate a quick breakfast and was working at his desk by nine. After lunch he made a couple of pastoral visits. But the whole day seemed to crawl along at a snail's pace; having dinner with Katherine was all he could think about.

He was back at the manse waiting until it was time to walk over to her apartment when she called. Her voice on the telephone sounded surprisingly flat. "I'm at the hospital."

"At the hospital? Are you all right?"

"Yes, I'm fine. I'm not the one that needs to be in the hospital."

"That's a relief! I've been distracted all day thinking about us getting together for dinner tonight. I'm sure the elderly church member I checked on this afternoon noticed that I was only half there."

She sounded more like herself when she answered, "Me too. It didn't help that I had two old hypochondriac guys and a screaming three-year-old with his inept mother all in a row after lunch. At two-thirty I was about ready to chuck the whole thing and call you and ask if you wanted to swap jobs."

He laughed under his breath. "No way! I'll keep my difficult church members, thank you." His laughter faded. "But I thought you weren't on call tonight. I'm surprised to hear you're at the hospital."

"I'm not on call; I drove over to be with Kristen. I'm concerned about her. She began to spot and came home from school early yesterday. Erin called the office and I stopped last night after I finished seeing patients and checked on her. It didn't seem like anything serious, but it got worse overnight. I checked her at the office during lunch hour today and sent her to the ER and they admitted her. I gave her case over to another doc at the hospital, but I still want to stay close to her, so I drove over here to check on her after I finished seeing patients. I figured if she's stable, I could zip back to the village and we could still get together for dinner tonight." She paused. "But I'm worried about her, Mac; she's a couple of weeks into her second trimester; if she miscarries it could be difficult. I'm going to stay here with her and her mom—at least for a while."

"You need to stay there so you can be close to her." She could feel the warmth in his voice. He paused. "Looks like our date tonight is off."

"Maybe not. I know Kristen thinks of you as her pastor; maybe you'd like to drive over here and visit her. I'm sure she'd appreciate seeing you. If she stabilizes, we could go somewhere in Saratoga and get some dinner."

"Great minds think alike! I'll do it! I'd already decided I would drive over before . . ."

She interrupted, "Can you hold for a minute? The charge nurse wants to say something to me." He could hear them talking in the background but couldn't make out what they were saying. When she came back on the phone she said, "It's not going well—looks like Kristen may miscarry; they're going to prep her to go upstairs to surgery. If you can get here soon, you might be able to see her before she goes in. You mean a lot to her,

Mac; I know it would help her to see you and have you pray with her. She asked me to be in touch with Marshall if something happens. Erin won't be happy with me, but I'm going to call him anyway. Kristen deserves to have him with her. Are you coming?"

"I'll be there in less than a half-hour."

After nearly eighteen years the tall Presbyterian pastor was a familiar figure at the hospital in Saratoga Springs. The floor charge nurse greeted him by name. "I suspect you're here to see Kristen Klein, Reverend Macdonald." He nodded. "You'll need to wait here for a few minutes; they're not quite finished prepping her. The last thing they'll do is give her a pre-anesthesia sedative. In a few minutes that will make her logy, but you'll have a chance to talk with her before it takes full effect. Her mother and Dr. Klein are with her."

"Thanks, Maggie. I'll to down to the front desk and check the list of new admissions to see if there's anyone else I should visit while I'm here. Then I'll come back here and wait in the hall outside Kristen's room until it's okay to go in and see her." He paused. "In case no one's told you, the baby's father may be on his way here. His name is Marshall. When he arrives, I know she'll want to see him right away."

Maggie nodded. "I'll watch for him."

In a few minutes he came back; the door to Kristen's room was open. Katherine and Erin were standing next to her bed. Kristen smiled weakly when she saw him. "You didn't need to come all the way over here just to see me, Mr. Macdonald. Aunt Katherine says it won't take them long to do what they need to do—that it should be easy."

"I'm sure everything will go just fine, Kristen, but I still wanted to see you even if only for a few minutes."

A tear ran down her cheek. "I'm glad you came, Mr. Macdonald. I know I shouldn't be scared. Aunt Katherine says they do these things for women all the time and it always goes well, but I'm still scared. I feel better just seeing you."

"It's all right to be afraid, Kristen; I would be too." He walked to the side of the bed and took hold of her hand. "If it's all right, I'm going to put my hand on your head and say a prayer. Is that all right? I think it would help you not be so worried." He watched her nod and close her eyes. "Dear God, Kristen is afraid, but so are we all—her mom, her aunt and me. We know deep in our hearts that she will be all right because she's in your loving care. Help her to relax so the doctors can do their wonders and then give her quick healing. Touch her with the strengthening Force of your love. As she feels the touch of my hand on her head let her feel your love inside her. Amen."

When they opened their eyes, Marshall was standing with Maggie in the doorway. Maggie smiled at Kristen, "Here's someone else who wants to see you."

The tears flowed out of Kristen's eyes. "Oh, Marsh, I'm so sorry I didn't take better care of our baby."

Marshall shook his head and walked quickly to the edge of the bed and touched her cheek. "Don't say that, my beautiful Kristen, you took wonderful care."

Kristen didn't respond right away, then she said, "I feel kind of funny."

"You will for a little bit," Katherine said, "and then you will drift off to sleep and when you wake up it will be all over and you will be fine." She looked at Erin. "The rest of us will go outside now so you can be with Marshall until you fall sleep."

When they were out in the hall Katherine said, "Are you all right, Erin?"

"I guess, thanks. I'm concerned about Kristen, but like you said, if they need to do anything, it should be pretty routine." She shook her head back and forth. "But it will take me a while to be all right with her Marshall." She looked at Walter, "I'm glad Katherine called you, Walter. You've been so helpful getting us through all this."

Walter smiled. "Thanks, I'm glad I have."

Katherine reached out and touched Erin's shoulder. "I know it's hard now, but in time I hope you will all right with Marshall. He really loves Kristen and that's what matters most. Once she's in recovery I'll come back here and let you know how she is. She'll probably be in surgery for about an hour. Why don't you go get something to eat and then come back here and wait for me? Right now, I need to go scrub. They know Kristen's my niece and they probably won't need me to help, but they're a little short-handed and I'll stand by just in case they do."

She looked at Walter, "Why don't you get a snack too and wait for me downstairs in the cafeteria."

"I doubt that I'll snack, but I'll meet you down there when you're finished."

After Katherine walked away Walter looked at Erin still standing in the hall, "I'm going to wait here for Marshall; he may need someone to talk with after Kristen falls asleep."

Erin forced a smile. "I'm not hungry, but I need to do something besides stand here for the next hour, so I'll get a cup of coffee—even if I don't drink it." She looked toward the doorway to Kristen's room; tears welled up in her eyes. She reached out and touched Walter's hand. "Thanks for asking God to take care of my little girl."

"Please don't worry; I'm sure she'll be all right."

She wiped a tear away with the back of her hand. "It wouldn't be good for me or for Marshall if I'm here when he comes out."

"I understand; I'll wait for him."

She reached out and touched his hand again, then walked down the hall and through the door into the stairwell.

In less than a minute Marshall walked out of Kristen's room and into the hall. He was obviously upset. "They're going to take her to surgery now. Can we go somewhere and be together for a few minutes, Mr. Macdonald?"

Walter nodded. "There's a small chapel at the end of the hall. We can go in there and be alone."

When they were inside the chapel Walter shut the door and they sat down together in the front pew. Marshall's body shook as he wept. Walter placed his hand on his shoulder. After a while the sobs subsided, and Marshall looked up at him. "All of this is my fault, Mr. Macdonald. I love her and I wanted so much to be close to her, but I shouldn't have made love with her. I hurt her."

Walter shook his head. "It's not all your fault, Marshall. You and Kristen made love with each other; you did it together. Kristen will get better quickly and then you can go on together. As hard as it is to lose a baby, most of the time when a woman's body doesn't want to keep it, it's for the best."

Marshall sighed. "I hope so." After a while he went on. "There's so much to think about, Mr. Macdonald. After we talked with you, we decided we wanted to be married in June right after graduation. Part of me still wants to do that and part of me says it would be better to wait. When we thought we were going to have a baby we put our college plans on the back burner; now maybe we should wait to get married and go ahead with what we planned to do before we thought we were going to have a kid to take care of?"

"You don't have to decide all of that tonight. I think you've done what you can do today. You stood by the woman you love. That's enough; the rest can wait."

They heard a gentle knock on the door. Walter stood up and walked to the back of the chapel and opened the door part way. George Morrison stood outside. He spoke softly. "Hi, Walter, I saw Erin Ellis downstairs and she told me that I would probably find Marshall somewhere with you." His eye caught Marshall's back. "I came here to be with my son—if he wants me." Walter opened the door wide. Marshall stood up and turned around. George looked directly into his eyes and held out his arms. "Does my son want me?"

Marshall held out open arms to his father.

Walter stepped into the hall, shut the door, and left them alone.

It was nearly eight o'clock when Katherine dressed in her green surgeon's scrubs walked into the cafeteria. Walter was sitting alone reading a newspaper, a cup of cold coffee on the table in front of him. He looked up at her and laughed. "You're dressed for work, not for dinner out." He watched her smile and then asked, "How did it go?"

"It went fine. No complications, I didn't have to do anything." The smile faded from her face. "How's the father?"

"Doing well. I left him in the chapel hugging his father about an hour ago. It was heartening to watch. I think George has finally let his feelings temper his believing." He looked at her face. "Even if you didn't have to do anything upstairs but watch and wait, you look tired."

"I am. I'm not up to a fancy dinner out—we'll have to postpone that, but maybe we could go somewhere and get something simple."

"Let's do it! You'll be hungry after you relax a bit and there's a nice neighborhood restaurant not far from here that serves delicious Italian food until ten o'clock."

She smiled. "Leonardo's! How do you know about Leonardo's? You were there with someone, weren't you?"

"It's a long story. I'll tell you about it sometime but not now. I think you've had enough trauma to deal with for one day."

"*Trauma?* There's *trauma* for me in your story?" Her eyes were open wide.

He laughed. "No, not at all! That was an overstatement. There's really no trauma for you in the story."

"Even if there isn't you can't make me wait long to hear about it."

"I won't; I'll tell you soon, but right now we need to go eat. How about if we take my Bronco and I bring you back here to get your car after we have dinner?"

"Sounds good."

He looked her over and tilted his head. "You are going to change out of that outfit before we go?"

She shrugged her shoulders and tilted her head to match his, a twinkle in her eye. "I can just wear my coat over it." She watched his face; he was on to her. "I'll change and meet you by the door to the parking lot in ten minutes."

It was almost nine o'clock when they walked through the restaurant's front door. Though Leonardo's hair was greyer than the last time he saw him, when he held the door open for them Walter recognized him right away.

"Ah, Dr. Klein, so nice to see you—and with a new friend."

Katherine held out her hand and Leonardo grasped it with both of his as she said, "Please meet Mr. Macdonald."

Leonardo frowned and pondered, "Macdonald? I may have met you before?"

"You have, Leonardo, a long time ago; it's nice to see you again."

Leonardo looked back at Katherine. "We do have your usual table in the alcove available, Dr. Klein, would that be satisfactory?"

"That will be delightful." After Leonardo seated them and walked away she looked knowingly at Walter. "He recognized you."

Walter smiled. "He did."

"So, was there another woman with you when you were here before?"

He looked sheepish. "Yes, there was."

"It was Mary Kerrigan, wasn't it?"

The concerned look on her face surprised him. He answered carefully. "It was Mary, but you already know I'm done with her."

She laughed under her breath. "Maybe. As we discovered that first evening we spent together, we're never completely done with a past lover. So, I'm jealous of her (her smile broadened) —but not a lot. I can wait to learn more. Right now, I'm off call and would like a glass of wine."

A server walked up to the table as she was speaking. "I am Riccardo," he said, looking at Walter, "and it will be my pleasure to serve you." He shifted his gaze to Katherine. "And would *Signorina* Doctor Klein and her friend care for some wine?"

She looked at Walter. "Riccardo knows I am a *signorina*, not a *signora*—and that I like Chianti. Will you have some, Mac?"

"Definitely; in fact, we should have a bottle." Riccardo handed him the wine list. There were at least half-dozen Chiantis. "What do you recommend, Riccardo?"

"The Castello Banfi is reasonable and delicious (he looked toward Katherine) and the *signorina* likes it very much."

"Then we shall honor your expert opinion and the *signorina's* taste and have a bottle, please."

Riccardo returned quickly and opened a bottle of Castello Banfi.

The dinners and the wine were delicious. As they lingered over coffee and bisque tortoni Katherine asked, "What do you think Marshall and Kristen will do now that she's no longer pregnant?"

"When they last talked with me they were planning a June wedding, but with no baby to be concerned about now I think they'll decide to wait."

Katherine pondered for a moment. "If that's what they decide, once her body recovers, I'm sure Erik will prescribe a birth control med for her. I know moral conventions would say they should abstain from sex, but by then they won't be high school students anymore. And once a relationship becomes sexual, especially when the two people are in love, it's hard to back away. Physicians have to weigh whatever they may think people should do against what they will do. Right?"

He nodded. "When you're their age passion can overwhelm conviction." He tilted his head. "Maybe even when you're our age?"

She laughed. "Speaking of conviction, when you prayed with your hand on Kristen's head you said something like 'Touch her with the Force of your love.' I never heard anyone use that kind of phrase when they prayed. I like it."

"I'm glad; it's full of meaning for me."

She sat back and relaxed against the back of her chair. "Say more."

"Are you sure you're up to this?"

"I'm tired, but I'm too curious to quit—and you're the one who has to do the work of explaining."

"Now that's an invitation I can't resist! Here's the whole thing in a sentence: I believe there's a powerful caring Force in the universe that can flow between people and between God and people. I use the word 'force' for a number of reasons. I think 'love' has become a weak, even cheap, term in our culture, so I use 'force' because it's a stronger word. I think this Force is a different kind of force from what physicists mean when they use the term, but I believe that this Holy Force can be just as potent as a mechanical force like gravity. It's both caring *and* potent."

She nodded. "Makes sense to me, Mac. We talk about the 'healing touch' in medicine. I often touch people when I speak with them about healing and I think, sometimes, the caring touch can help them heal as much as any medication I prescribe. If God is alive like you say, why wouldn't God do the same when you pray?" He laughed boisterously. She stopped abruptly and asked, "What's so funny?"

He sounded apologetic. "Sorry for the outburst, but it took Wilson Morton and me three hours to get to the level of understanding that you and I got to in three minutes."

She grinned. "Well, that's not hard to believe. He's a philosopher and you're a theologian. Your heads may handicap you when it comes to matters that involve the heart. I don't think people reason their way to faith, it's more like falling in love. You just have to reason away the barriers and then let nature take its course."

He gave her a sober look. "Is that true of us? Can we reason away the barriers and let nature take its course?"

She matched his look. "I sure hope so." She hesitated before she went on. "As a relationship develops you sense there are things you need to talk about that might do it in. You put off talking about them, hoping they'll just resolve themselves. But usually they don't, and if you don't talk them out, they come back to bite you."

"Is that what was holding you back the other morning when you said you drifted into bed once and won't do that again?"

"It was part of it. I want to make this journey to the end with you, but I have some baggage I need to unload before I can let myself do it. I suspect you may have some to get rid of too, but it's twenty-five after ten and we're both too tired now to start that kind of conversation. Besides, I don't think we want to talk about that kind of thing in a public place (she glanced around the restaurant) even if we are the only people left in here."

He looked straight at her. "We need to do it soon."

"We do."

"Your place or mine?"

"Mine, it's my turn to cook."

"I'll bring the wine."

"I could do Friday or Saturday, but I know Saturdays don't work for you."

"That's especially true when we're together because it always gets late and I'm a lousy preacher when I'm tired. Let's do Friday."

She smiled. "You preach better than the rest of them even when you're tired."

22. HIS FEAR

The following Friday the sun was still making deep shadows as Walter walked up the driveway alongside the doctor's office where Katherine kept a second-floor apartment. A delightful aroma greeted him when he opened the back door and started up the inside stairs. When he rapped on the door at the top of the stairs he heard her shout, "It's open." He opened the door and shouted back, "Something wonderful is cooking!"

He heard her voice from the living room. "It's the beef stew that's your favorite! I made it early this morning and it's been cooking all day in the slow cooker."

He set the bag he was carrying on the table as she walked into the kitchen. "Thank God it's Friday! I'm so glad to see you!" He took her in his arms and kissed her warmly.

She touched his cheek with her hand. "I can tell! What's in the bag?"

"Two bottles of Louis Jadot Beaujolais."

"*Two* bottles? You must be planning some evening!"

He shrugged his shoulders. "You never know what might happen when it's just us."

She tilted her head and grinned at him. "Then, let's not delay! The corkscrew's in the top drawer over there. I just put some hors d'oeuvres and wine glasses on the table in front of the sofa. Bring the wine, sir. I'll await you in my parlor."

As he brought the uncorked bottle of wine into the living room his eye caught a bowl of dip and some crackers. "I know what that is; it's that crab dip you make."

"And that you love—which is why I make it."

He took a small plate and spread dip on several crackers. He tilted his head as he handed one to her. "I think you have designs on me, madam."

She raised her eyebrows. "Could be."

He noticed some tiredness in her eyes. "How'd your day go downstairs?"

"Busy! There's some kind of GI virus going around the school again. It doesn't amount to much for most kids—they get by it in a day or so, and there's really nothing you need to give them other than OTC stuff like Pepto-Bismol. But there's always a few overly concerned moms who insist on us seeing their kid anyway. So, we have to squeeze them in, and Friday is always packed to begin with because the office is closed on the weekend. How about you?"

"Since I already kissed you, you'll be happy to know I haven't had the GI virus!"

She nodded knowingly. "I probably wouldn't get it from you anyway. When you have my job, you've been exposed to just about everything and built up immunity to most of it. So, what did you do besides finishing a sermon?"

"Actually, I finished that yesterday. The kid I usually coach on Thursday afternoons was home with the infamous virus, so I used the found time to wrap up everything for Sunday. This morning at just after six I was standing in the middle of the Schuylerkill in my waders, fly rod in hand."

"And?"

"I caught a couple of brookies."

"So, where are they?"

"Back swimming in the creek; they were too small to keep. Actually, I rarely keep a fish—mostly I catch and release so they can go back to their fun and I can go on to see if I can fool one of their cousins with one of my fake bugs." He looked sheepish. "But luck was with the fish this morning. I'd been fishing for just over an hour when I stepped into a hole and water flowed into the top of my waders—not a lot, but enough to give me a good soaking. I crawled up onto the bank and took them off and dumped the water out of them and put them back on and tried to keep fishing, but I was too wet and cold."

She laughed carefully. "So, did you drive home in your waders?"

He grinned. "You can't do that! I took them off and threw them in the back of my Bronco. Fortunately, there was a leftover trash bag in the back compartment. I spread it out on the driver's seat before I sat down so I wouldn't soak the seat cushion with my wet clothes and drove home sitting straight up so I wouldn't get the seatback wet. Even if it was an unusually warm spring morning, I was glad for the heater."

"I wish I'd been there to help; I could at least have driven." She was barely suppressing her laughter.

He put the last of the dip onto a cracker. "Okay, that's enough levity at my expense. Your famous dip is delicious, but my stomach is hungering for some of that stew I've been smelling ever since I opened your door. I'm ready to eat!"

She stood up. "That's one of the things I like about you, Mac; you're right out there and say it like it is. I'll bring the stew pot to the table while you bring our glasses and the bottle of wine."

An hour later as she filled their coffee cups he looked up at her and made a face. "I ate too much."

She tilted her head and looked askance, "You're not going to get sick, are you?"

"From that delicious stew, not a chance."

"Then you're probably not going to pass on the fancy dessert I made early this morning?"

He laughed. "No way! I'll have space for it—in a while." He sat back in his chair and feigned a look of concern. "You do need to know that my doctor says I should pay more attention to my weight. It's been creeping up over the past couple of years."

"I'll have a word with him; you look fine to me."

"You don't think that would be a violation of professional ethics?"

"Probably, but I'll take the risk."

He sighed and crossed his arms in front of him, a serious look on his face. "This is fun, Dr. Klein, and I don't want to be a killjoy, but when we had dinner together at Leonardo's and talked about tonight we said this would be an evening with a purpose—that tonight we would talk about some things we've avoided talking about."

She nodded and sighed. "We did, but now that we're up to it, it feels scary."

He relaxed his arms and looked directly into her gentle eyes. "It always feels scary to take your clothes off the first time with someone you love. I want us to get to that soon—very soon, so I'll take the first risk and tell you what I've been afraid to talk about with you."

"Whatever it is, it'll be okay for me to know about it."

He relaxed against the back of his chair, looked at the floor for a moment and then looked up at her. "I'm afraid, Kate, that life for you, the free-thinking doctor, would be too confining, even oppressive, if you married me, the Presbyterian minister. I know that this feeling is partly old baggage from my time with

Mary Kerrigan. I knew she could never even get close to traditional believing, and worse, that she couldn't keep still about her disagreements. I know you're different. You don't have the same need to tell the whole world what you don't believe, but I'm not sure whether you could be comfortable, or whether it might even be painful for you to be constantly with people who will expect you to believe like they assume I do. I don't know whether what you believe is even close to what Presbyterians are supposed to believe; we haven't talked about it enough for me to know." He paused and watched her face carefully when he continued. "Could you make peace between what you believe and what they would assume you believe?"

She didn't answer right away. "Probably—though when you put it out there like that, I'm not sure."

"That's what I've been afraid you'd say, that you don't know whether you could—which is why I've been uneasy talking about it with you. The night we met at Erik and Becky's I was a little, maybe more than a little, concerned about what you said about your believing. You said you had a Jewish-Lutheran heritage. You talked about doing a Jewish Bat Mitzvah and then going through Lutheran confirmation. You described yourself as 'eclectic.' You said, 'I chose what I think is the best of both—I'm a selective believer.'"

She shrugged her shoulders. "That is what I am, but why should it frighten you? Within those two faith camps—which is how I think of religious groups—when it comes to beliefs the doctrines are different, but the metaphors are similar. Both Jews and Lutherans speak of God's 'Spirit,' 'Blessing,' 'Shalom.' Both believe that God is on our side—not in any partisan way—but that God is unconditionally for us humans."

She watched him settle back and relax in his chair as she spoke. "That's how I practice medicine, Mac. When someone comes into my examining room I don't think about whether they can pay or whether they are to blame for whatever malady they may have. I don't look for blame or payment; I think about how I can touch them with whatever I have to offer that will help them get better." She smiled. "From a theological perspective I suppose you could say I dispense forgiveness."

He gazed at the tenderness on her face for a while. "I like what you believe."

She tilted her head. "But it's not strictly Presbyterian, Mac. I think Presbyterian Calvinism is much more confining, much more specific, than what I believe. When it comes to knowing what God is like I think we're lucky when we get it half right. Calvinists seem like overly confident theological hair-splitters to me. Maybe that's why Calvinists worry about God more than Jews and Lutherans do?"

He laughed cautiously. "You may be right."

She paused and looked at him carefully before she went on. "What I am, Mac, may not be what Presbyterians are, but I think it's close to what you are."

He looked surprised. "Why would you say that?"

"On Monday when we had dinner, we talked about the prayer you prayed with Kristen and then about your conversation with Wilson. When you prayed you asked God to touch Kristen with 'the Force' of his love. Is 'Force' a Presbyterian thing? Where'd you get it? I think it's yours."

He answered quickly. "It's not Presbyterian; it's mine."

"So, you're not a pure Presbyterian, Mac; you're a 'Macsbyterian.' You've moved beyond sixteenth-century Calvinism to form a coalition of convictions. What you are is a mixture of what you inherited and your own experience. But that's no big deal; it's the way it needs to be. You've done what most of us have; I bet at least half the people in your church have done the same—even if they don't realize they have or are afraid to admit they have. You haven't completely abandoned the old ways of believing, but you're not confined by them either."

"No, I'm not."

"Then why are you so uneasy about being married to me who has done the same? Is it because I'm a reminder of what's happened to your believing—and you're uncomfortable with what's happened to your believing? Maybe we've both fallen into the water and will have to swim together? Am I right?"

He didn't say anything for a while. Then he said simply, "You are." She waited for him to continue. He stood up. "I have more to say about why I'm uneasy, but I want to go into the living room where we can sit close to each other on the sofa while I say it."

She smiled and stood up. "Bring the wine bottle, sir and I'll bring the glasses."

They walked to the living room and sat down on the sofa. He poured some wine into their glasses, took a sip from his, set it on the coffee table and leaned back against one of the sofa's arms. "That soaking I got this morning was the second soaking I've gotten when I was fishing. The one this morning reminded me of the first one. I was twelve years old and at our family's camp on the Sacandaga Reservoir. It was early June; the water in the Reservoir was still high from the spring rains and melt-off—almost even with the dock in front of our camp.

"I'd gone down to the dock early in the morning to go fishing. When I was a kid, I'd often wake up early and go fishing on my own; I was a strong swimmer and always took a life jacket with me, so the family didn't worry about me being on the water by myself. I'd put my fishing pole and tackle box in the boat and was reaching back onto the dock for the oars. I had one foot in the rowboat and the other on the dock, and as

I leaned over to reach for the oars the rowboat began slipping away from the dock. I tried to stay upright, but the boat quickly moved too far away from the dock and I fell backwards into the lake. The water was only up to my shoulders, so I grabbed the boat with my left hand and the dock with my right hand and pulled the boat back to the dock."

She laughed. "So, you got a bath!"

"I did!"

Her laughter waned and she looked sober. "So, other than getting wet both times why is that memory significant?"

"Because it's the story of my life as a minister now. On the one hand, I face unwavering Calvinists like George Morrison who never venture off the dock; they just stand there year after year 'looking forward to the past.' In seminary I was taught to be like them: I was taught what I should believe, not helped to discover what I could believe. As a Presbyterian minister I'm expected to keep both feet planted firmly on the dock; I'm expected to profess and promote only what people on the dock believe and only in the ways in which they are supposed to believe it.

"But that's not enough for me anymore. I've encountered too many Wilson Mortons who have left the dock behind and don't have any convincing experience of God. The old words and the old images by themselves don't speak to them. I want to say something helpful to them—and I think I could. But when I try to keep one foot on the dock and the other in a boat, the boat keeps drifting away from the dock—and I keep falling into the water."

She reached out and touched his knee. "But you can swim! Why can't you just swim to the boat you want to reach?"

"Because I have to leave the dock to reach boats like Wilson's, and I'm not supposed to go away from the dock." He looked away from her.

"But Mac, you can always swim back. You can swim back and forth between the dock and the boats." She took hold of his hand. "Look at me, Mac!" He turned toward her. "You *need* to swim back and forth between the dock and the boats! It's not just the boats that have moved away; the dock has moved away from the boats by standing still. The people on the dock need to hear what you learn from the people in the boats just as much as the people in the boats need to hear what you've learned on the dock.

"*All* believing, no matter whose it is, is like fiction." He looked startled. "I saw you flinch when I said 'like fiction;' but hear me out before you try to respond. Fiction can point to fact; that's just being real: pointing is as close as humans get to perceiving what God is like. Even the most inspired belief is like fiction. Our vision is always partial, never perfect. *Every* glimpse of God is someone's fiction. Even what the people on the dock believe is like fiction. Even if they don't realize it's fiction, it still is—no matter how inspired it may be. They need to know that."

He stood up and walked to the window that faced toward his church. He could see the church steeple towering over the rooftops. He gazed through the window at the steeple for a while and then turned back toward her. "That would be a hard reality for most church believers to accept. Most people in organized religions are partisan believers. Sacred texts and doctrines that embody the beliefs that members of their group are supposed to believe, they're told to take as fact—and that's it for them. Christians have their Gospels; Jews have their Torah; Muslims have their Koran. Each group believes that their text alone embodies the real truth about God—and that the others are myths." He paused and shrugged his shoulders. "But even St. Paul in the Bible discovered that's not true when he ventured beyond his Jewish heritage and came across some Gentiles who weren't part of any Jewish or Christian group but were obviously already inspired by God." He walked back to the sofa and sat down next to her.

She watched his face carefully as she spoke. "You're like St. Paul, Mac. You have the Scripture, but you also have encountered the Force. You have what you inherited, but you also have what you've discovered. The fiction you've discovered may come as close to reflecting the reality of God as the fiction you inherited." She raised her arms, hands upturned in a gesture of openness. "Sometimes, maybe closer? Who knows what inspired wisdom awaits you in the spiritual experience of a Wilson Morton or Molly Hutchins? Physicians have learned the importance of listening to patients. Maybe practitioners of faith need to learn that too—to learn from their parishioners as well as preach to them? Maybe God inspires lots of people, not just the officially-credentialed ones on a dock?"

He nodded reluctantly. "That's what I want to believe, but it's not the way I was taught to believe—and I doubt that many, maybe most, members of my congregation could make the stretch." He sat back down next to her.

She took a sip of wine and set her glass down on the coffee table. "I can probably make the stretch easier than they can because I was brought up as a Jewish Lutheran, straddling two faiths. You can straddle too, Mac, and still keep your integrity. When you stand on the dock and preach to Presbyterian Christians you can use the conventions that you know will nurture people in your faith group. But you can also sit in a boat and talk the talk of different listeners; you can honor their fictions so you can nurture their faith, or, like Wilson, their might-be faith. You can swim back and forth between the dock and the boats.

"It's different out there on the water now, Mac. People expect you to talk their talk—to say what you want to tell them in a way that's meaningful to *them*. Fewer and fewer people are willing to sit in church pews week after week like their grandparents did and be hit over the head with theological concepts that have little or no meaning in the world they live in. You're not waffling when you choose words that match the variety of metaphors different people embrace, you're being multilingual—you're speaking both to those inside your box and those outside it. You help people believe when you speak their language. Your new doesn't negate the old; knowing Force is real makes Spirit more plausible." She paused and smiled. "You may even convince me that God is more than a word. You've got hold of my boat."

He didn't say anything for a while, then he took her hand in his. "It matters more than you know to hear you say that."

She smiled gently. "I may understand more about why it matters than you think I do."

He watched her carefully as he spoke. "It's so hard to admit that fictions are as close as we can get to perceiving what's beyond the edge—that there's always more than we can know. Likening what we believe to fiction would horrify most of my minister colleagues and scare lots of people in my congregation." He paused and laughed under his breath. "I'm doing a risky dance here. The Presbytery could judge my new believing to be heretical. I could get locked out of the church, but I want to make God a believable reality for some of those who are left out." He let go of her hand, relaxed against the back of the sofa and spoke with determination. "I won't deny the reality of the Force I have discovered—even to keep my job, Kate. That's the fear I've been afraid to tell you about—that I may be inviting you to share a life I won't be able to keep on living."

She spoke softly, "I know that." She turned and lifted her feet onto the sofa and lay across him; she reached up and pulled his head down to her and kissed him. After a while their lips parted and she looked into his eyes. "You may be Walter when you talk about God to your congregation, but Mac is where you feel God's Force touching you. Mac needs to get through to Walter. People who risk faith don't stay either on the dock or in the boat. They swim. If they throw you off the dock, Mac, I'll jump in the water and we'll swim together. God's Force is with us."

He reached out and touched her cheek and said, "Thank you." He wrapped his arms around her and held her tightly to him. As they lay together in the quiet, she could feel the movement of his breathing against her. They drifted off into sleep.

23. HER FEAR

She was looking up at him when he opened his eyes. He spoke softly. "We fell asleep."

She nodded. "I could feel your heart beating against my breasts, and if we keep going where that leads, we won't finish the conversation we promised we would have tonight."

He stroked her hair. "I could say it doesn't matter whether we do, but that wouldn't be fair. We've talked only about my stuff, not at all about yours."

She laughed and kissed his forehead. "You're too damned responsible, Reverend Macdonald." He raised up against the back of the sofa. She sat up and sighed. "Well, I guess corruption will have to wait!" She eyed the empty wine glasses on the coffee table. "Maybe we need to switch to coffee; it should still be warm in the coffeemaker. And how about one of the brownies I made?"

He chuckled. "Do you think you can put me off with sweets?"

"Only for a while!"

They held hands as they walked together to the kitchen. He looked at the brownies on the tray on the counter and let go of her hand and pointed to the largest one. "I'd like that one, please, with some coffee—and then I want to listen to you."

She placed a plate with the two largest brownies on it in front of him, refilled their cups and sat down.

He took a bite of one of the brownies and then held out the rest of it toward her in the gesture of a toast. "This is absolutely delicious." He grinned at her, "And I bet you suture as well as you bake."

"I hope you never have to find out how well I suture—but if you ever need it, you will get the best." She took a deep breath and looked at him intently. "Okay, enough procrastination; my turn to confess!" She laughed awkwardly. "Actually, my worry has nothing to do with believing—at least not to begin with. Like yours it's partly a trauma left over from childhood, but I didn't have to fall into the water to bring it back." Her laughter faded. "I thought about it the other night when we sat together in the cafeteria at the hospital after I was done standing in with the surgeons helping Kristen.

"When I was a kid my father was in a solo practice. He was a superb doctor, totally committed to his patients right from the start. Actually, he was too committed: he believed that patients should be able to reach him whenever they needed him. The downstairs telephone at home had a long cord on it and we ate every meal with the phone sitting on a chair next to his chair at the table. It always rang at least once, usually several times, during a meal. Most of the time he would just answer it and tell the patient what to do or ask them to call the office the next morning to make an appointment.

"But, sometimes, the conversation with a patient went on for a long time, and he would say, 'I'll be right over,' and hang up the phone and say to us at the table, 'I'm sorry, but I have to go,' and zip out the door, half of his meal still sitting on his plate." She looked gloomy. "What I didn't know then was that most of the time it really wasn't necessary for him to rush off to check on the patient, but *he* felt like he needed to do it."

Walter watched her carefully. "How did your mother deal with that?"

"She was young when they married and in the beginning I suspect she just assumed that it was part of the package you get if you marry a physician. But as we kids came along and she got older she complained more and more about it to him, and he kept promising he would do something about it, but he didn't and she began to lose patience with him. Though we weren't supposed to know, she even threatened to leave him if he didn't protect his time with her and us. So, he finally got an answering service and took on a partner."

"And that helped?"

"On the outside it did, but inside he still felt the same way. His head was still preoccupied with his patients all the time. The telephone wasn't on a chair by his chair at the dinner table anymore, but he would call the answering service at least once every evening to see if anyone had called for him, and, if someone had, he would call them back and, sometimes, still go out and make a house call."

She paused, a pained look on her face. "There were never times when my father devoted himself unreservedly to my mother—or to us. When she was in her last sickness and I sat with her late one afternoon in the hospital she looked at me with tears streaming down her cheeks and said, 'Katherine, you know I haven't been happy with your dad for years, but I couldn't leave. Don't ever let yourself get trapped like I did.'"

He reached out and took hold of her hand. "I'm so sorry—such a terrible way to live."

She nodded. "It was. Hardly any physicians live anymore like my father did. Patients, especially older patients, still want us to function like he did; they talk about how dedicated the old doctors were to their patients, and complain that younger doctors are 'too professional,' but we think we have the right to a personal life apart from our practice. My father was a hero to his patients, but that heroism came with a price, and his family paid the price—and so did he."

She looked at him carefully. "I'm one of the new breed of 'younger doctors,' Mac. We don't think we need to be always-on-duty heroes. When I'm treating someone in my examining room they have my full attention, but after they leave and I enter information about them in their chart, they're gone. I've done what I can do, and unless the case is unusually serious and I'm on call and have to follow up on it after hours, I don't think about them after I leave the office. They never come unannounced to my apartment here or to my condo when I'm in Saratoga. And if they call after hours, they get my answering service, and the people at the service know whether I'm the one on call, and, if not, who is."

She moved her hand away from his and sat back in her chair. "It's not the same with you. That's what I was thinking about when I was with you the other night and you wanted to make love. I wanted to make love with you, but I said I wouldn't do it because we weren't together somewhere where we could be sure that no one would interrupt us."

He spoke quickly. "That's the way I want it to be too. We need to be somewhere where we don't have to think about anyone but us."

She looked straight into his eyes. "Okay, here's my trauma straight out: I don't see how that would be true if I marry you. We wouldn't have the assurance of that kind of protected space in your manse. Your doors are never locked; people walk in unannounced all the time. Most of them are not dangerous like Gary Shanahan who threatened to kill you the other night. You laughed when you said you were working in your study the other day and the chairman of the property committee went into the basement through the outside bulkhead doors to shut the water off so he could replace a leaky faucet, and went up the interior stairs from the cellar, walked through the kitchen, yelled 'hello' and then walked right on up to the second floor bathroom. I wouldn't have laughed. Suppose we'd been in bed!"

He shook his head back and forth quickly, a pained expression on his face. "That would have been awful!"

"Yes, it would have! Please don't misunderstand me, Mac. It's not that church members call you occasionally in the middle of the night when someone's been in a terrible accident that bothers me. I could live with that; it happens in my practice too. But everyone in your congregation feels free to crash into your life at any time of the day or night even for something that's not at all urgent, that could wait, and you let them—like last month when we were going to meet in Saratoga for dinner on a Thursday night and one of your parishioners called you at five o'clock and asked if you could come over around seven to talk about the baptism for her baby. She apologized for calling at the last minute but said the godparents had just dropped in and were going to stay for supper. It was no emergency, yet you thought you had to give in to her and meet with them because she's a parishioner—and we lost out on our dinner."

He sat back in his chair. "I was really sorry about that."

"I know—you said you were, but that kind of disruption happens to you all the time—and being sorry afterwards is not good enough. You don't seem to have any protected time or space that is exclusively yours. Members of your church don't feel any need to ask whether what they want from you is an intrusion. I don't think it even occurs to them that it might be." She sighed and shook her head side to side. "It feels like déjà vu to me, Mac. For years my father's patients took advantage of him at my expense—and his. If we were married, I think your church members would do the same."

She leaned across the table. "Though my father's issue had nothing to do with God—and I suspect yours may not either—for some reason he felt like he needed to let his patients rule his life. My big fear is not whether your church members can live with what you believe; I know you will figure out how to make that work. I'm scared that if I marry you, your church members will still own you. I'm afraid I would end up living with you like my mother did with my father." She paused and looked straight at him. "And I won't do that."

He nodded reluctantly. "I hear you."

She reached out, took both of his hands in hers and looked deeply into his eyes. "Everyone admires Walter, the man of God, and so do I, but I'm in love with Mac, the man. I don't think most people in your congregation have ever considered how you could be someone's husband, as well as their minister. I know you're committed to your calling; can you also be devoted to me? Can you be both Walter and Mac?"

He bit his lower lip and looked away from her for a while. Finally, he looked back at her. "When you say it that way, I'm not sure."

She let go of his hands and sat back in her chair. "I need you to be sure before we get in any deeper, Mac. Passion is addicting; once you start it with someone it's horrible to have to stop. I went through withdrawal once when I was young and in love with David and had to break it off because he couldn't fit me into his life. I don't want to go through that again; it's too painful. I won't tell myself that it might not be as hard this time because I know it would be worse." She reached out and touched his hand. "I want you, Mac. God knows how much I want you, but before I let myself go with you, I have to be sure I can have you."

For a few moments he didn't say anything, then he said. "I understand. I know what I need to do and I want to do it. I just don't know how. I have to figure that out."

She looked into his eyes. "I'll wait for you."

He tried to smile. "I guess there's nothing more to say now."

"I guess not."

He stood up slowly and retrieved his jacket from the hook by the stairwell door and put it on. She sat motionless in her chair and watched. He stood opposite her for a moment and then gently touched her cheek. She turned her head and kissed the tips of his fingers. He saw the tears in her eyes through the tears in his own. He spoke softly. "Good night, Kate." He tried to smile. "By the way, you look awful."

"Good night, Mac. So do you."

When he reached the bottom of the stairs he walked through the old kitchen to the outside door. He pushed the locking button in the center of the doorknob, opened the door, walked through the doorway onto the side porch and shut the door. He tried the outside knob; it wouldn't turn. He stood and watched the lights going out in the upstairs windows and thought, "I've locked myself out."

24. QUANDRY

Walter slogged through the days that followed the late-night conversation with Katherine. Her nonnegotiable ultimatum played over and over in his mind like an earworm. Could he build fences the way she needed him to? He wasn't sure. It was one of the few times in his life he felt immobilized.

The following Friday afternoon he drove to Saratoga Springs to visit a parishioner in the hospital. It was almost dark when he arrived back at the manse. He scrubbed two large potatoes, wrapped them in foil and placed them on one of the racks in the oven. He turned the oven on and set it at 350. In three-quarters of an hour when the potatoes were about half done, he'd start cooking the chops he bought at Jim's Market at noontime. Now he had time to watch the news, sports and weather on television.

As he walked from the hall into the parlor, he glanced out a front window and noticed a vintage 1947 black Fleetwood Cadillac sedan parked in front of the church. Only one person in Schuylerkill Falls owned a car like that: Butch Chichester. One day years ago when he stopped at the garage and it was one of those rare times when Butch wasn't busy, Butch guided him to an unused bay at the back of the garage, lifted the canvas covering and showed him his "baby." It was gorgeous.

Sure enough that was Butch's Cadillac, and when he turned around and looked through the doorway and out the window behind the desk in his study he could see Butch walking up the manse driveway wearing a suit and tie. He'd never seen the mechanic so dressed up. He walked back down the hall, into the kitchen, opened the door and stepped out onto the porch. "Hi Butch, nice to see you. Would you like to come in?"

"Thanks, Reverend, I would!"

When they were inside, he motioned Butch toward a chair at the kitchen table. "Have a seat and tell me what brings you here all dressed up."

Butch sat down and looked directly at him. He sounded nervous as he spoke. "Margie Marchetti and I would like you to marry us."

Walter tried to mask the surprise in his voice. "You want to marry *Margie?*"

"Yes, we love each other and we want to make it official."

Walter looked away. The mention of Margie's name cast him back to the winter's evening he met her. It was the only time he had seen Margie face-to-face.

When he turned into the manse driveway, he noticed an old pick-up truck parked in front of the house. As his headlights flashed across the truck's windshield, he could see a woman and two older children seated inside it. Two guns were locked in a gun rack hanging in front of the truck's back window. The glimpse he caught of the teenagers led him to believe they were Butch Chichester's kids, but the pick-up was not Butch's.

He walked up the walkway, climbed the steps that led to his side porch, opened the door to the kitchen, switched on the porch light and then the kitchen ceiling light as he entered. He was about to shut the door when he noticed the woman walking up the walkway. He opened the door and faced her. The woman was dressed in a well-worn jacket, jeans, and work boots. She was pretty, but there was nothing weak about her.

"Are you Reverend Macdonald?" she asked.

"Yes, I am."

"May I have a word with you?"

"Of course, but it's cold out here in the wind. Why don't you come in? You're welcome to bring your young people in too, if you would like to."

"That won't be necessary. I prefer to stay out here; what I have to say won't take long." He stepped out onto the porch and closed the kitchen door behind him. The woman looked directly at him. "I'm Margie Marchetti."

When he heard the name, he felt like he was facing a myth come to life. He had known Margie Marchetti only by reputation—which was as close as most people cared to get to her. Margie's farm sat along a dirt road south of the village. No one knew when or how it had become Margie's farm. She had no known local lineage; one day she was just there. Mostly she lived in the old farmhouse by herself and raised beef cattle that she bred and butchered and sold to local markets. Her beef was excellent—and men were attracted to her; there had been a parade of them through her life. They all came away with the same report: she was hot, and she was a crack shot. She could take down a rabbit on the hop at thirty yards.

Men stayed only as long as Margie wanted them to. When she was ready for them to go, they left. They'd seen her take down a few rabbits—and butcher steers.

Margie was only a passing curiosity in local gossip until Walter heard that Butch Chichester had moved in with her. Several years had passed since Marilyn, Butch's wife, died and left Butch with two preschool children. Everybody in Schuylerkill Falls knew Butch and Marilyn; Marilyn's death was a tragedy the whole village felt.

It was especially hard for Walter to watch life slip away from the beautiful young woman he had married to Butch only a few years after he became pastor of the Schuylerkill Falls Presbyterian Church.

One early fall afternoon several months after he officiated at Marilyn's funeral Walter happened to stop at the garage when business was slow. It was the first time Butch talked with him about Marilyn's ghastly dying from breast cancer. Walter seemed like someone a man could share his grief with without being ashamed. Butch broke down completely. Walter stayed with him long after closing time. His care that afternoon forged a bond between him and Butch; the mechanic and the minister became friends.

Every once in a while when Walter drove by and noticed that there wasn't anyone else at the garage, he stopped and talked with Butch while he worked. He got acquainted with Butch's kids who often played in the paved lot next to the garage after school. One Saturday afternoon he and Butch put up a basketball hoop and backboard above the side door that faced the paved lot next to the garage. Villagers smiled when they drove by and saw the Presbyterian minister playing a pick-up game of basketball with Larry and Hattie Chichester and their friends.

Walter was more than a little concerned when he heard a few years later that Butch and his two kids had moved in with Margie. For a while he said nothing. Then one morning there was no one else around when he stopped to pick up his Bronco after Butch serviced it. He made small talk with Butch for a while and then told him he was uneasy about Butch and his kids moving in with Margie; given Margie's way of using men and then casting them aside, he wondered whether moving in with her would be best for Butch and his kids in the long run. Butch listened and said nothing, but Walter could see that he took his words to heart. After he left the garage he wondered whether he had overstepped—Butch was not a member of his church. Still, he was glad he had shared his concern; he would have felt even more uncomfortable if he had said nothing.

"Butch says you told him he shouldn't have moved in with me," Margie continued.

"I did."

"I don't think what Butch and I do is any of your affair."

Walter watched her eyes as she spoke; they were softer than her face. "I only want what's best for Butch and his kids, Margie."

She stared back at him. "What's best for Butch and his kids is ours to determine. Understand?"

"I understand what you think."

She folded her arms in front of her. "You need to understand he's my man now. You won't meddle; I don't tolerate anybody meddling in my life. Do I make myself clear?" She kept staring at him. He said nothing. When she realized she wasn't going to stare him down she turned and started down the walkway.

He called after her, "Margie." She stopped and turned toward him. "Don't hurt him. He's already been hurt too much." She paused for a moment, then turned toward the street and walked down the driveway to her truck. When she opened the door of the truck and the cab light turned on he could see Larry and Hettie Chichester in the truck and two guns locked in the gun rack in the back window. He stood and watched Margie drive past his driveway and out of sight.

Walter sat back in his chair. "I'd be happy to talk with you and Margie about a wedding. You know what I usually do; you and Marilyn sat with me years ago before I married the two of you. When are you and Margie thinking of getting married?"

Butch gave him an uneasy look. "Right now; I've got the license in my pocket." He reached into the inside pocket of his suit jacket, pulled out a business-sized envelope and laid it on the kitchen table. "It's right here."

Walter wasn't sure how to respond. "I like to meet with people ahead of time and listen to what they're looking for in their marriage and give them a chance to choose what they would like to include in the wedding ceremony so I can prepare it." He could see that the suggestion made Butch uneasy.

"I don't think there's much Margie and I need to talk about before we get married. She told me she came to see you one afternoon a while back and told you to stay out of our lives. That's her way; you never have to guess what she wants. When I came home that night after work she said you told her not to hurt me, that I'd already been hurt too much.

"Reverend, she heard you. She's tough, but she can be as gentle as she is tough. She's helped heal my pain from losing Marilyn. A few weeks ago, I had that old dream where I'm looking at Marilyn's wasted body just before she died. When I woke up shaking like I always do Margie held me close to her. After a while she told me I'd done enough shaking and that it was time to go back to sleep—and while she held me I went back to sleep. Margie may not be a shrink, but I haven't had that dream again since. That's worth a lot, don't you think?"

Walter nodded. "It is."

"And she's as good for my kids as she is for me. She treats my kids like they're hers. She's never had kids of her own. Who knows why? But she's taught my kids how to be tough and gentle. It may sound funny, but I think you have to be tough to be really gentle—otherwise you're just weak. She's taught them how to survive on a hill farm. Even my thirteen-year-old girl can put down a hopping rabbit with a .22 at ten yards and take it home and clean it and make the best rabbit stew you ever want to eat. Margie's a tough and gentle woman and she loves me, pastor. You can't ask for more than that in a wife."

Walter sat back in his chair. "You're right; you can't."

Butch reached out and picked up the envelope. "Two months ago I decided I was ready to make our arrangement permanent. I convinced Margie to go with me and get this license from the town clerk. But when we got home I got cold feet. I'm ready now. I'm ready to be married again, and Margie's the one."

"But why right now, tonight?

"Well, to be perfectly honest, this license we bought two months ago runs out at midnight tonight. We figured why spend three bucks to buy another one when we can still use this one? We got Ed Hutchins and Lauren Shanahan to agree to stand up with us; they're out in my fancy car with Margie. My kids' grandma has agreed to keep track of them for the rest of the week so we can get away. Ed can keep the shop going while we're gone. So, we're ready to roll, Reverend. All we need is the right spiritual mechanic to jump start us." He grinned at Walter. "Three bucks is three bucks, Pastor."

Walter was pensive for a moment, then he smiled. "Sounds like an easy fix to me, Mr. Chichester. I'll do it, but you need to know it's cold inside the church."

Butch shrugged his shoulders. "That's all right; probably won't take that long anyway."

"No, it won't. I'll get my service book and meet you at the church door."

"Sounds good!" Butch stood up, opened the door and walked out the drive toward his car. Walter pulled the service book from the bookcase in his study and was almost out the kitchen door when he remembered the oven. He walked back into the kitchen and shut it off.

The two couples stood behind Walter as he unlocked the front door to the church and switched on the lights in the vestibule and the sanctuary. When he asked Butch and Margie what they would like anything special included in the service, Butch said, "Just the usual—but not long." Then Margie said, "I want Butch and Ed to stand in front of the church with you, Reverend, and then I want Lauren to walk down the aisle toward them and then I'll walk down the aisle after her like a real bride."

Walter looked into her eyes. "You are a real bride, Margie."

"Can I light the candles on the communion table?" Lauren asked.

Walter nodded. "That will add a nice touch. If you need matches, you'll find some on a back shelf on the inside of the pulpit." She walked to the front of the sanctuary and lit the candles with a cigarette lighter she took from her purse.

Walter started to lead the two men toward the front of the sanctuary. He stopped suddenly and turned to Butch, "What's your real name, Butch? I can't use "Butch" in the ceremony; I have to use your real name."

"You do?"

"Yes, I do; it's a rule."

Butch hesitated for a moment and then said, "Arthur."

"Arthur?!!" Ed said, a big grin on his face.

Butch looked at him solemnly. "Yes, Arthur. Now get that shitty grin off your face or I'll have to wipe it off myself later when we're outside!"

When the men reached the front of the sanctuary, they all turned and faced back toward the center aisle. Lauren walked slowly toward them. When she reached the front of the sanctuary, she walked to the left, turned, and stood facing the back. Margie entered, walking slowly. There was music in the silence as she walked to join them. It took only a few minutes for Margie and Butch to make their vows to each other. Walter stood with Lauren and Ed outside the church door and watched as they drove to the end of Church Street and turned onto Main Street, blowing the vintage Cadillac's horn loudly as they went.

When the sound of the horn faded away in the distance Ed turned to Lauren and said, "Maybe someday that will be us?"

She looked at him carefully. "It could soon, Ed; you know it could. We've talked about it a lot—but you always say, 'I'm not quite ready.' Are you ready now?"

He looked at the ground. "I'm still not sure it's fair to lay my crap on you."

Lauren spoke in an insistent voice. "Look at me, Ed!" He raised his head. "I want you, Ed, crap and all. Butch and Margie just said, 'for better, for worse' to each other in there. Everybody has a worse. I know you'll never forget what you did that day in Vietnam. I love it that you are enough of a man to suffer when you hurt someone." She gestured toward Walter with her head. "He's told you over and over that the Big Guy up there thinks you're okay. You know he knows; he's a no-bullshit preacher. You need to forgive yourself and move on." She emphasized each word as she spoke: "*Please just do it*! Forgive yourself! I love you and I want you in my life—all of you."

Walter interrupted softly. "I don't think the two of you need me to be here. I'll just go inside and put out the lights and close up."

Ed laughed under his breath. "We may need you sooner than you think, Coach." He reached out and took hold of Lauren's hand. "It took two of you, but I think I finally get it. I will still remember, but it's different now. Let's go home, Thursday girl."

Walter went back inside the church, blew out the candles and turned out the lights. As he walked along the sidewalk toward the manse his thoughts went back to Kate. "I can't believe that what I just did with Butch and Margie is what Kate's not willing to live with." He shook his head side to side, "But they did barge in and interrupt supper—and I let them do it."

He stopped walking and looked down the street in the direction of Katherine's apartment, then back at the church building. He thought, "I just can't believe Kate wouldn't have wanted me to do what I did for them; it was fun and beautiful! And they would have wanted her to be there, and she would have gone to the church with us. There's something I'm not getting here—like it's been with Ed. There's something not getting through to me."

It was nearly eight thirty when he finished baking the potatoes and grilling the chops. After he cleaned up the dishes he thought, "Maybe I should talk with Erik. He's a doc who grew up in a manse—and I'm sure there was no interrupting telephone sitting on a chair next to the dining table in that manse when they ate supper."

25. BOUNDARIES

During the coffee hour following the worship service Sunday morning nearly everyone had left when Walter saw Erik Peterson walk past the door leading from the church parlor into the hallway. He stepped into the hallway and called to him, "Got a minute, Erik?"

Erik turned. "Sure, as long as it's just a minute. I've got a grandkid waiting to go fishing. He's too young to be patient."

"Well, actually I need more than a minute, but it doesn't have to be right now."

"What's up?"

Walter motioned to a door leading into the sanctuary, "Let's go in there." Once inside the empty sanctuary with Erik facing him he struggled to find the right words. Finally, he just started speaking, "My . . . ah . . . personal life is moving on in a new way and," he paused, "I'd like to talk with you about how you protect space for your home life with Becky and still maintain your commitment to your practice."

Erik grinned. "So, things with you and Katherine are heating up."

Walter cocked his head to one side. "Has she been talking to you?"

Erik folded his arms in front of him. "Now, pastor, you know that doctors don't gossip—except with other doctors. Can you wait until Wednesday afternoon to talk about it? That's my afternoon off and Becky will be gone all day, so I'll just be doing some long-overdue maintenance on the hay mower to get it ready for first cutting. Could you come by around three?"

Walter nodded. "Thanks, Erik. I'll be there—and I'll throw some work clothes in the back seat of my car in case you need help with something."

Erik laughed. "I'll find a dirty job for you to do. See you Wednesday."

Wednesday afternoon as he approached the long drive that led to Erik and Becky's farm Walter recognized Jack Rivenburg driving out. Jack waved and smiled as he drove past. Walter drove along the line of Maple trees and parked his car in the turnaround. The dog recognized his Bronco and barked to welcome him. He patted the dog's back and ruffled the hair on his head as the two of them walked to the barn. The large sliding door on the front of the barn was open and he could see Erik inside staring at the hay mower, tools scattered on the floor next to him. "This looks like the start of something big!"

Eric sighed in disgust. "The damn thing wasn't tying bales right when we did the last cutting at the end of last summer. I had all winter to fix it, but you know how that goes."

"I do! The spring-loaded line retractor on my fly reel didn't work right on the last day of trout season last fall. I had all winter to fix it and I still haven't done it. Last week when I fished the Schuylerkill I ended up standing in the creek with line all over the water yanking on the reel trying to get it to retract."

"Did you have a fish on?"

Walter shook his head. "No, but the guy standing a few yards away laughed when he saw the tangled mess all around me. That was enough humiliation. A fish on too would have been over the top." He paused. "That looked like Jack Rivenburg driving out when I drove in."

"It was Jack Rivenburg."

Walter looked concerned. "I hope he doesn't have something serious."

Erik shook his head laughed. "Depends whether you're the one that's got it. He's got a bad case of poison ivy. When I checked my answering service early this morning Ellen at the service told me Jack called last night from the Grill. She said he told her he has a really bad case. I see lots of people with poison ivy this time of year; the stuff is easy to overlook before it leafs out completely. You probably know that sometimes Jack still drives truck for Price Cutter Supermarkets. He told the service he had to leave early this morning to pick up a load of produce in the City but hoped I could see him this afternoon. He somehow got the stuff in his crotch and the itching has kept him awake most of the night for the past two nights."

Walter cringed. "How'd he get it there?"

"Just being careless. Sunday morning it was so nice he decided to clean out some brush behind their trailer. He didn't notice that some of the vines he was pulling up were poison ivy, so the oil from it got all over his hands. That would have been bad enough, but he had to take a leak while he was working and didn't realize his hands were covered with poison ivy oil. You can guess what he's got it on, and he's got it there really bad. I didn't have the heart to tell him to go to the office this afternoon when Katherine is the only one working. She'd be all right with it, but he wouldn't. So, I told them to tell him to come out here and I'd take care of him.

"When he got here I took a look at the rash and gave him some Benadryl to help relieve the itching. The blisters on his you-know-what look terrible." He paused and chuckled. "He'd be better off if he'd come to church on Sunday—don't you think? Maybe you can figure out a way to use that in a sermon?"

Walter laughed under his breath. "I'll work on it. Can I quote you?"

"Sure."

Walter eyed the mower parts strewn around the floor. "Can I help with that thing? I threw some work clothes in the back of my Bronco just in case."

"Nah, I've spit out all the swear words I know at that wretched machine and none of them have worked; I need a break. I'd offer you a beer, but I suspect you'll still be on duty after you leave me so you wouldn't want someone to smell beer on your breath." He watched Walter nod and then shrugged his shoulders and smiled. "Well, even if I am off duty today, I don't want to drink alone; we'll have to settle for leftover coffee."

"So," Erik said as they sat at the kitchen table and he poured reheated coffee into their cups, "you're moving ahead in your relationship with Katherine, and you're wondering how you're going to keep living the fishbowl life of the minister in the manse and be the kind of mate she wants."

Walter laughed. "You never dance around anything, doctor; you just go right at it!"

Erik shrugged his shoulders. "Most of the time I have to because there's a roomful of patients waiting to see me." He paused and then continued more gently, "The truth of the matter is that I know that what you need to do won't be easy. When you practice medicine—or ministry—in a small town you're vulnerable; people track you down all the time and try to barge into the middle of your life. It took a while for Becky and me to work out a way to deal with that. I had to build fences."

"But you did it."

He nodded.

Walter took a sip of coffee. "Well, as a minister I'm not sure I know how to do what you did as a doctor. Maybe it's easier for physicians?"

"I doubt it, but, then, I'm the doctor."

"Well, let me give you a for instance. The other night at suppertime I'd just put some potatoes in the oven when Butch Chichester and Margie Marchetti showed up at the manse and wanted to be married. It was funny in a way; when I asked Butch why they were so anxious to do it that evening, he said they'd bought a marriage license two months ago and it would run out at midnight."

Erik chuckled. "That's Butch—always practical. So, what'd you do?"

"I shut off the oven and went over to the church with them and did the service. It was fun to see them so happy. But after I got back home and finished cooking my late dinner I wondered how Katherine would have felt if she had been there when they showed up unannounced at the manse door at suppertime wanting to be married right then." He paused and tilted his head, "Suppose Becky had been here this afternoon when Jack wanted to see you about his poison ivy, would you have still seen him?"

Erik cocked his head to one side and shrugged his shoulders. "Maybe. Becky knows that sometimes that kind of thing happens when you're the village doc. Once in a while I let a patient interrupt my personal life, but if I do, it's always when it's something serious and they really need me, never because they crash in.

"So, my response to a request like Jack's would depend on how Becky and I had agreed to spend the afternoon. If we had agreed to spend the afternoon with each other, I would have asked the office to tell Jack I couldn't see him until tomorrow morning. Then he would have had to decide whether he wanted to see Katherine today or wait until tomorrow to see me." He grinned. "When people want to crash into your life you have to put things in perspective. Poison ivy can be pretty aggravating, but to my knowledge no one has ever died from it!"

Walter sighed and then stood up and walked to the other side of the room. "I get your point, but I've established a seventeen-year pattern of not putting 'things into perspective' when people want to get to me. I've lived like a priest married to the parish. People feel free to barge into my life without warning any time of the day or night and expect me to respond right away, not just for something major like a death or serious illness, but even for something that's not at all urgent.

"Case in point: one night a few weeks ago Katherine and I had plans to go out to dinner and Ann Shields called just before five o'clock and asked if I could stop over that night about seven to talk about baptizing her baby. The baptism isn't scheduled until two months from now, but Ann hoped I could come by that evening because the godparents were in town unexpectedly and she had invited them to have dinner. So, I had to choose between responding to a parishioner's request and keeping my date with Katherine. Ann's request wasn't an urgent life-and-death thing, but since it was a request for ministry, I felt I should make the pastoral call—so I phoned Katherine and told her we'd have to postpone our dinner date. After the hard conversation I had with her the other night I can see that in the future when I make choices like that I'll need to find a better way to balance what I feel obligated to give to church members and the home life I'll share with her."

He shifted around in his chair. "Yeah, I see the look on your face. I know I'm mostly to blame for the fix I'm in; I've let people do it. If church members think I'll be home, they don't assume they should call ahead and set up a time to see me, they just come by. I told Katherine about Ken Rawlings coming to the manse a couple of weeks ago to fix the bathroom faucet. He just pulled his pickup into the drive, got out, opened the outside cellar-well door, went into the cellar and shut off the water, and came up the inside stairs into the kitchen, yelled 'Hi' as he walked by the open door between the kitchen and my study, and then walked right on up the back stairs to the second-floor bathroom."

Erik shook his head in disbelief. "He really did that?"

"Yeah, he did. And Katherine said, 'Supposed we'd been in bed!'"

Erik laughed under his breath. "Sorry for laughing, but Ken has a big mouth. I couldn't help thinking how that would have gotten noised around the parish!" When he saw the pained look on Walter's face, the smile faded from his own. "I know I shouldn't have laughed, but you do understand why Ken did what he did. I *invited* Jack to come out here today; he came by only because he called the office first and they told him it was all right. Ken didn't call ahead of time because like you said he didn't think he needed to."

Walter grimaced and sat back down at the table. "And that's my problem."

Erik nodded, and took a deep breath. "You've never had a wife or a family you needed to protect, Walter. No one's had to be concerned about walking in when you were in bed with someone—or for any other reason.

"But if you marry Katherine, things will have to change. If Becky and I want a matinee, we just lock the doors. You ought to be able to do the same. If you and your wife want to make love in the afternoon, you ought to be able to do it without worrying that some parishioner will show up unannounced at your side door—or come up from the cellar and walk up the back stairs that end in the hall opposite your bedroom."

"That's exactly what I want! My question is not what but how to get it." He sighed and shook his head.

Erik thought for a while. "Maybe before you try to *do* anything you need to take a hard look at what's inside your head."

"Which means?"

Erik took a sip of coffee. "I grew up living in parsonages. My pastor dad was a good role model for me and I think he could be for you. Dad was a genuine outspoken earthy Lutheran. Nobody ever considered taking advantage of him. If he had looked out the window of his study like you did the other day and seen the chair of the property committee go into the parsonage cellar, he would have gone immediately down the inside cellar stairs and confronted him. After he said hello, he would have said something like, 'I'm grateful that you're here to fix that leaky faucet, Ken, but next time you need to come into our house please call ahead and let us know when you would like to stop by, and give a rap on the door when you get here so we know you're going to be going into the cellar.'"

"Seems reasonable enough but Ken's a volunteer; he's doing something for the church for nothing. A comment like your dad made would probably would have made Ken angry."

"It might have, but that's no reason not to say it. If Ken looked angry, my father would have shrugged his shoulders and said, 'I'm sorry, I didn't mean to offend; I really appreciate what you do for the church. I know this house belongs to the church, but it's our home. All I'm asking you to do is to treat it as our home.' The key point here is that my dad believed in his head that he and we had the right to protect that space as our own."

Walter sat for a while and looked out the kitchen window. "And you wonder if I think saying something like your dad did would conflict not only with what people expect of me, but with my picture of how I should be as a pastor."

"I'm guessing that you're not sure, based partly on what you've told me and partly on my own experience—and that not being sure makes you vulnerable."

Walter looked away for a while, then back at Erik. "You're right. I do think I should always be accommodating."

Erik sat back in his chair and smiled knowingly. "When I was about to finish my residency and Becky and I were going to be married, my dad and I took a walk. I think it would help you to hear what he told me on that walk. He said that when he began practicing ministry as a young curate assisting the pastor in a large church, the pastor's wife invited my mother to have tea with her. When she got back home dad could see that mom was upset. He asked her why. She said that while they drank tea earlier in the afternoon the pastor's wife told her, 'Your husband's calling is from God, Cynthia, and you must always put that first; when someone wants him, no matter what the reason, no matter how small what they want may seem to you, you must never intrude or interfere. You must never let what he may have promised to do with you get in the way of his ministry. It's the Christ-like thing to do.'"

Walter sat up in his chair. "And what did your father say?"

Erik leaned forward. "Dad said, 'I told your mother that Jesus was a martyr, not a lackey. A martyr is never a victim. Martyrs sacrifice for a purpose, not because they let someone take advantage of them.' Dad stopped walking and looked straight at me and said, 'Erik, you're a good doctor and you'll soon have a busy practice. You'll need to protect your life with Becky. When someone you didn't invite wants to intrude into your life at home always ask yourself, "Is there a real need here that *I* need to respond to *right now*?" When you sacrifice for someone, be sure it's for a purpose.'

"My father didn't feel like he needed to be either a hero or a lackey to his congregation, Walter. Neither do you. You have the right to protect your personal life with Katherine; you just have to do it. It may take a while for people to get the message, but they will." He took a breath and grinned. "Some of our church members may have difficulty envisioning their pastor as a lover, but they need to get a life. They need to know that you have the right to make love with your wife on your day off without worrying that some church member will walk in and interrupt you. Unless they bring news of a catastrophe, if they knock on your doors and no one answers, they should just go away and come back later. If you can't say that out loud, I will."

Walter sat up and laughed under his breath. "Really?"

"Yes, really." He paused and then continued in a gentle voice. "You're not the only one who will have to struggle when you bring Katherine into your life at the manse. If you marry her, there'll be a learning curve for us like there is for you, but in the end having her in your life will be good for all of us. When you treat your personal life and your marriage as sacred and protect them, by example you're telling us that we can do the same. There's a sappy kind of religion that turns people into lackeys, Walter. Lackeys are not godly, they're suckers. You don't prove you're godly by pleasing people; you show you're godly by doing what matters—and that includes what you do with the person who shares your bed."

He stopped talking, stood up, walked to the sink, rinsed out his coffee cup, filled it with water and drank it down slowly. He turned and faced Walter. "Prayer and sex are both supposed to be practiced in private, Walter. As the Good Book says, 'When you pray, go into your room and shut the door and pray . . . in secret.' The same apt advice applies to making love; it's a holy experience that should be done behind closed doors. And you shouldn't have to worry that someone is going to come up the stairs and end up outside your bedroom when you're in the middle of it. Sex with someone you love is as sacred an act as prayer. Sacred acts deserve sacred space."

Walter sat for a while looking off into the distance. Finally, he leaned back in his chair, looked directly at Erik and said, "I get it. I still don't know exactly how I will make it work, but I get it and I damn well will make it work. And I believe what you say: that I won't have to make it work all by myself."

Erik walked back to the table, sat down opposite him and smiled warmly. "Now, am I going to see you at my surprise sixty-fifth birthday party on Saturday?"

Walter responded slowly. "You're not supposed to know about that. Did someone tip you off?"

Erik grinned. "Well, someone did, but except for that one innocent little person you're the only one who knows that I know, and I know you can keep a secret for three days. Eri and Melanie and the grandkids are coming on Saturday for the party and to stay overnight. Emily, my four-year-old grand-daughter, spilled the beans when she and I talked on the phone last Sunday. Apparently, everyone else had left the room when she said, "See you at your surprise party on Saturday, Grandpa."

Walter laughed. "So, now you have to pretend."

"I can do it, Walter." He cocked his head to one side. "I know you usually don't go out on Saturday night, but I'm sure Dr. Klein will be at the party—at least for part of the time. She's on call for the weekend so I can be free on my birthday. We've got new pagers so we don't have to sit home when we're on call, just have to be in the area where we can get to a phone. If you luck out, you might end up here when she does." He grinned. "Will I see you at my surprise party, pastor?"

"Yeah, I wouldn't miss it even if it is on Saturday night!"

26. CAN AND WILL

The invitation to Erik's surprise birthday party read, "Hors d'oeuvres at 6:00—Dinner at 7:00—Birthday cake at 8:30." Walter arrived at just past six thirty. Before he drove into the driveway he could see that there was no space left to park along the drive or in the yard so he parked along the road, walked to the house, went in through the back door that everyone used and walked through the kitchen into the crowded dining room. He chatted with people gathered around the table and filled a plate with hors d'oeuvres and poured himself a glass of red wine.

As he made his way from room to room, talking with friends, he searched for Katherine. By seven o'clock when a buffet dinner became available in the dining room he realized she wasn't there; she must have had a call. He decided he would stay until Erik cut his birthday cake and then go home so he could get a good night's sleep to prepare for Sunday morning. At eight-fifteen he glanced into the dining room and saw her filling her plate at the picked-over buffet. He came up behind her and said softly, "Hi, Kate."

She turned around and smiled broadly. "Hi, Mac."

"You're late. You must have had a call."

"I did."

He motioned toward the kitchen with his head. "Becky will light the candles on the cake soon. When she does people will gather in here to sing 'Happy Birthday.' Want to go into the kitchen and find a corner where we can be by ourselves while you eat some supper?"

"Good idea!" He followed her out of the crowded room into the kitchen. No one was seated in the alcove by the turned-off television set. They sat down and she placed her plate on the coffee table that was covered with magazines.

She saw him watching her taking rapid bites of food and laughed. "I'm starved—as you can see; I've been going non-stop since lunch. I just spent the last hour with a new mother whose one-year-old has the croup. When young kids have croup they make a honking sound when they breathe; the honking makes them sound sicker than they really are. So, I was reassuring as much as treating. Anyway, the honking finally moderated and I told her I was sure with a good night's sleep he would get better—that she could call the service and have them page me back if she needed me—and managed to escape." She noticed the concern on his face and smiled. "I'm really all right, Mac— just hungry as hell! I wish I could have some of that wine you're having, but I can't drink when I'm on duty."

"That makes me feel guilty because it's really good."

"Not guilty enough to deny yourself!"

He looked a little sheepish. He sat and watched her eat for a while. "I'm really glad to see you; it feels like years since we were together. So much has happened since we had that tough conversation. I've moved along—a lot; I think I've discovered some stuff about me that could help *us* move along." A squealing noise inside her purse interrupted him. "What's that?"

She sighed. "It's the pager." She reached inside her purse and shut it off. "I'll need to use that wall phone. She stood up and called her answering service. "This is Dr. Klein." She listened and then said quickly. "I'll go right over." She hung up the phone and shrugged her shoulders. "Well, I almost got to eat some supper. Adele Simpson is having one of her spells. She has angina, as you know; usually a nitro calms it down, but her housekeeper doesn't stay over on Saturday and Sunday nights, so she's alone and afraid. I need to check on her." She looked at him and smiled. "You want to come? She's your patient too. You check on her every Saturday and Sunday night, don't you?"

"I do; I just unlock her back door and yell up the back stairs to be sure she is okay." People in the other rooms began to sing "Happy Birthday." "Let's go now while everyone is occupied. We can just slip out the back door. In the morning after the church service I'll explain to Erik why we left; he'll understand. Why don't you drive your car straight to Miss Simpson's house? I'll drive mine to the manse and walk over. Do you know where the back-door key is hidden?"

"I do—on the ledge above the kitchen window that faces out onto the porch."

He stood up. "Let's go."

By the time he had parked his Bronco in the manse driveway and walked through the path that led alongside the carriage house and past Miss Simpson's garage to her side porch Katherine was already inside the house. He opened the back door and stepped inside. He could hear Katherine and Miss Simpson upstairs laughing. He called up the stairwell, "Doesn't sound like a sick room up there!"

"It's not; she's fine. The spell's gone by." He heard muffled voices, then Katherine said, "Miss Simpson wants you to come upstairs. She said she feels safe inviting you to come to her bedroom because there's another woman present!" He heard them laugh.

"All right, I'll chance it."

He walked up the narrow back stairs and through the hallway to the front bedroom where lights were on. Katherine sat in a chair she had pulled up next to the bed. She was holding Miss Simpson's wrist. She smiled at Walter and said, "Her pulse is fine now; not too fast, just nice and steady."

Walter stood next to Katherine. "Well, that's a relief. Treatment that requires prayer I can deal with; irregular pulse is beyond my scope of practice."

Miss Simpson gave him a serious look. "Praying is efficacious even when there is no pulse."

Walter laughed. "'Efficacious,' an adjective that I believe means 'capable of having the desired result or effect.'"

Miss Simpson raised her head. "I suspect it is from the Latin *efficaci,* usually rendered in English as 'efficacy' meaning powerful and effective. Your prayers are efficacious, Mr. Macdonald." She relaxed her head against the pillow.

Katherine looked back and forth between them. "I think this is a familiar game the two of you play."

Walter nodded. "It is. Miss Simpson hasn't been in the classroom for more than twenty years, but she is still a walking unabridged Oxford English Dictionary. Give her any word and she can tell you its history. In almost eighteen years I have never stumped her."

Katherine thought for a moment and then said, "Catawampus."

Miss Simpson responded immediately, "Positioned diagonally, cater-cornered." She paused and pondered for a moment. "It could have roots in the Scottish word 'wampish' which means to wiggle or twist. But it's a colloquial word and they can be hard to trace. I think it may stem from the cater-cornered way numbers are placed on dice. In that case, I would have no further information. I have no experience with games of chance. I prefer Providence."

Katherine smiled knowingly. "I almost stumped you, didn't I?"

Miss Simpson looked directly at her. "When I am next up and about and downstairs, I shall trace the word's origins thoroughly so as to be informed completely if anyone should ask about it in the future."

Katherine nodded, "All right, Miss Simpson, you can count on me to ask for the results of your research the next time I see you." She turned and looked at Walter. "I think we can go along, Reverend Macdonald; this patient seems quite recovered."

Miss Simpson looked at Walter and then at Katherine. "Not before *the* Reverend *Mister* Macdonald offers an efficacious prayer."

Walter turned toward Katherine and smiled. "'The Reverend Mister' is the correct usage; as I just noted Miss Simpson is the ever-alert grammarian." He walked to the opposite side of the bed. Miss Simpson reached out her hands, one to Katherine and the other to Walter. Walter prayed, "Heavenly Father, you know it is always comfortable for me to pray in this home. You and Adele are good friends. We are grateful for your grace that sustains her every moment of every day. We thank you for bringing her safely through another spell. We thank you for the healing ministry that Dr. Klein brings to her. And now we ask that you will give her a night of quiet rest and good energy for the day tomorrow. We pray in the name of Jesus. Amen."

Miss Simpson opened her eyes and said, "Amen and thank you to both of you." She held tightly to both of their hands and looked back and forth between them. "I hope you won't think me too forward, but I have a word of advice I want to give to you." She paused for a moment and then looked first at Walter and then at Katherine. "I have never called you 'Walter,' Mr. Macdonald;" she turned her head toward Katherine and said, "nor have I ever called you 'Katherine,' Dr. Klein—as you know I am stickler for proper address, but I am old enough to be your mother and I want to speak to you as a caring mother would. What you, Katherine, and you, Walter, feel for each other is a gift from God. God's gifts are meant to be enjoyed." She drew their hands across her and placed them together. Her voice took on a soft intensity. "Don't delay your enjoyment like I did mistakenly when I was your age." She let go of their hands. "And don't forget to lock the door and place the key in its hiding place on your way out."

Walter reached out and placed his hand gently on her head. "God bless you, Adele."

The light from a streetlight flickered across their faces as they stood outside Miss Simpson's locked kitchen door. Walter suddenly felt weary and noticed that Katherine looked the same. "I'm tired and you look like you are too, but maybe we can follow Miss Simpson's advice anyway. Why don't you stop at the manse, even if just for a little while? All I have to offer is the usual reheated coffee (he smiled), but I buy very good coffee." He paused and looked serious. "I want us to move ahead, Kate—right now."

She reached out and touched his cheek. "So do I; I'll drive around the block and meet you in your kitchen."

In a few minutes they sat together at the table in the manse kitchen. Walter laughed a little under his breath as he spoke. "Miss Simpson can be so stern, but she's become a dear friend. She's kept me in line theologically and grammatically all the years I've been here. I've grown very fond of her—and I know she cares a lot about me."

Katherine nodded. "There's something beautiful about what you have with each other." She paused and then spoke carefully. "About what you have with lots of people here." She took a sip of coffee. "As I drove around the block and into your driveway, I wondered how much longer you will be content to stay here doing the kind of thing we did tonight? Especially after that hard conversation we had the other night I wonder, will that always be enough for you?"

He looked puzzled. "I've always assumed it would be. I've never really thought much about that question. Why do you ask?"

She set her cup on the table. "How you would answer that question is important for both of us. You said earlier that you have discovered some things about yourself that could help us move ahead together. I'm not sure what that means. Most ministers change churches and relocate several times during the course of their ministries. Is that what you'll do? I wonder, because I want to stay here in Schuylerkill Falls.

"Though no one knows besides Becky and me, Erik plans to retire at the end of this year. When he does, I want to give up my Saratoga Springs practice and practice here full-time; I like being the village doc. You've been the minister here eighteen years. That's a long tenure for a preacher. You're very good at what you do, but I know your mind is restless, filled with questions and challenges. Will you be content with a ministry to the Adele Simpsons and George Morrisons and Molly Hutchins and Wilson Mortons and all the rest here for another twenty years?"

He looked away for a while and then looked back at her. "One late spring afternoon during my senior year at seminary I sat in a practice of ministry class. We were all eager young candidates panting to charge out and start doing ministry. Seminary had inspired us to visions of greatness. I don't remember exactly what we were talking about in the class, but the professor paused like he always did when he was going to say something significant. He leaned against the chalk board and looked at us carefully and said, 'You people think you're going to save the world, but you'll get over that.'"

He sat back in his chair. "I've gotten over that, Kate. I know I'm not going to save the world, but I am going to help a few people find enough faith to make their way through life. Doing that is enough of a challenge for me. The Adeles and Georges and Wilsons and Mollys and Eds and Laurens and Eriks and Beckys—and Kates—and all the rest of those I care for here are a microcosm of what's out there.

"I can swim back and forth between the dock and the boats as well here as I could anywhere; I don't need to go somewhere else to be that kind of minister. As time passes, I will learn how to help some others—maybe more than a few—stretch old ways of believing to include new perceptions in their believing like God's Spirit as the Force. I'm well aware that it will be a real challenge to help most of them to do it. At the very least I can broaden the spiritual vision of kids who grow up here so they will hang on to their faith when they encounter astrophysics and evolution in the college classroom. There's more than enough to do right here to keep me sprinting for the next twenty years."

He paused and she watched him closely when he went on, "Now about us. On Wednesday afternoon I talked with Erik about protecting space for you and me here in this house. I will do it, Kate. I know what I need to do and I'm ready to do it. It will take some members of my congregation a while to understand how they need to change the way they deal with me when you're here with me, but they'll get it. Erik and a few others who already understand will help them get it."

Tears began to well up in her eyes. He leaned toward her and extended his open hands. She laid her hands in his. "Here's the bottom line, Kate: I am determined that we will be comfortable here in this house—time will tell if we can, but if we're not, then we will find space of our own somewhere else—like Erik and Becky did when they moved out of the house where your office is." He paused and looked carefully at her. "I love you, Kate, and I will do whatever I have to do to have you in the rest of my life. I'll be Mac to you even when I'm Walter to everyone else. I'm not exactly sure how I will do everything that I need to do to make that work, but I know I will not be anyone's lackey. There will never be a telephone on a chair next to our dining room table when we eat a meal together." He closed his hands tightly around hers.

Tears ran down her cheeks as she spoke. "I believe you. The answer is 'yes.'"

He let go of her hands, stood up, walked around the table, knelt in front of her chair and enclosed both of her hands in his. "A man should kneel before the woman he loves when he asks her to marry him, even if she has already answered 'yes.' Katherine Esther, will you marry me?"

She withdrew her hands, leaned toward him and placed her hands on either side of his face. "Yes, Walter Liam, I will." She drew him toward her and kissed him.

After she relaxed her hands from the sides of his face; he stood up and pulled his chair up next to hers. "I wish we could run off and do it tonight, but you're on call and I have to preach in the morning. Such bad timing. And next week I'm off for my annual continuing ed week. I'm registered for a seminar at Union Seminary in New York. It runs the whole week, until Friday morning. I have next Sunday off and I planned to stay over in the City for the weekend and go to Jimmy Ryan's with some old seminary buddies to listen to jazz Friday night. My minister friends don't have next Sunday off, so they all have to leave Saturday morning, but I don't. I figure I can take in a Yankees game Saturday afternoon, go to the service at Riverside Church on Sunday morning and hear Bill Coffin preach and take the train back to Albany Sunday afternoon. I'd happily give all that up if we could just drive away together after the church service tomorrow morning."

She looked incredulous and laughed. "This is either fortuitous or providential—depending on your beliefs. *I'll* be in New York City next weekend too. My younger brother's a partner in a City law firm. My nephew, Mark, turns twelve and his bar mitzvah is next Saturday. They're practicing Jews so they won't have the party on Saturday because it's the Sabbath; they've planned a big Sunday brunch that will go on long into the afternoon. I'll go to the Shabbat service Saturday morning, but that's it. I don't keep the Sabbath and I could skip the brunch on Sunday." She tilted her head and leaned forward. "Where are you staying?"

"In a not-fancy room in a small hotel near Columbia University. It wouldn't do for two of us."

She smiled. "My brother has reserved a block of rooms at the New Yorker Hotel. You could join me there on Saturday. I doubt there will be anybody else there from here except Kristen and her mom and stepfather. Erin and Matt wouldn't have a problem with us being together in a hotel, but we should probably honor your ministerial appearance for Kristen's sake. I could reserve a room that adjoins mine for you for Saturday night. Adjoining rooms sometimes have a door that goes between them." She paused and looked into his eyes. "Will you go away with me next weekend, Reverend Macdonald?"

He spoke slowly, his voice filled with conviction. "Nothing in this world will stop me, Dr. Klein. I'll meet you in the lobby of the New Yorker at noon, baseball tickets in hand, dinner reservations made at a great restaurant I know about on the Upper East Side, ready to live out a lifetime's fantasy with you for the rest of the night."

She spoke softly. "I'll be there waiting for you, Mac." She sighed and stood up. "But now I better go home to my apartment. You have a big day tomorrow and who knows how much uninterrupted sleep I will get tonight."

He walked across the kitchen and took her coat off the hook. When he turned around she had begun to laugh. He looked puzzled. "What's funny?"

She shook her head and said, "You wouldn't understand."

"Try me!"

She kept on laughing as she said, "No!"

He wrapped his arms around her coat, a mischievous look in his eyes. "I'm not going to let you leave until you tell me what's so funny."

She took a breath and said, "Okay. You probably don't know that women fantasize about getting the minister into bed."

He shook his head in disbelief. "Really, they do?"

"Yes, they really do. It's the ultimate conquest, Mac; if you can corrupt a minister, you could corrupt anyone." She stopped laughing, looked straight into his eyes. "I'm going to seduce you next weekend, Reverend Macdonald."

He laughed under his breath. "Only if I'm vulnerable."

"You will be."

27. DAREDANCE

The days of the following week crept by. Not that either of them had nothing to do: a steady stream of patients at the office, plus two babies making their appearance in the middle of the night kept Katherine running. The seminar in New York City was exactly what Walter had hoped for: a no-holds-barred yet responsible look at the tension between traditional theological and emerging scientific worldviews. But the overnights were unbearably long; they both spent hours awake longing to be with each other.

At noon on Saturday Katherine was sitting in a chair facing the registration desk when Walter walked through the revolving door into the New Yorker Hotel lobby. As soon as she saw him she jumped up and ran toward him. He dropped his suitcase to the floor and put his arms around her and kissed her. He looked into her eyes. "I'm here for you."

"I have no doubts about that, Reverend Macdonald. I already checked you in. I put your room on my credit card. It's next door to mine. There's even a connecting door between them." She shrugged her shoulders and grinned. "What a surprise, huh? Here's the key. Would you like to leave your suitcase in your room before we take off for the ballpark?"

"Am I dreaming, Kate?"

"No, we're both awake and alive, Mac. And we're going to live the dream: the Yankees will win, dinner will be magnificent, and we will float together across the dance floor." She paused. "And then I will seduce you."

"Can we go right to the last part and skip the rest?"

She laughed. "No, actually it's all part of the process. It's a dance of anticipation. So, let's get your suitcase to your room and head for Yankee stadium."

The Yankees won, the dinner was delicious, and they floated over the dance floor. He inserted the key and unlocked the door of his room at quarter to eleven. "Would you care to stop here for a while, Dr. Klein? I have some stuff to share with you. Would you like to see my stuff?"

She nodded and tried to look innocent. "How thoughtful of you, Reverend Macdonald. I would be delighted to see your stuff."

They walked into the room and he pointed to a bouquet of flowers and a bottle of champagne sitting in an ice bucket on top of the dresser.

She held up the bouquet and turned it around and looked at all sides of it. "They're beautiful. How in the world did you get them in here?"

"I called the hotel this morning, told the front desk I would check in by noon and ordered them to be delivered to my room by eight o'clock this evening."

She set the flowers down and turned the champagne bottle around in the ice bucket until she could see the label. "Besserat! It doesn't come any better." She looked at him with a look of disbelief, "I didn't expect anything like this."

He gestured toward her with his hands outstretched and said, "It's . . . all part of the process."

She smiled knowingly. "I see." She lifted the bottle from the bucket and held it out to him. She giggled and tried to look coy. "Would the gentleman like to pop my cork?"

He laughed out loud. "I would be delighted to pop your cork." He brought a towel from the bathroom, wrapped it around the bottle and worked the cork out. The cork came out with a loud pop. He set the bottle down next to the ice bucket and looked at her apologetically. "I goofed; the only glasses we have are these two that were in the bathroom."

She shook her head. "It doesn't matter."

"Well, at least they're real glass." He held one up and turned it around. We'll pretend they're crystal." He set the glasses on the dresser, poured champagne into them and handed one to her. He raised his glass to her. "To Kate, my soon-to-be wife, for whom I have waited a lifetime—and tonight the waiting is over." They clinked their glasses together and sipped champagne.

"They do sound like Waterford crystal." She watched the expression on his face as she ran her tongue around her lips. "I want more." She took a second sip and held out her glass to him. "To Mac, my soon-to-be husband." She paused and then said, "'Mac,' the most wonderful word that has ever touched my ears." They clinked their glasses together again and took another sip of champagne.

She sat down on edge of the bed and he sat down next to her. "Okay, Kate, there's one question I don't know the answer to."

"Which is?"

"Have you thought of how we're going to elope?"

"Of course, I've been thinking about it all week."

He gave her a quizzical look. "You have a plan?"

She nodded decisively. "I do."

He tilted his head. "Well?"

"Tomorrow when we wake up I'll call my brother and offer my regrets about missing the bar mitzvah brunch. We'll check out and catch the noon train back to Albany. We'll drive our cars to Saratoga and leave one of them at my condo. Then we can go shopping for a ring—or two?" She paused, a questioning look on her face.

"Two."

"That's what I told them at Batchelder's, that fancy jewelry store in downtown Saratoga."

He looked puzzled. "We already have rings?"

She looked a little apologetic. "Early this week I picked out the ring I want; I think you'll like the one that matches it."

He laughed. "I'm sure I will—if you're going to put it on my finger."

"I've known Brent Batchelder for years. I had to guess your ring size, but if your ring needs resizing, I told him we'd need to have it first thing Monday. He can get it ready. Then we can go back to my condo and I'll call Louise Springer, who was one of my high school classmates and who is the Saratoga City Clerk. I'll tell Louise what's going on with us and that we will come by her office Monday morning for a wedding license but would like it backdated to today. She'll have no trouble making that happen. Then we'll stop at the hospital and I'll get the lab to do our blood tests. I'm a doc so they'll give me the report in less than a half-hour. Then we can go to Leonardo's for dinner and afterward go back to my condo and spend the night there. We can pick up the license at nine o'clock on Monday morning when the clerk's office opens. We'll get Louise and someone else in the office to sign the license as witnesses and you can sign it as the officiating minister, put today's date on it and file it right then."

He laughed loudly. "I can sign it?" He looked awestruck. "I can sign my own wedding license as the officiating minister? Do you think that's legal?"

"Why not? I can't imagine there's anything in the statute that says you can't. I even asked Louise if you could and she couldn't think of anything in the law that says you can't."

He shook his head and looked at her. "You're one amazing woman!"

She smiled and nodded. "Thank you."

"I suppose you've figured out a way for your office to deal with the patients you're supposed to see Monday morning."

She leaned back against the bed-pillow. "I told them last Thursday that they would need to reschedule my patients this coming Monday because I wouldn't be in that day." She held out her glass toward him, "Now that we've settled the details, would you fill my glass with some more of that Besserat and do the same for yourself?"

He shook his head in feigned disbelieve, reached out to the dresser and picked up the bottle of champagne and poured some into their glasses. He set the bottle down and took a sip of champagne. "All right, Kate, only the most basic question remains: where and when will our eloping take place?"

She smiled and motioned with her head toward the door between the rooms. "In there, in the next room, in . . . I would guess, about ten minutes."

He tilted his head to one side. "And how is this marriage going to become official?"

"We will satisfy God tonight and the State of New York on Monday."

"We can satisfy God tonight?"

"Yes, we can satisfy God tonight. You can marry us. I'm sure that you've done enough weddings that by now you have the essential words memorized. We can say them to each other, and you can pronounce us husband and wife." She paused and nodded, "And then as husband and wife we can do what lovers do when they dance over the edge. Okay?"

He took a deep breath, "Okay, very much okay. I'm ready; I'm very ready."

She sighed. "Suddenly I've lost interest in champagne." She stood up and set her glass on the dresser. "I will go out the door to the hall and hang the Do-Not-Disturb sign on your doorknob as I leave. I'll unlock the door to the next room and hang the Do-Not-Disturb sign for that room on the outer doorknob as I close the door. Then I'll get ready for our wedding. When I'm ready I'll unlock the lock on my side of the door between our rooms and knock three times. Give me about two more minutes and then your bride will be ready."

She smiled and kissed him gently on the lips. He watched her pick up her purse and walk to the hallway door. She smiled again as she plucked the Do-Not-Disturb sign from the inner doorknob. She held it up and said, "See you soon, Pastor!" She opened the door, placed the sign on the outer doorknob and shut the door. He heard the hallway door to the next room open and shut. He sat on the bed for a while listening to the sounds of the city. Then he said out loud, "I should have bought new pajamas."

He undressed, washed, put on his pajamas, brushed his teeth and sat back down on the edge of the bed. When he heard three raps, he picked up his watch from the dresser and pressed the timer button. He watched the secondhand creep around the watch face twice, then stood up, walked to the door between the rooms, unlocked it from his side and opened it.

Her room was dark except for the flickering lights of the city coming through the window. He heard her voice. "I'm over here—in the bed. Come and sit on the side of my bed." He walked over to the bed and sat down. In the flickering light he could see her face and her hair spread out on the pillow. She grinned. "Those are quite the pajamas."

He laughed. "A little while ago I thought I should have bought new ones for the occasion. But maybe it doesn't matter?"

She shook her head. "No, it doesn't; you won't need them very long. I didn't dress up either." She waited for him to say something, but he didn't. "So, Reverend Macdonald, are you ready to marry us?"

"I am."

"Then we need to hold hands." She slipped her arm and hand out from beneath the covers. He could see that her shoulder was bare.

He took her hand in his and spoke slowly, with conviction, "I, Walter, take you, Katherine, as my wedded wife, to have and to hold, from this day forward, for better, for worse, for richer, for poorer, in sickness and in health, to love and to cherish, till death us do part."

He let go of her hand and she took his hand in hers. "Help me, please, if I forget my lines."

He nodded.

"I, Katherine, take you, Walter, as my wedded husband, to have and to hold, from this day forward, for better, for worse, for richer, for poorer, in sickness and in health, to love and to cherish, till death us do part."

They were quiet for a moment. Then she said, "Well, finish; pronounce us married."

He held her hand between both of his and looked into her eyes. "By the power vested in me by Almighty God tonight and the State of New York on Monday I pronounce us husband and wife."

He leaned over and kissed her. He raised his head slightly; his lips brushed hers. "I love you, Kate; my heart is yours."

She whispered, "I know. I hear it inside me."

After a while he sat up and gazed at her. "I just thought of something funny."

"What?"

"When your friends ask you what you wore to your wedding, what are you going to say?"

"Nothing."

He looked surprised. "You're really going to say that?"

"Yes, I'm going to tell them that I wore nothing—that I *un*dressed for the occasion. And when they meet you and hear how we did it and see what you look like, they're all going to be envious."

He looked straight into her eyes and spoke slowly. "So, you haven't worn *anything* for this occasion?"

"No, I haven't. Now, Reverend Macdonald, please take off those garish pajamas and get into this bed with me. I'm freezing in here by myself."

About the Author

Douglas Alan Walrath has worked as an insurance investigator, musician, factory worker, pastor, teacher, farmer, and seminary professor. He holds degrees in history, theology, and sociology. He finished a long teaching career as the William Edgar Lowry Professor Emeritus of Practical Theology at Bangor Theological Seminary, now the BTS Center. He is the author or co-author of a dozen books in the fields of religion and culture, church leadership, literary criticism and, most recently, literary fiction.

At Bangor Seminary Walrath taught sociology of religion and developed mentored practice programs that helped students translate theory into practice. He was awarded grants from the Pew Charitable Trusts and the Lilly Endowment to support his innovative curricula. Prior to joining the faculty at Bangor, he taught sociology of religion and practical theology as adjunct faculty for Drew University and the Hartford Seminary Foundation.

After a dozen years as a local church pastor Walrath served as a regional and national church executive with the Reformed Church in America. As a national executive he developed demographic criteria for choosing new church development sites. As as an independent strategic planning and conflict management consultant he travelled throughout the US, Canada and England working with national church bodies and non-profit organizations. He served on several national task forces studying the impact of social change on the future of American churches, and consulted with a variety of futurists and research organizations studying the future of religion and spirituality in American culture.

For forty years Doug and Sherry, his wife, have raised their food organically on a farm in western Maine. They grow vegetables on land they have lovingly cared for and sell hay to neighboring farmers. For fun they play traditional jazz at local venues, photograph wildlife, critique each other's writing, and enjoy challenging conversation and watching deer and their fawns frolic in the field at dusk.